A Telling Experience

Richard M. Trask

ISBN 978-1-953223-07-4 (paperback)
ISBN 978-1-953223-09-8 (digital)

Rushmore Press LLC
1 800 460 9188
www.rushmorepress.com

Printed in the United States of America

Contents

1

The Tickle of Life: Tales Short and Tall

THIS BOOK IS AN ILLUSTRATION of life as anecdote, showing how a bunch of little nothings actually add up to something. Experience is not a story until it is set in a pleasing and interpretable form. Putting our experiences into story form can make better sense of our otherwise chaotic lives. The telling of my story will, I hope, help you to appreciate the heroic adventures of your own life in your own artful way. As Emily Dickinson wrote, "I'm Nobody, who are you? Are you Nobody too?" But every Nobody is also Somebody. Let's together follow this transition of nobody (you and me) to somebody (you and me squared). It's a wild ride and I promise you'll like it. Trust me. You'll laugh your head off and cry your eyes out but otherwise no harm done.

I have four children, three boys and a girl: Tom, Dick and Mary, and Danny. Two of them had significant birth defects. Danny was born with an aplastic hip. Had it not been corrected, he would have hardly been able to walk. The treatment, in his first year of life, was for him to sleep at night with a brace that spread his feet and legs apart, knees out wide flat, toes of the feet pointing outward away from each other. That allowed the separated hip joint and bones to knit into the ball and socket mode. It was, after a year, a complete cure.

My daughter Mary had eyes that did not focus in tandem. The ostensible result was a lazy eye, wandering off to the side. That eye was strengthened by means of a pirate patch affixed to the non-wandering eye, forcing the lazy eye to work. After several years of the patchwork regimen, the eye no longer wandered, though the two eyes never learned to work together in depth-perception focus. Her brain alternately looks through one eye, then the other, but doesn't fuse images from the two eyes into a three-dimensional view. It disqualifies her from being a fighter pilot. Other than that, there were few lasting consequences. I myself was not quite so fortunate. I'm still recovering from my birth. Maybe you are too. So let's talk about it in story form. We'll stick to the world of fact and tell the truth mainly, like Huck Finn and Mr. Mark Twain did but without the stretchers.

Everybody has a story—many stories actually—fit to serve forth for human consumption and delectation, not simply spat out to the wind. In this book I will tell experiences that may seem random and inconsequential on the surface. It is up to my mind and my words to make them really "tell," to give them their due, to make the casual consequential, to create something of nothing, to play the god of my microcosm. Life (any life—yours, mine, ours) is like a war—long lulls shot through with moments of fear and trembling, pain and pleasure. The doldrums tend to be ordinary, but some unaccountably dramatic moments are extraordinary if we ponder them (haven't we all had one or more near-death experiences, for example?).

Each of our lives, maybe even each day of our lives, is replete with the telling incident, if only we might recognize it as such, tie it up into a neat package or bottle it for enjoyment later on. That is the premise, illustrated a score or more times, in this collection of tales short and tall: *A Telling Experience*. Within the larger maze beyond ourselves, we run our wayward mind-boggling personal routine. "Why did I do that?" we think. "What do you mean?" we say. The silly things that continually rise to nick us from without or ache us from within are both annoying and significant. There is a scheme to things even though we get perplexed about it all. Like, you are enjoying a joke during a hearty dinner, bite your tongue almost in half by accident while laughing, and have the emergency room instead of dessert. There was a reason for that sequence despite its unpredictability.

Reality and philosophy blend and unroll in tandem. You are brushing your teeth, and a tooth--or two--falls out, not in childhood but in middle age. So the crush of your own mortality hits you with a rush after this close "brush with death." You wonder why we should have teeth rather than a continuous upper and lower enameled ridge for biting and chewing, a design that would eliminate the need to floss. Is it because Wisdom comes with the big back teeth? But they too often get uprooted or root-canaled. So irony is everywhere.

It's hard to know what to make of things. What the hell is going on here, there, everywhere? A euphemistic bumper sticker paraphrases a well-known salty lament this way: "It Happens." (A related joke: Southwest Airlines flight attendants say that during a flight, after you have stowed your bags overhead, "Shift Happens.")

The truism about life being hard is a theme within this work, *A Telling Experience.* Life is not only hard, it's "hard as nails." What do events symbolize? We live and move in metaphor all the time: a walk in the park, a turn for the better (or worse), the brink of disaster, the edge of night. Everything is both itself and something else. Our mind is restless and relentless in relieving tedium. One thought leads to another. In the 1950's TV show, Richard Carlson's character Led Three Lives. Maybe someday my neighbor will have wed three wives. You know?

But then, also, you never know, so they say. Confusion reigns, sometimes. Yet if you can figure out your own plot for your own life, you can guard against its being a diabolical plot.

The tales in this book constitute a combination of short stories and philosophical reminiscences. It's a concentrated effort, a selection of emblematic experiences in childhood and in the nearer past and present. It is true life, my life actually, packaged in a form that often mimics the dramatic construct of fiction. In a good portion of these stories the action is as much mental as it is physical. It's about how the mind creates reality out of what goes on around it, or sometimes what doesn't go on except within the self, our illusions and delusions, which is funny stuff generally, and also in particular. Did your first encounter with your spouse, or your best friend, or your worst enemy happen by accident or by design? We like to think the world we experience is largely of our own making as individuals. Events are the props upon which we attempt, in a fumbling way, to impose our will, though we may make even more a mess of things than before. Maybe we don't control things themselves as much as we just stick our foot into them.

Often a story herein will begin with a generalization about life (a wry twist of a cliché, for example, "Where did the time go?" referring in this case to when you got knocked unconscious and lost several minutes or hours). The generalizations I give stem from a personal experience, and then I tell the experience to illustrate the point or the "lesson." But there are many meanings to what transpires around us, and our brain seizes upon an interpretation that is often partly or maybe even totally wrong. Like, breaking my wrist cured my tennis elbow in the ensuing fallow period, but does that explain the "purpose" of my broken wrist? We pretend to make sense of things when things don't make much sense in their real form, as if we could somehow determine what that "real" form might be.

We can strike to uncover the riches hidden beneath the dross of our daily grind, stir the depths of our inner wellspring, find the nexus between breathing (existence) and inspiration (transcendence). At their best, our fantasies are what John Keats called "a waking dream," like his *Ode to a Nightingale*. Keats's plaintive nightingale sang to him in music that symbolized his own poetic gift easing the burden of his terminal tuberculosis. His philosophizing about the timeless beauty of poetic song transmuted a lament about his passing away into a serenade of the immortality of his poem. His poetic ode was like the song of a nightingale—in effect eternal, ubiquitous in the human consciousness. Keats was, at that point, a living work of art in his mind. On a lower, earthly level--in the cold world of fact--all too soon in his own life he gave up the ghost, whistling in the dark. But his story, and his art, lives just as he dreamed and bespoke it. So, too, our own story is fit material for art.

Life, fully comprehended, is a condition of unrest, a "dis-ease" so to speak, cured by its end in the "resting place." It begins in "labor" and cries of anguish from both child and mother. This trauma is the original syndrome (not an "original sin"), the initial squeezing of each little life out and into the baggage of its parents and station. The sustaining and vivifying tonic on the consequent journey is laughter, and the only roadworthy vehicle is love. To tell this odyssey we, the human race, invented language, and although it is a common story that we all share, the different form it takes for each one of us is what makes it interesting.

The differences give us something to talk about and figure out. We find that our umpteen various experiences resemble somehow those of each other. And we also suffer and rejoice uniquely in our own person, because each of us is special. The collective comedy and tragedy of human experience, felt in so many ways by all of us personally, we express through language in equally telling terms in our own stories and anecdotes, homely or grandiose, in the form of epic or joke. The more stories, either funny or sad, that we can learn and tell, the better we can know each other, and ourselves too. In a true light, each of us is a weirdo it would seem. At least, extrapolating from myself, I hope so.

From birth (our first jolting loss of unconsciousness), our most abiding sensation is that not only are we alive now, we feel like we have always existed. Yet we can say, if our life is a one-shot deal, it is a very long shot. Why me? Why now? It's a stimulating brainteaser, a creative catalyst. So we will play upon that conundrum at some point.

Life is a funny thing, and so is the language that tells of it. Almost any word has multiple meanings, as we see from their definitions in any dictionary. Take the word *funny*, for example. It has three main meanings: amusing, odd, tricky—sometimes with opposite connotations. Like, "funny business" is not amusing. Two things can look alike but be very different, like onions and bunions. In life as a whole, appearances can be deceiving, as Adam and Eve first found out. That can be disquieting but on the whole is a plus. It's what made Cracker Jack popular: the prize and the surprise inside.

The stories in this book are mainly funny because life is funny, in all three senses of the word. The word "Tickle" in this chapter heading is a paraphrase from Chaucer's *Miller's Tale*: 'The world is now ful tikel sikerly,' that is, "the world is really precarious, certainly."

In Chaucer's tale, the speaker of those words doesn't get the point of his own warning about cheating spouses and conniving guests. In the context of this chapter heading, I use the word "Tickle" in the hope that many of these stories will tickle your funnybone and even touch your heart. At the same time, they will show the little world of our own life in its topsy-turvy aspect: what you see is not necessarily what you get. And sometimes we don't get or understand what we see.

This book had its genesis a few years ago at a workshop, "Writing the Land," at Ghost Ranch, Abiqueue, New Mexico, conducted by Professor Robert F. Gish, at that time Director of Ethnic Studies at Col Poly, San Luis Obispo. I had been a professor of English for a good many years, a medievalist, writing papers and articles about Chaucer and redoing the great old epic *Beowulf.* I hadn't written a story since my teenage years, and precious few back then. In working with Bob and our group, "the dam broke" for me, as Bob put it, and the stories shot forth, first in a gush, then sporadically in ebbs and flows after I got back to the academic grind and the humming daily run of life. Eventually I retired and picked up the pen in the newly rediscovered mode, to produce a full collection of "tales short and tall." Thereupon the tales were honed and buttressed through a workshop, "Writing Your Memories," at Trinity Center in Salter Path, North Carolina, conducted by poet Agnes McDonald, M.F.A. from University of North Carolina at Wilmington. So my two greatest debts in this work, *A Telling Experience*, are to Bob and to Agnes.

In composing the tales I chose both ordinary and not so ordinary situations that played upon my mind as a revelation. The stories leapfrog from childhood to adulthood, which is one dimension of their being both short and tall, that is, tales of youth and age. They are also "tall" in the sense that they stretch to reach the absurd aspect of life that we all encounter and are dumbfounded by from time to time.

The nice thing about writing what really happened is that, though it may at times strain credulity, we know that life can be, and is, like that, because we have encountered it personally, entered the twilight zone on our own. Everybody's life is mundane in some ways and bizarre in others, I would say. And so although this is essentially my own story, I hope it will strike a common chord with all who share my experiences vicariously in them.

As the tales unfold to the mind's eye, a larger story is seen to emerge throughout the collection, namely, the struggle we all experience in losing and finding our way on our separate and shared paths of life. Every person's story, mine as well as yours, is in some way universal. The trick, and the beauty of it all, is in figuring out how: A sand dollar is, in fact, priceless. The cosmic and the comic are almost interchangeable. *Marital* and *martial* are anagrammatic (implying that marriage is a battleground). We see that relaionships are amazingly multidimensional, and it is tons of fun working them out.

There are great and long gaps of weird experience not treated in these particular stories, and many of the most intriguing people and events in my life are scarcely mentioned, including my brother and sister, my four children and their mother and the family years from my early adulthood to middle age, the wallowings and wanderings of my vocation, and so on. The work is not intended to be a full chronology of missteps. The tales first took shape from happenings about Ghost Ranch, then about post-Ghost Ranch, with early life episodes provided for context. The rest that is silence for the moment is still being jabbered about locally. There are many tales yet to be shouted from the rooftop. What is your own "telling experience"? Let's ponder now a few of mine.

2

It's a Long Way to Santa Fe

MY FATHER WAS MY ROLE model in life. When I was a kid, I vowed that everything he was I wouldn't be. All I had to do was the opposite of what he did and I would be okay. I determinedly rejected him as an act of the will, an enforcing of an emotional revulsion that I had toward him. I would not have felt this way if I had understood him, or maybe I would have felt so anyway. There was little chance of me feeling otherwise. He was incomprehensible, not just to me but to everybody. My mother married him because she was young, naive, inexperienced--in other words, a sucker. She was abused by him to her dying day, a day which came prematurely for her because of him. She martyred herself and her children because she thought it was her duty, her calling in life. She took consolation in religion, stuck in there for the good of the family as she must have rationalized--a tragic irony.

It's unhealthy for a boy to grow up hating his father, and indeed in this sense I grew up unhealthy. So did my brother, three years older, and my sister, three years younger than me. We had defense mechanisms. My brother was never around. My sister to this day cannot remember her childhood. For me, I found something that my father represented to me that I could love. It was trains. He took me by myself with him on train excursions during my pre-teen years. From Washington, D.C., where we lived, we would go to Minneapolis, where his family lived. It had become safe for him to go there. His father, Birney, had recently died, whom my father out of inferiority hated. For the first seven of my years that my grandfather was alive, till he died, I and my brother and sister had been prevented by my father from ever seeing or knowing this good man, who might have been useful to me as a proper rather than an anti-role model. The family lore, reported by my mother, was that not only was Birney the salt of the earth but that he had never had so much as even a common cold in all his life and seemed untainted by the world. So now my father was free to take me back to the old homestead and the innocuous relatives, unknown nonentities to me.

I fell in love with the trains on that first trip and my subsequent rail excursions to places near and far that my father would take me to: Philadelphia, Norfolk, Grafton, Green Spring, Romney, Petersburg. No place was too podunk or obscure for a train trip. In loving the trains, I could love my father who introduced me to them.

Then for a while every summer (it seemed like every summer though it was only for two years), I would go to camp alone with my brother on the train to Tunkhannock, Pennsylvania. And it was just the train that was the highlight of this two week juvenile experience. Having become hopelessly neurotic by the time I was seven, I have few other than horrible memories of those lonely summer exiles on the Susquehanna River--incidents like being shot in the mouth by a water pistol filled with some bullyboy's urine; or of being spooked by the graphic maiming of a Confederate soldier in the classic comic version of *The Red Badge of Courage.*

But the train trips to and from summer camp were a rail highway to heaven. I remember the finest little details from first to last: The old fashioned, even for then, coaches on the B&O's Royal Blue which my brother and I boarded at Union Station in D.C.; the fancy diner with the blue china engraved with a scene of an archaic locomotive at Harpers Ferry; the inviting, dawnlight haven of the interior of the coach that we settled into; the crisp embossed head-napkin draping over the top of each seat, with a beautiful dark blue perfect circle emblem of the image of the Capitol and the big letters B&O under the dome; a choice of window seats; the eyefilling maze of rails fanning out from the depot; the swing-swaying of the driving engine while merging onto the main line; the soothing deep undulating of the cluckety cluckety cluckety cluckety lullabying from the linked caravan of the superheavy six wheel carriages in full momentum; and later on, watching the big, black-boned smoke-chugging steamer charging by us on the platform, so thrillingly vibratingly close, at the Wayne Junction transfer to the Reading; then a second change of trains at Bethlehem; next, ogling on the final leg, from the rearward coach we sat in, the Black Diamond diesel snaking around the curves of the Lehigh Valley. A melancholy feeling, like the end of the line, would hit me when the conductor called out "Pittston" just before we had to get out at Tunkhannock. I loved to hide inside those long funnels to other vistas.

I progressed in my training to the privilege of going it alone to visit my only surviving grandparent--my mother's mother--who long was one of the most important people in my blighted young life, by train to Phoenix. I was by this time pushing fourteen. The Sunset Limited carried me off into the sunset, into the land of the sun, the western rim of the world, like another planet to me. My first palm tree. My first flowering desert. Camelback Mountain. Ornamental orange trees. Big sky. Sunny streets lined with those magical tower high palms each topped with its green cap of plumage, the silver studded deep black night lit up as with tiny pointed white Christmas tree lights all over straight up and sideways; the way everybody wore just splashy colored shortsleeve shirts even downtown; the red, brown, and orange colors of the sandscape, the spaciousness of the horizon in every direction.

Maybe there was heaven on earth, from a train. Arizona was Nirvana. I had never seen any landscape so exotic, any sun so glittering. The air was new blue and bright, and I had a train that would take me there. Life might be worth living after all, even for one so young.

Now in old middle age, I still take a train whenever I can, wherever I can. If a train goes where I'm going, that's how I go. And the longer it takes, the better, the more lingering the ecstasy. When I go to Santa Fe, I take the train even though the railroad is no longer the Santa Fe, and it doesn't even go to Santa Fe--just to Lamy, fifteen miles short. With the locomotive following the Santa Fe trail up and down the Raton Pass to 8,500 feet, at forty miles an hour for hours, you would think the least the train could do would be another fifteen miles along high plain to its namesake. But I forgive this train for its shortfall. It got me close enough. And I forgive my father for his innate shortcoming. He got me to the train.

3

The Phantom Dogs of Ghost Ranch

Do you ever hear an old car whose creaky engine and loose-jointed parts make squeals that rattle your ear in a haunting way? Keep your ears open. What might its sounds resemble? The ears are the brain's side windows on the world.

There's an old legend that at Ghost Ranch, New Mexico, wild cattle can be heard stampeding unseen at night, flattening the landscape, their hoofprints visible at dawn under the dust of the rising morning mist. This legend would shortly inspire another one, created by me. We were on our way, by train, to Abiqueue, New Mexico, to a participatory seminar called "Writing the Land," conducted by Professor Robert Gish of Cal Poly, San Luis Obispo, to be held at Ghost Ranch. I needed inspiration to write my own Western quest, my desert trek.

Before this region was the Wild West, it was in olden times considered a Wild Waste. Then romance set in and every venue acquired Bunyanesque scope. Emptiness became big sky, vast horizons. I knew beforehand that Ghost Ranch was set in mountainous terrain near Santa Fe, and I had been to Santa Fe, but I was glad not to have seen any pictures of the Ranch ahead of time, so as to heighten the suspense, deepen the first effects of the experience upon arrival. Whatever was on the horizon for me, it would be big as all outdoors.

The train ride to Lamy, the terminus fifteen miles outside Santa Fe, was in itself new. I had been west on the Southern, the Southern Pacific, the Burlington, the Rock Island, and the Milwaukee Road, but never to Santa Fe on the Santa Fe route. Next to trains, I like a good old pioneer trail, and that made this Santa Fe trip special to begin with, following along parts of the rutty-ruin Santa Fe Trail through Kansas and Colorado. I was having fun already, the rocking roll of wheel on rail in high Superliner style in fastforward mockery of the gyration of trail wagons, the hum-clickety of rails superseding the bumpety-splat of dirt-road ruts.

I'm a fun guy in a deadpan sort of way. I like to kid around with my better half, Karen, as we travel. She was opposite me in the compartment, and I was facing forward to the direction of travel. We approached a concrete bulwark that only I could see. I flinched suddenly.

"Dam!" I cried. She looked up at me in concern.

"Did you forget something?" she offered.

"No," I said. "I don't mean 'Damn it,' I mean 'It's a dam.' And it's not a mirage, it's a real lake."

Karen shot back, "That damn joke of yours is more like a mirage."

Mirage or no, the imagination, and the words to frame it, were already taking shape from the features of the landscape.

At Lamy, we were picked up by a waiting, dust-beaten van for the ride to Ghost Ranch. Karen and I were in the back seat of four double seats, behind several teenage-type girls. The driver was a nice windburned looking lady, hair blown breeze-dry, bleached blond by the sun, a true daughter of the West.

As we got on the road, we heard a familiar but fantastically placed sound, insistent, staccato, high pitched but unmistakable.

"I hear dogs barking," Karen remarked.

"Yes, I hear them too," said I.

Karen is a dog fancier. She goes to dog shows, requires mastiffs or yellow Labs as pets at any given time.

"What kind of dogs are those barking?" I asked. "I mean, what breed?" Karen is an expert on dogs and has the discrimination of a gourmet, just as she can describe the ingredients in any exotic recipe she tastes in a restaurant. But this encounter baffled her.

"I don't know what kind," she said. "I just know there is the sound of dogs barking, here in the van."

"I agree with you," I said. "But since there are no dogs in the van, it must be the squeak of barking dogs from some moving or flapping parts of the van."

We stopped for a traffic light on the approach through Santa Fe. The barking continued while the van was at idle.

"Yes, the barking dogs are still with us even though the van is not moving or flapping at the moment," I noted. "They must be very small dogs caught in the hidden machinery of the vehicle."

And so it went, throughout the hour and a half trip to Ghost Ranch--the weathered woman, the freshlooking girls, Karen and me, and the barking dogs still without explanation.

Mesas and bluffs loomed, dipped, lumbered past in huge, slow motion as we--humans and dogs--sped along. I looked for Camel Rock, wondering if Mother Nature and Father Time had abused any of its features since last I saw it a few years ago. There it was, coming up on the left, not much a camel at first, but finally very like a camel--even more like a camel than before: eyes, lips, nose, mouth, an incredible likeness, hardly a better facsimile of man or beast this side of the erstwhile man in the mountain on Profile Rock in New Hampshire, infinitely better than the hollow eyed, rock sucking Man in the Moon. The more I thought about it, it seemed that phantoms were a natural part of this landscape: a fantastic camel more real looking than Joe Camel ever was, a pack of invisible dogs barking in the van, all even before we got to Ghost Ranch.

Finally, we did take the right turn onto the hardpacked dirt road, the dogs ever more frantic in their raucous chorus. Into the compound we came. The dogs were roaring with anticipation. What did we ourselves see? A nondescript field with a few scrubby trees and shrubs. Some medium-high cream-colored but nonvariegated cliffs, all in all less picturesque than travelogues or *Arizona Highways*. A place without much face, but with a name and a history. An expanse for my mind to play on. I knew something good would come from this nothingness; I was charged with being my own creative eye, ear, and voice, *ex nihilo*. From now on I would be a writing fool.

Up the Mesa we drove to Bluebird Cabin. Karen and I got out. The dogs went off, still in the van. We looked around Bluebird Cabin. No bluebirds to be seen, just our little room.

"Damn!" I said.

"Did you forget something?" said Karen.

"Not a thing," I said. "It's all here. The illusion is the reality. That's what the dogs were telling us. And I'm their ghost writer."

4

The Worst of Sins: A Tale from the Crypt

I HAVE A POINTED HEAD. It got that way when I was about six. David (my older brother), Marian (my younger sister), and I were walking around the National Zoo in Washington with my parents when David started chasing me like in a game of tag. In the good old days of 1947 the sidewalks of the zoo were not finished items. They were of an uneven, cindery gravel. As I tried to bolt away from David, one of my feet tripped on a rock, my other foot slipped on loose stones, and I fell bodily onto my forehead, bloodying the ground crimson and peppering the skin of my forehead with the shot of grimy pebbles. I lay there, red with blood and pale with shock.

It was a central wound--right in the middle of my forehead-- and it was horrid. My parents took me to the nearest doctor they could find, right across from the Zoo park entrance on Connecticut Avenue. The doctor was a woman, whose name I have reconstructed in adulthood as Dr. Chickering, though at the time I remember being ministered to by a Dr. Chicken. So I learned early that women could be doctors and not just mothers untainted by the real world. I wore the badge of a large, inwardly soggy, square bandage patch just up from between my eyes, prominently displayed for a couple of weeks. The wound scabbed and stiffened, irregular and ugly. I think Dr. Chicken had to do a lot of digging in the subcutaneous layers. It left a spiky, blotchy scar, a scarlet inkblot as if marking for me the life of a bruised childhood. Over the course of many months, the splotch dimmed pinkish, then off-white. But the grainy grime had not only got under the skin, it had gone to the bone. You can't splint a forehead. The crumpled cartilage triangulated forward forming a projecting, fossilized bump.

It was my personal stigma. Its proportions acquired tremendous dimension in my imagination--like a prow of an antique steam engine's cowcatcher. I spent much of my spare time feeling it with my fingers, finding a perverse fascination with my uniquely broken brow. I'm sure, now, that it didn't look quite that prominent, but I can still feel the edged cleft, eroded down, as I to this day peruse its subtle undulations under my by now crinkly skin. Yes, it's still there, pointing my memory to my brother's doing in of me so long ago.

My mother also did me in, I decided sometime later in life--a heavy burden put on her by me to bear upon my mind. We had to pay for her sins by getting up at 6 a.m. to go way over across town on Sunday, ten miles into the deepest of ghettos in northeast D.C. to St. James Anglo-Catholic parish--extra early so we would have time to go to confession. Anglo-Catholic means rosaries, incense, an ascetic, shriveled up priest, lectures on heaven, hell, purgatory, and on mortal versus venial sins, leading to that most dreaded of all consequences, the torture chamber of the confessional box.

Yes, here would be sorted out your destiny: would those mortal sins damning your soul eternally be washed away or not? Your fate was all up to you--meaning me. I had the power to damn myself by what I would or wouldn't say in that incantatory rite. Certain sins were mortal because they killed the soul, condemning it to burn forever in hell--a fire feeding upon itself and upon you, meaning me. Yes, this was the drama unfolding every Sunday, for my sensitive soul, although one had to go to confession only once a month, unless under pain of mortal sin.

But I, then, was always under pain of mortal sin, even if I only could bring myself to go to confession once a month. And this was long before I even knew there were, for example, words so evil as masturbation much less any acts so unutterably foul. No such nasty things were ever explained or even mentioned by my parents or by Father Plank. And my brother never told me his secrets. Anyway, in my early youth I was sexually nonprecocious. Yet even in sexual innocence, I suffered the wrack of a guilty conscience, perpetually. I had committed, according to my religious instruction, the gravest sin--worse, so I was told, than murder. Indeed, I had on a momentous occasion stolen money from the church.

This crime occurred when I was age nine or so. To steal money from the church, Father Plank had said in Sunday school, was worse than murder because it in effect hurts people's souls who are ministered to by the church. To place another soul in jeopardy is more serious a transgression than any bodily crime, more evil than killing someone.

My family used to spend a week at a farm in Pennsylvania on summer vacation--the Rouses' farm, a hundred acres, big barn full of hay for jumping into from a high platform, cows mooing and milking, homemade tomato juice thick and mushy. I had some fun there, but I paid a high price for it.

One evening we drove to a nearby church bazaar, a carnival atmosphere but for charity. There were games of chance, fixed in favor of the house, in this case the local church, of unknown denomination. There was a roulette wheel. I had a dollar or two in change. I could barely see over the ledge where bets were placed on numbers and colors. The colors were red and black--the devil's own colors, as I would learn later in life. I put down a quarter on red. The wheel spun, and came up red. My lucky day. I knew my money was doubled: the church owed me my quarter back plus another. The man put money on my square to pick up, and I did. I counted it up: seventy-five cents, a quarter more than I had won. I kept it all, knowing I should return the extra quarter. My ill-gotten gains in hand, I left the game and proceeded to worry about that incident the rest of the night, the rest of the week, and the rest of the month. I had stolen money from the church, the worst sin, and I would have to confess it sacramentally.

The month passed by and it was time for confession. My saintly mother woke David and me and Marian up at 6 a.m. that Sunday as usual, and with my drone-like father along for the ride--of course he by custom drove (or careened--he was a dangerous, thwarted menace behind the wheel)--we sped across town to that holiest of shrines,

St. James, C Street Northeast, in its hellish ghetto. It was the highest Episcopal church, meaning the most arcane in doctrine and trappings, on the East Coast, and therefore my mother insisted on this place. It had not only rosaries and incense, it had medieval icons of saints, stations of the cross, a Tridentine mass ritual, litanies, vigils, votive candles--red for the living and blue for the faithful departed-- and, most ominously, the funereal booth of the confessional.

We were supposed to write down our sins to make sure we wouldn't forget any. I usually used the back of an old envelope, like Lincoln did for his Gettysburg Address. I think I brought one along out of habit and scribbled some stuff on it--like I was mean to my sister, I dawdled about taking out the trash, I lost my temper at friends, and so on--not real deep matter. But I knew what the real sin was, and I knew I had to confess it. It was mortal, it was prime, it was the ultimate--yes, my warped little mind believed this grotesque fantasy to be true. I stalled as long as I could but finally genuflected and made my stooped, stupid way to the back corner of the church and the terror awaiting in the isolation booth.

"Bless me, Father, for I have sinned. It has been a month since my last confession. Since then I've been mean to my sister, I put off taking out the trash, and I yelled at my brother sometimes." The rest was silence.

Father Plank waited a moment and then said, his aquiline nose curving toward me, probing in the gloom of that narrow house, "Anything else?"

"No, that's all," I said quickly. After all, how could I admit to committing the worst sin possible?

"Fine," he said. "Just say the rosary twice and pray for the souls in Purgatory."

Then came the usual mumbo-jumbo of "I absolve thee from all thy sins, in the name of the Father, the Son, and the Holy Ghost, Amen. Go in peace."

All that, of course, exacerbated the problem. I had also been taught by Father Plank in Sunday school that the only unpardonable sin is knowingly withholding a sin in confession. So now I had not only committed the worst sin, I had confirmed myself in it by concealing it. I was now doubly damned.

Do you see the general nature of the problem? I was conditioned to suffer guilt chronically and to require and wallow in the disquietude. So yet another month passed. Confession time rolled around, as it always did, first Sunday of the month. What was I to do? I was bound to confess that I had committed the worst sin and that I had compounded it by hiding it in confession. It was a pretty hopeless situation for a kid like me to be in. Like I always wanted and needed to do the right thing, for conscience' sake--and let's for the sake of argument acknowledge that I had a rather overwrought conscience.

On that ghostly early-hour ride to the dark, creepy cloister, the accustomed game that David and I played was relished less than usual at the thought of the impending doom looming for me--either now in the confessional or hereafter and ever. We would play an alphabet game—more structured than the "I see something green" game that my own children would eventually play in the car when I got a car and family of my own: "I see something green" (or blue or brown, etc.), like grass, or your big brother's eyes, or a passing shirt or skirt, which you had to guess at ad infinitum. No, in my rule-oriented childhood days, my brother and I would try to get through the whole alphabet by finding, in sequence, an *A*, a *B*, a *C*, a *D*, etc., on passing license plates or road signs, billboards, etc. Joe Apollonio Sheet and Metal Works near LaFayette Park was always good for a *J*, I remember. The letters I obsessed on inwardly this chilly Sunday were *D* for damned, *H* for hell, *M* for Mortal, *S* for sin, and *R* for wretched, or however you spelled it.

In the bowels of that cursed sanctum once again, I genuflected and groped my way rearward to meet my fate.

"Bless me, Father, for I have sinned. It has been a month since my last confession. Since that time I yelled at my brother, was mean to my sister, and didn't take out the trash as much as I was supposed to." Pause. Silence.

The voice behind the grate intoned, "Yes, anything else?" Pause. Silence.

Finally, in an act of superchild courage, I managed to blurt out, shaking inwardly and trembling even on the surface with tingling skin and halting breath, "Yes, I withheld a sin in confession."

Quick as a shot, the curving nose jolted up behind the pattern-pierced perforations of the screen and the tremulous, agitated voice in a bellows-whisper wheezed with utmost urgency, "What WAS it?"

With equal rush but in diminished tone, my voice as if by an automatic reflex quelled the suspense with the words, "I forget."

Incredibly, my words ended the inquisition. Without further probing of conscience, or question, or counsel, Father Plank accepted my patent lie and left it to rot in me inwardly. I left the confessional disappointed and, in my heart, unshriven--literally, doomed.

Trivial and silly as that drawn out episode seems to me, the adult, I recall it with explicit vividness and some existential bitterness. That specific guilt was subsumed by the more general, pervasive sense of unease that haunted my growing up and which found obsessive transfer to many equally absurd incidents and faux pas in later life. But I still remember it, and you might say I'll probably never absolve Father Plank or his church high and mighty for not sticking his hooks in a little deeper to root out some of my anxiety at its core, or for not, more agreeably, anointing me with some magic balm to soothe somehow my still tender and aching forehead.

5

We Don't Talk About Things Like That

WHEN I WAS LITTLE, I got a lot of my education from *The World Book*. It was easy to pick out a favorite letter of the alphabet for that day and flip around in it. You could pick a big-book letter or a little-book letter depending on your mood. *S* and *M* fit into the big category, even before I learned what those letters really meant. Some letters were combined so you could get two in at one sitting, like *U-V*. And toward the end of the alphabet things just kind of ran together in a jumble, like *W-X-Y-Z*. But that was a good one because there were a lot of maps and pictures with the war articles. World Wars One and Two loomed large in my mind, based on that volume.

Otherwise, I was not into sex and violence at all as a child. Sex was an unknown country with no maps, and I didn't like to fight. I have both sensitive skin and nerves. At day camp one summer, when boxing gloves were forced on me against another young punk, I learned that the pain of getting punched in the nose was not worth the pleasure of hitting somebody else. And as far as sex goes, I was one of the 144,000 innocents who know of only the spiritual side of heavenly bliss.

The World Book was downstairs next to the dining room table, so I often read it either in the dining room just next to my mother in the kitchen, or on the living room floor, under the feet of my mother sitting on the sofa, or davenport as my father called it. When I would come to a word I didn't understand, it was easy for me just to ask my mother rather than going to another big book to look it up. The first word I remember asking my mother to explain was *so*, so you can see this was a habit established early and often. Not that my mother's explanations were always sufficient or even correct.

One time I remember riding in the car next to my mother in the front seat. We passed a service station. *Esso,* the sign said, big and red. I worked it out, out loud, saying to no one in particular, "Three-ess-ess-oh." She was quick, however, to correct me. "No," she said, maternally. "You just pronounce the last two letters: *S - O.*" "Oh," I said, glad to be set straight.

Mercifully, she stopped there rather than countering with "Not *Oh*!! *S - O!*" Always good natured, she was never sarcastic and never tried to be funny at someone else's expense. But you can see how my education through her was partial, and lacking in context. She took the short cut of avoidance.

One afternoon, when I was a bit older, maybe eleven or twelve, pushing puberty, I was into *U-V* on the living room floor, my mother alone on the sofa hovering just above. I got to an article accompanied by a fascinating picture graph. One of the great things about *The World Book* for a kid is the visual symbols used for data. There was a graph using symbols of hospital beds--the more beds, the more sick people having the specific diseases listed in sequence from top to bottom on the left side of the chart. There was maybe a half-column-width of beds for tuberculosis (say, five small bed-icons), a quarter column or two-and-a-half beds for typhoid, just one bed for diph-theria--all of them long and hard things that I had been protected against by education and inoculation. But at the top of the chart was a category and graphic that intrigued and mystified me. It looked like there were enough hospital beds, each with an inert male stick-fig-ure in it, for every student of Alice Deal Junior High School if they would ever get this disease, whatever it was. It was a word I had never seen in print or heard spoken, as I tried to sound it out. What was this secret plague? Without looking up from the book, I matter of factly referred to my easiest prime resource, my mother:

"What does 'veen-reel' mean?" I routinely asked, expecting the usual gracious, uncomplicated answer. Her response was shocking to me in its offended, almost violent tone.

"Oh!" she gasped as if spotting for the first time an unwanted stain on the carpet. "That's something very bad! It's just a thing that shouldn't be! It's JUST awful!" End of explanation.

Her manner and agitation right away put me off of the subject. I didn't like to see my mother hurt or distressed, and Lord knows I had seen, heard, and felt enough of that over the course of my childhood from her living with my father. The picture that I was left with was just that maybe a quarter of the population in the U.S. was in bed with veen-reel disease. Which of course is true, but in a different way than I imagined or knew of. So I ceased my perusal of *The World Book* for the day. And I got no other sex education in my own household.

Not that I didn't try. But self education only goes so far alone in one's own room. And, as I was to discover, even that sanctum was not my private preserve. My main research tool consisted of *Playboy* magazine. This was at a time when I no longer shared a room with my brother, for my parents had built an extra room on the house as an addition, to be their bedroom. I have only just this moment figured out that it was so they could have a room big enough for separate beds to sleep in alone. Their old bedroom, which became my sister Marian's room, had the heirloom double bed which they had to use perforce.

The new one had twin beds too narrow for more than one person at a time. And my father almost never slept in that room at the same time as my mother anyway. He stayed up late at night into the early morning hours sitting at the davenport vacated by my mother, under the antique metal-ribbed skirt-shaped shade surrounding the three-way reading light, endlessly snipping and clipping items of no account from old newspapers which he had stacked up in closets and in his corner of the bedroom. He would snip and doze, snip and doze, then just doze till the snoring became a continuous whistle-rattle. Upstairs, when I would get up to pee, the light that seeped up from downstairs ushered my way to the bathroom. It was a remotely haunting nightlight for me, and Marian and David.

When Marian moved into what had been my parents' room, David moved out of the room that he and I shared, which was the biggest upstairs bedroom, into Marian's old room, the smallest of the three bedrooms upstairs. The room's being so tiny gave him an excuse not to spend much time in it and not to accumulate too much excess baggage into this garret, for he was hardly ever home. He did, however, have a requisite supply of softcore pornography. And I took advantage of his chronic absence by steeping myself in it. The lowest, most ancient stratum of this curious archive was pre-rock & roll, pre-*Playboy* titillation. The convention of this primitive part of the collection was that a woman could expose breast but not nipple, butt but not cleft. In as prudishly prurient a manner as possible, all kinds of contortionist bending with decolletage were dreamed up, obsessed upon, and snatched by photographers, and then by me. Uplifted T-shirts were used as nipple bras. It was fascinating, and educational. I never knew how many strange poses it was possible for a woman to strike, to hide what should by nature be revealed.

Still, there was a naturalness to it all. It was about good feelings. The settings themselves were pretty, pastoral, even reverential: Lady Godiva's bareback riding of her horse under the loose flapping tent of her hair. Lily St. Cyr in half her underwear, who obviously had God's approval, if only in name. The litany of lovelies paraded past, page after page, smiling sunshine faces unspotted by acne, skin pure and smooth, goddess bodies, every curve in due proportion, and all this forbidden fruit so delicious, this Garden of Eden, awaited my delectation, unbeknownst to their provider my brother, or to anyone. Delight was at my fingertips there in this room whenever I chose to venture in. All this pleasing reverie was available inside the house on random occasions, constituing a change of pace from the mental exertions of chess club after school or the exhausting exhilaration of baseball with my friends outdoors. It rounded out the recreational life of my magical, innocently prurient adolescence. I made my big brother's place also my own. I could be a big boy, like him. I, too, had a right to this room of dreams.

With rock & roll came *Playboy*. This was vintage stuff. Hugh Hefner, David, and I together (in our own time and place) viewed these new vistas as pioneers. I found visual fulfillment in David's room, and on occasion I imported a new model to my own room for an hour or two. I didn't read *Playboy* much, but I looked at it a fair bit.

One afternoon, when I was of early teen age, I was perusing *Playboy* quite innocently, centering my focus on the current object of contemplation, comfortably lying on my bed as was my wont, and with my door closed, or almost so. Unannounced, my mother opened my door and caught me red handed--no time to stuff the offending tome under a pillow or blanket, which I would without guilt have done gladly to shield my mother's sensibilities. Too late. Whatever errand my mother was upon, she must have instantly forgot it at sight of the spectacle before her. Her shining little boy was being defiled! Quick as an aroused scorpion, she seized the glossy pages with her long, white fingers and, standing full upright at the foot of my bed, she proceeded to rip apart, page by page, section by section, fold by fold the naked beauty within.

"That's what we do with that!" she intoned with emphasis, highly incensed. She left, taking my treasured fantasy in scraps, which I surely would have done my best to paste together if anything had been left of it.

I continued to raid David's room, more furtively and inhibitedly than before. I continued to fantasize, though not now without guilt. And my mother's impassioned but wholly shattering violation of me, in my room, even today clouds somewhat, for me, the saint's image that she earned to bear.

I must say that my mother was my only parent who tried to attend to my needs. She considered to provide for my sex education by sending me, one evening when I was in sixth grade, by myself down the block to St. Columba's Episcopal Church--the lowest Episcopal church on the East Coast--for the sake of that lowest, most degrading aspect of the human condition, the topic of sex, strictly meaning the biology of reproduction in this instance. I, as my brother David before me and my sister Marian after me, would get the single dose of medicine to last us our whole lives through and protect us from overexposure to this contagious threat. The preventive? An animated but deadly nonentertaining half-hour film called "Human Growth," with all the appeal and interest, as implied by the ominously clinical sounding title, of a film on cancerous tumors. I can remember, vaguely, cross sections of a thing sticking into another thing, and that's about all I remember of it. It didn't look like anything human to me and I learned nothing of practical benefit, use, or application present or future.

It does currently call to my mind, however, a remark my mother made to me sometime previous when I must have asked her where babies came from. She told it this way, as I recall: "Mommy loved you so much that she let daddy put his wee-wee in her to make you." This news, supposed to be reassuring, was disquieting and ridiculous to me in concept. In retrospect, it revealed her attitude to sex. It also served the purpose of squelching my normal and natural interest in this primary area at least for the moment. And that was the extent of her lecture. She left it for me to figure out how babies were made out of pee-pee. For many years after that, I was under the illusion that babies were made in the bathroom and that it was done standing up. How else could father's wee-wee be stuck in mother in such straits? It puzzled me some how the wee-wees could match since fathers were taller and mothers shorter, till I began to notice that women's hips were higher up on their legs than men's hips, and then it seemed to come together as a picture in my mind: one of the most sexless sex fantasies ever imagined, I bet.

But I did quite early find out from my mother how and why boys are different from girls in large disparity above the belt. One day when I had my shirt off I asked her, "Why do boys have these two big pimples on their chest?"

"Well, dear," she confided, "both boys and girls have those things on their chest, before God decides whether you will be a boy or a girl, so that you can be whichever God wants you to be. If God makes you a girl, they grow to give milk to your babies."

That made sense to me then, and it still does in a crude sort of way, but it's wrong in that God doesn't procrastinate in making this decision about gender.

As I got older and absorbed from the more open atmosphere outside the house some droplets of wet truth about sex, the most unthinkable, ungodly thing about it was the hypothesis that my father and mother had done this, not just once but at least three times. What's sad about my apprehension is that, I conclude, my mother had the same horror but as a married adult. And I sympathize with her. Eleanor and Alfred were worse than a mismatch. They were almost not of the same species. If some marriages are made in Heaven, that one was made by collusion of Hell and Purgatory, regarding my mother. At no time was there a mutual love in this arrangement, because my father had a condition that blocked his access to human love.

I did not know the technical nature of his problem until I was fifty years old. It was in a book Marian had gotten about psychological disorders, including Asperger's syndrome. While Marian, David, and I were growing up, we experienced Daddy as childishly crude, bad tempered, mean and inconsiderate, given to tantrums and tirades unpredictably and unprovoked. I didn't consider that he was perhaps mentally ill. For even as children, we are encounter-ordered people, and we abstract from such meetings or acquaintances not only an idea of orderly behavior but of patterns of disorderly behavior. And Daddy fit no such scheme, was incomparably out of touch.

There seemed to be no other such kind of person in the world of experience. A spilled glass of milk was a catastrophe loosening a demon: "God damn son of a bitch!" not spoken but yelled as if a warning to run like hell, which we would have done if we had had the wherewithal to do so, but the string of profanity dumbed down to an infantile potpourri of bathroom words from a long dead idiot's idiolect: "Schmuck! Pot! Doodoo! Stink!" spat out directly toward the offending toddler, usually David or me. I could go on, and I will presently, but this example typifies the nature of his disorder, which in general terms was an inability to connect to others in context, a total incapacity for human empathy, an emotional shut-in. It was an intense sort of autism in adulthood, and there is a growing body of documentation of this syndrome detailing symptoms similar to Alfred's.

You could see it in his eyes. They were dull, almost as if filmed over. They were not evil eyes, but nobody was at home on the other side as you tried to look into their window. The voice, powerful enough to be an opera singer's, if he had had any control over it, languished in long yawns over his do-nothing life at home, and was abused in a ludicrous, infantile way around the house. He trumpeted his presence, a call to the only attention he knew how to draw, that of disgust, but at least an acknowledgment of his existence, through belching. He elongated the burp and liked to sing body-odor smell words within the belch: "Beeee-oh, Beeee-oh, Beeyo-Beeyo-Beeeeee-oh." He accompanied too often these vocal abominations with modulated and extended farting. He paraded from room to room doing this, upstairs and down.

It was an emotional disability, not an intellectual one. He had a degree in electrical engineering and a graduate degree in law. He could do not only advanced math but write urbane and cogent letters to the editor of *The Washington Post,* usually on issues of mass transportation, and almost all of them were duly published. And of course it was that part of him that attracted and fooled my mother into this farce of a marriage. He didn't burp and fart and yell and cuss in baby talk when they dated.

And now she was stuck with him, on religious grounds. For her it was a fast track to Heaven--a quick exit from this vale of tears. And she shed more than her share. But to stay with Alfred, she obviously, ironically, had to turn her back on sex. And that big denial deprived her children of an essential part of their development in the facts of life, as life and love should be lived.

I remember one Sunday as we were all in the car going down Massachusetts Avenue on the way to St. James, the high (Episcopal) church experience. Past the traffic light at the intersection of Reno Road, I began complaining in some vague way about having to get up early to go to church. My mother had a ready, prepackaged answer for that foray into blasphemy, heresy, and sloth. Half turning her head toward me in the back seat, where I was between Marian and David, she instructed me: "You don't know. You might be dead in two weeks." I still find those to be frightening words to a child of tender years and feelings such as I was. I have by now guessed, however, that she was speaking those words for herself rather than for me. Her destiny was not here. She was building a mansion in the sky.

That's the home she really wanted, and she wanted me there too, in the most innocent of ways. For there is no sex in heaven. And, more the pity, for her there wasn't any worthy of the name on earth either.

It was Elsie, my grandmother, who was there when I needed to be confirmed in the belief that sex is a big part of what adult life is all about. I married Barbara K. in January 1964. She was Roman Catholic, the "universal church" not in those days being quite so obstinately "catholic" as St. James Anglo-Catholic parish in its downtown timewarp. Good Pope John, with his then-recent encyclical which I recall by the title "Human Growth," though I probably misquote, had reaffirmed the Church's ban on artificial birth control. Elsie knew the burden of too many children. Long ago, she had determined in her case that two were too many, for when a young widow she gave up her infant second born daughter, my mother's sister, to family friends to raise. So to me, the bridegroom, she gave a double pack of Nonoxynol for unbridled use and, without a word of instruction or advice from her own mouth, packed it up in a box with marital sex manuals, as a special gift for me to study for myself into the night.

I was gratified at this prospect. Barbara's sex education, however, was from nuns, and she hadn't yet quite arrived to readiness for self discovery through the unfettered sexual bonding which, in my opinion, is what lifts marriage up from the bondage of earth to the realm of the shooting stars into the Empyrean and beyond. But I loved Barbara beyond bounds. She was that miracle of miracles, my saintly mother in nubile form. Barbara and I made a good go of it for twenty-five years. Not bad for two people who had known little of the opposite sex but each other. As it turned out, we both eventually had to find out about the wider world on our own, take a separate path, and go down that lonesome road with somebody else.

6

One Shoe Off and One Shoe On

LIFE IS HARD ENOUGH WITHOUT having to work at it to make it harder than it already is. Live and let live is a useful precept too often unheeded. Like when I got a speeding ticket for twelve miles over the limit on an open road at 6 a.m. (67 in a 55 m.p.h. zone). Nobody was hurt by that violation and nobody was helped by that correction. Society was not improved by the authorities' intervention, and I was diminished by it, or my wallet was anyway. Likewise, in the daily round, one's work is hard enough without having a mean boss to make it unbearable. My rebellion against such a situation sometimes has taken unusual forms.

My first job after college graduation was as a technical writer for the Atomic Energy Division of Allis-Chalmers Manufacturing Company, Bethesda, Maryland, beginning February 1964. It was sort of fun at first, a new experience correcting others' written work instead of having one's own efforts red-penciled, or red-penned, as had been the case for my previous ten or fifteen years at school. A-C's Atomic Energy Division had a number of existing reactors generating an endless stream of technical progress reports and updates. Two of the most productive were the La Crosse Boiling Water Reactor in Wisconsin, termed LACBWR (pronounced "lackbarr"), and the Air Force Nuclear Engineering Test Reactor in Dayton, Ohio, known as AFNETR (pronounced "affnetter"). We were learning to speak acronymese, one of the linguistic requirements of the job, early in the game.

The work at Allis-Chalmers tended to come in fits, a period of overload followed by indeterminate lulls. When there was no work in the hopper, you were supposed to sit at your desk and "look busy." My office mate Jim would, for example, take out a technical manual and immediately insert into its middle a recent or vintage copy of *Playboy* magazine to surreptitiously pore over.

I myself might pull out the *Webster's Collegiate Dictionary* on my desk and read snatches at random, perusing and pondering its infinite riches, boning up for the next esoteric assignment I would imminently have to launch into, learning old words new to me, like *alembic*: "something that refines or transmutes as if by distillation." *Alembic* described my own function, really, namely transmuting mush by distillation into more spirited stuff with my alembic, namely a Bic. And since I was a newly minted college graduate, my transmuting, distilling instrument was, so to speak, my "alum Bic." Oh, I'm ever so clever, thought I, trying to fortify my ego strength in the new arena opening up after Commencement. In retrospect, that word *alembic* still comes first now to my memory, implying that I may have attempted to read that good book of Webster's through, starting with *A*. This enforced killing of time also marked the onset of a killing period in my life.

At yawning times like these I began to exude symptoms of not having hit upon my true calling. The rhythms, constraints, and vagaries of the time-bound corporate world seemed out of sync to me inwardly. I thereupon developed a grotesque habit beyond mere fidgeting or twiddling, to me humiliating in retrospect as a novel display of the uncouth.

I've seen colleagues extract impacted tubes of their own ear wax with half untwisted paper clips, but my little trick outdid any such quasi-purgative routine. When I tired of reading the dictionary, I put it aside, pondered the smooth even green of the oversize desktop ink blotter, which was maybe a twenty by thirty inch rectangle covering the central space of the faux wood that I leaned my elbows on. And then I would further pass the time by running my fingers through my hair, a luxuriant thick dark brown pompadoured mat billowing down into those moderately long fashionable sideburns of the 1960's.

As my fingers dug deeper into and under my hair, fingernails would search out and scrape miniscule excrescences from my scalp.

This mother-lode of dandruff produced flakes of assorted size and shape, settling snowflake-like upon the green felt, eventually covering this pseudo-lawnscape with an even drift side to side and corner to corner, an off-white dusting of the expanse. Then gingerly I would lift up the blotter, poise it dead center over the trash can beside my desk, and bemusedly shake a downy cascade into the bin.

That I could do this chronically despite a daily shampooing with Head and Shoulders vexed and fascinated me, this shedding, this sloughing off. The undercrust was thankfully invisible to the world at large; my hair showed no dandruff whenever I looked in a mirror. So, was my innermost brain going to seed in this downtime, drying up to eventually blow away like chaff in the wind? Jim seemed too absorbed in *Playboy* to notice what I was up to by way of keeping busy with my otherwise idle hands. I hasten to add, parenthetically, that I no longer foul the environment around me in this wretched way. In fact, only during this one year of tears did it happen. Now, not enough hair is left on my head to be worth scratching, and the shampoo I use anymore is Shed and Holders, which sweeps clean and sets firm.

I also recall, with more nostalgia and grace, the coffee breaks that would sometimes even begin our day in the office before we dug into the pile of manuscripts waiting to be ripped to shreds by our editorial acumen. We would ease into our professional tasks by pre-professional preparation such as studying the morning newspaper, comics and all. The Jumble was the highlight of those diversions. Technical editors, production editors, secretaries would all crowd around the Jumble page, and we would apply our collective heads to each scrambled entry in sequence. I recall with pride being the first, one morning, to decipher the string GUREBO, namely, *brogue*. That success was not only the high point of my day but also perhaps of my entire career of just under three years as a technical writer. I had entered upon a journey that would become an agonizingly protracted false start.

My first boss in this job was a dwarfish, round faced fellow with bottle-bottom-thick red-rimmed glasses, a man whose name I don't recall perhaps because he seemed insignificant, a nonentity albeit a genial, benign sort of sprite. The only correction I recall him ever making to my work was in a description of some concrete settings for an atomic reactor. The text I was editing referred to a certain pouring of concrete called pour number nine. He matter of factly suggested to me that since it was the name of a particular pouring of concrete it could be dignified as a proper noun and graced with initial capitals as Pour Number Nine. That struck me as a reasonable though entirely inconsequential suggestion. I have a thin skin and do not take criticism well, so inconsequential reasonable suggestions suit me just fine.

Tragically, boss number one (I revert to lower case in deference to inconsequential nonentity) died within a couple of months of my taking the job. He took sick and kicked the bucket, just like that. Cause of death: undiagnosed terminal colitis, it was said. All of us in the office were shocked and saddened by this unexpected calamity. This nice little man was not at all elderly. What other, unlooked for catastrophe might next befall? The answer to that unspoken question came soon enough, as it turned out. It took the form of an apparition in the flesh, an ogre from the realm of nightmare. It was boss number two, whose name I actually do recall. To my mind his signature took the form of John Crotchforth, though whether that was his true name or just a poison-pen-pal name will go unsaid. I hope he's dead by now, after the lapse of these more than four decades, lest he be offended in the flesh by me at this point. He wasn't all bad, actually. Nobody is, so they say, hard to believe as it is regarding some folk we all have known. He even sent me a Christmas card once. Whoopee!

He walked in mincing steps, pigeon-toed. His face was stubble, the only manly aspect about him. Shot-glass-thick spectacles, wire-rimmed, pinching into his temples and behind his ears. A stooping, drooping gait, paunchy gut, shirt half pulling out up from the belt. Voice a half lisping high drone, Capote-inspired. Had a master's degree, so they said. Taught a course at American University, part-time instructor, providing at least a one-case example of "Them that can't, teach." So they hired this guy because of the master's degree and the teaching credential, let's suppose. We felt sorry for students that fell afoul of him. The office was demonstration enough that he couldn't teach. One day he paraded around showing off his editing bible, a booklet titled "Take the Fog Out of Your Writing." It prescribed to write by formula, and he took it literally.

Jim and I heard him, from his office next to ours, counting out the syllables in each sentence of text, adding and dividing to compute ratios and quotients of every string of letters and words that crossed his desk. His myopic method of close analysis was in due course applied to a piece that had slipped through my hands into his, or rather been snatched away by him as I was working on it. From the interior of his sanctum the clack of the adding machine could be heard crunching the words and syllables into numbered bits and pieces.

After many minutes of clacking and crunching, from the abused machine's grinding away underneath Mr. J. C.'s audible heavy labored breaths, came a staccato, almost obscene summons: "Dick!" In effect, this four-letter epithet seemed like cussing, altogether a quite improper noun as it tore into my ear and ego. Gad, he was asking for and challenging me to come in and defend myself, if I could.

So I entered into his little world. With a mocking smile he bade me come closer up to his desk so I could see what he was doing to my work. Early in the first paragraph of text he honed in on a compound sentence, one with two independent clauses, like "Prices rose and profits fell." Pointing to the words on the page with a stubby, crooked finger, he intoned, "See this sentence? See this conjunction? PUNCTUATE!"

That word, spat out and punctuated by his own sputum on the *p*, took me aback, violated my space and my rightful place as a professional wordsmith. I knew the rule he alluded to, and I also knew the exception to the rule obviating the punctuating in this case. Maybe his pusillanimous universe was too circumscribed to admit of qualification or expiation. Really, no punctuation is needed in a terse compound sentence; for example, *Birds fly and fish swim*. No pause, no suspense, no confusion. Why bother with clutter? Less is more in this instance. But I didn't argue. He was imperious, impervious. I beat a hasty retreat and vowed to make myself as scarce as possible while searching for another job, any job but this.

I had opportunity, means, and motive to absent myself from my desk for long forays into the corridors of the five-story office building on Arlington Road. I expanded my horizons hourly, exploring and staking out every available nook beyond the dreaded lair where that jerk lurked. As a technical writer, a large part of my job, indeed the backbone of it, was to get context and detail accurate according to the intent of the scientist or engineer who drafted the original text. In short, our job was to translate the jargon of highly educated and sophisticated but too often semi-literate technocrats into more or less plain English or at least understandable English while maintaining fidelity of content. It was a fine line. Ordinary English is often not adequate to advanced technology.

Yet the polysyllabic jargon handed down to us was typically overloaded, an abomination of obfuscation so to speak. So the tech writer or editor logged several miles a week, it seemed, walking the halls hunting down the chemists, physicists, nuclear engineers, computer systems analysts responsible for the gibberish that we had to squeeze meaning from. Some scientists are easy to work with in this vein, some not. Some are even good writers, but not most. Yet, unlike our own big cheese, all were at least reasonable facsimiles of human beings, and I enjoyed hanging out evermore around them, getting to know them better, hearing their side of the story, and learning more and more myself about atomic reactors.

And I became increasingly abstracted, ever more lost in a daydream world. I had gotten used to escaping emotional disaster by that means from my earliest years anyway. Actually, my mind was easily preoccupied by science, which is what attracted me to this company in the first place.

On my own time, from schooldays onward, I cheerfully had memorized the eras of geologic time, from Cambrian to Pleistocene. I found I could make up clever mnemonic devices, more literary or at least more lexical than mere acronyms, to call everything to mind in sequence: Cambrian, Ordovician, Silurian, Devonian, Carboniferous,

Permian, Triassic, Jurassic, Cretaceous, Tertiary, Pleistocene. Or, in initial cap vernacular, Can Old Souls Drive Cars Peeling Tires Just Crazily To Pieces? And the fact that strata, for example, contained the successive fossils in layers, like multicolored pages in a colossal cosmic book of life, endlessly fascinated me. Still does.

And I continue to find refuge in reverie, pondering time-scapes and picturing landscapes beyond the personal microcosm. Anytime I drive through the big cut in Sideling Hill, west of Hancock, Maryland, on Interstate 68, I behold the syncline of the exposed layers that open to view a miltidecker concave sandwich squeezing a dozen U-letter shapes of compressed rock together top to bottom like so many giant sized Dixie party cups or immense bowls stacked inside each other and cut through vertically—a black layer curving down and then up, laid above but tucked inside the next layer of brown supporting the black layer and hugged underneath by the grey layer which is cradled by the tan layer just below, and so on, all piled high in evenly bent stripes mirrored on either side of the roadway that runs through the huge gash of the cut: layered folds stuck together as if forever.

But the edges of the strata on the outward sides of the mountain disappear into the open air. How did the continuation of those layers get taken away? Clearly these interlocked U-shapes constituted the primeval valley between old Appalachian peaks that towered above them on either side eons ago, that out-topped the height of today's Rockies. The old valley now peaks up on its own as today's Sideling Hill Mountain. The old ghost mountains straddling both sides of that valley, which is now a precipitously sloped mountain, got washed away by rains and snows of yesteryear. Science in this manner proves out even the Old Testament prophets: "Every valley shall be exalted and every mountain and hill laid low."

In the mid-1960's, atomic reactors seemed the way of the future, the answer to the looming energy crisis. Later, after the Chernoble and Three-Mile Island emission accidents in particular, they languished particularly in the U.S., and Allis-Chalmers no longer maintained an Atomic Energy Division. But I have always been hot for atomic matter, then and now. Protons, neutrons, gluons, quarks--new cutting-edge theory and technology, new quirky terms emblematic of creativity at its highest and latest advance. New theories of Everything, and of Nothing. Ultimate philosophy.

Why, for example, is there not Nothing everywhere? An empty cosmos. How do we explain pre-Big-Bang? Eventually I found a metaphorical linguistic solution to this scientific and existential conundrum, in a noncompound, noncomplex two-word sentence of my own devising, my own interpretive deep structure. It is, simply, this utterance: Nothing Matters. Meaning, in the action sense of the verb, that Nothing does Matter; Matter is made by No Thing. It reconfigures the old theological argument of God's Creation *ex nihilo*: something, i.e., everything, from Nothing. Current atomic physics claims to demonstrate the same anomaly mathematically and experientially. Subatomic particles are found to flit in and out of existence in a void, from a dark vacuum. Another verbal form of the same idea, the same paradox, is Nothing Can Not Exist. In other words, matter is created *ex nihilo*. And Nothing is denied as an entity. It does not exist. Only Everything, or Anything, can exist.

The Einsteinian matter enabling Allis-Chalmers Atomic Energy Division was thus, for me at first, a manifestation of the mystery entrancing my being. It was science, philosophy, linguistics in action. I had invested my waking energy, my intellect, and my good will into this worthwhile enterprise. And now that lofty thing was being trounced upon, degraded, finally shattered to smithereens, atomized in the most nihilistic sense. I had been exiled to walk back and forth from hall to hall, pillar to post, toiling up and down the endless stairs, a latter-day Sisyphus on a fool's errand for Mr. J.C., my Anti-Christ.

On an occasional day off I could pursue my desperate job hunt by dint of personal interview, following up leads from various sources, announcements, and contacts. Meanwhile, my workaday world was transmuting surreally into a kind of death-in-life pageant, a make-believe go-through-the-motions holding pattern for the sake of a paycheck. I became not exactly a zombie, an undead, but a nonperson in the sense that I felt so ill at ease that I was no longer my own person, was no longer myself while tiptoeing around that office.

I managed to spend much, even most of my time at work, outside of my and Jim's office by haunting the offices of the scientists and engineers, talking with them about their manuscript which I was editing, their own background, their own wanderings. I even learned, by dint of unstinting questioning, that some had graduated from the college of life rather than an accredited institution. "There is no sheepskin," one of them said to me once when I asked which degree he had received from the university he attended, listed on his resume. It mattered not. He was obviously competent, sheepskin or no, which my own boss, with two sheepskins, wasn't.

One fine-seeming morning, weatherwise, in the midst of this malaise, I dragged myself out of bed later than usual, each day's attempt to rise above it all being harder than the last. Glancing at the clock again, I realized I had little or no time to dress and get ready for work. Eyes still half closed, I slapped on the nearest suit to-hand, grabbed under the bed for my shoes, and bolted out the door and into my little old English Ford, which I had paid a cool two hundred dollars for, still a significant chunk of my annual salary of $5820. I felt unusually leaden that day, cared little for what was in store at work, and wondered why I even bothered to try to arrive on time, though it was requisite that I at least make an initial appearance in the office at 8:30 a.m. before undertaking my now accustomed corridor-odyssey escape.

Perhaps about halfway into my commute from North Arlington, Virginia, across the Potomac River at Chain Bridge to Bethesda, Maryland, I became aware of an anomaly in my work outfit for the day. In this era the workplace was a formal venue: sartorially rigorous, equally for men and women. For men, a tailored suit, button-down shirt, Windsor-knotted necktie. Nothing casual or offbeat factored into the dress code. As was my custom I had on a suit jacket with matching trousers, white dress shirt, conservative dark blue tie, solid black dress socks, and, lo and behold, nonmatching footwear.

One foot was shod properly enough—a crisp looking fashionable oxford hard leather dress shoe, recently polished to an ox-blood sheen. On the other foot, inexplicably, a rubber-soled hourglass-shaped protruding and curvilinear-toed red and white basketball shoe. I marveled at the incongruity. Unfortunately, this was not Freaky Friday. That hadn't been invented yet.

True, I had a choice. I could turn around, go back home, call in sick or something. But that was the coward's way. No, I would bluff my way through the day, somehow. It offered after all a challenge to be creative. At least it was something different, not just the same old same old. How would I pull this one off, I wondered. I was unhinged enough to try.

I pulled my English Ford into the parking lot on time. Well, I accomplished that first task of punctuality just fine. No one yet knows I'm a world-class jackass. The first hurdle was the security guard's desk. I sauntered in, affecting gaiety. "Good morning, Joe," I ventured, all smiles, hoping to attract his gaze into my face rather than down to my feet. I was already learning to alter my walk a bit so as to hide the nontraditional shoe from view till the last possible second. It seemed feasible to do it with one giant step with the right or good foot and an inline catching-up step directly behind it with the non-kosher foot. A pause midway up the aisle might perhaps facilitate regaining balance a bit, while leaning or bending casually against a railing as if to make small talk, concealing the clown shoe by lifting it behind the opposite calf. Then when the interlocutor's glance turns aside momentarily, a bold advance with the good foot followed by a quick whisk of the basketball foot to maintain equilibrium and keep pace, arms held straight and low, palms spread to aid in screening the red and white flash before your greeter can take it all in. Yes, I may have fooled old Joe. He's sworn to secrecy anyway, to protect his friends and coworkers from all enemies foreign and domestic. My scruffy foot is no threat, although not according to protocol. I'm cool so far.

Luck is with me. Nobody in the immediate vicinity past the guard desk down the hall to my office. My desk is at the far wall, below and against the window, opposite the doorway entry. Jim's desk is halfway between the door and my desk, facing the door, its left edge flush to the wall ahead on my right. Jim is already there, unfolding *The Washington Post*, just about to lift his eyes to greet me.

With bravado I sweep through the door, prominently displaying my one good oxford. Quick as a cat I jolt almost in one bound into my waiting swivel chair and swerve it deskward and window-ward, jamming the basketball foot deep under the farthest recess of the desk's central cavity. Safe at home, or what should be my home away from home, though of course that was no longer so. I turn my shoulders sideways and thrust my head and neck over my back to return Jim's truncated greeting. "Hey, Jim. How's it going?" You may understand that Jim was already a bit accustomed to weirdness from me, and yet this prelude to the daily grind was a novel twist. "Hey, what's new?" he said.

Did he in fact perceive, even at this early juncture, something more out of the ordinary than usual? I forewent that morning's Jumble and lost myself as long as I could manage in *Webster's Collegiate Dictionary*, researching ever more abstruse words to befit the uncanny nature of my plight: *exiguous? occluded? besmirched? unbeknownst?* Finally, I could stall no longer and had to take up some work left over from the previous day. It was a nearly finished job that was due to the typist that morning. How would I get through that?

I waited till Jim got up and left his desk. I picked up the prepared manuscript and negotiated my way, so far unseen, toward the secretarial suite where our typists' desks were, and they were almost always at their desks, slaving away, martyrs to the modern machine age. Our main secretary-typist was in fact a wonder woman, Joan, as much the equal to any man as was Joan of Arc. Short raven-black hair, deeply tanned skin, slim athletic figure, student of human nature, a kind, empathetic person, salt of the earth. Sensuous tenor voice, would inevitably greet me with the ingratiating salutation, "Hello, Dolly!" in dulcet, satirically unctuous tones. I loved her purely and truly as a kindred spirit, a platonic soulmate, though really I knew her hardly at all, just sensed a warm deep benevolence radiating out from her.

She, if anyone, would be able to understand my ridiculousness in any form. Why not show and tell all, to her at least? Well, I couldn't. It was too humbling for my ego to undertake such a dare. No, I would go down in flames trying to hide the obvious, that I was a fool of fools.

From outside the door I calculated the distance between the doorway of Joan's office over to her desk, peering out from around the corner as if up to no good. Only about ten feet. One good lunge and I'd make it. She seemed momentarily to look off in the other direction. Now or never. I fairly leaped ala John Wilkes Booth onto the stage and in a single bound, ala Superman, over to the front of her desk, half breathless with the tension, and cleverly thrust my offending appendage into the dark haven of the undercarriage of her desk, as if that were acceptable.

"Well, Hello, Dolly!" she opened, unruffled. "Here's the goods for today, just for you," I countered graciously. Apparently she suspected nothing. After all, what had she to fear from me? "Thanks a bunch, Mr. Richard," said she, rhetorically affecting gratitude though with all the good will in the world.

She resumed her labor. More bouncy than quicksilver I hop-scotched deftly back and out, careful to shield the untoward part of my getup by pretending a limp, as if from the strain of a recent backyard touch football brawl.

Well, that was three hurdles tried and made: the guard, Jim, Joan. One more to go and I was home, really home, free. Next was Strawson, the nuclear physicist author of my newest assignment. I would have to run the gauntlet from my office up three stories, into, through, and out of Strawson's office, back to my office, and finally back out past the guard and then on to home, which I could get to and from on a mildly extended lunch hour, thereupon a quick change of footgear and no one the wiser, maybe, though why should I care anyway, such was my current hatred for the place. On to Strawson and damn the torpedoes, nevertheless.

Strawson had advanced sheepskins and all the class I lacked. But we had mutual respect for each other and I enjoyed working with him more than with just about anyone else. I certainly didn't want to betray to him the current clunkiness of my essence. I would do my utmost to save face and put my best foot forward.

I snuck again out of my office into the empty hallway, up the end-of-corridor stairs—much safer for me in my condition than the elevator where I could be trapped like a rat—to the fourth floor and slyly down to Strawson's office, door open as always. I paused outside the doorway a second or two to plan my entrance and exit strategy. None of the technical staff offices were large. I could make it to the front of his desk, conduct our business up close while hiding my foot underneath the desk as I had trained myself to do, then, lightning-like, flash back and out before realization of anything out of the ordinary could register.

Concealing my bad shoe as best I could, I swung my good foot into the door first, struck a sideways pose to bring the trailing foot along in parallel, choreographing the move to try to block the shoe from view. But at this point I was only halfway to the desk, in an awkward sort of profile, stuck in limbo. I couldn't hold like that for long, so I took a half sidestep with my good foot and, focusing all my athletic abilities and sleight-of-foot into one deft effort, I swung my basketball shoe in a slide as if having slipped so that my body half falling could mask that foot while the gym shoe lurched toward the bottom edge of Strawson's desk. I thereupon stood straddle-legged, odd foot just under the desk, good foot stretched out in full display for effect, almost pridefully. "Did you hurt yourself?" Strawson offered, genuinely concerned at my faltering. "Oh no, I'm fine. Waxed floor, I guess," said I, lamely.

Strawson looked bemused, mildly confused at my plight. But my calm smoothness in sliding his manuscript over across his desk toward him momentarily eased his alarm. "Your writing's pretty good," I assured him, and that was indeed true. Strawson was one of the few Renaissance persons on the technical staff, good at everything, even writing, and it was a pleasure and an education for me to read his work.

We made some small talk while I brandished my good shoe around, basketball shoe still secured at an oblique angle below. He answered a few minor questions I had about the text, and yet all this contrived normalcy of exchange only served to unnerve me. I was putting on a sham show with my shoe and all. My mind and both my feet were out of joint in this facility which had collapsed my psyche so utterly, blasting me in my need to succeed in the world at large. I felt I must take leave even of my best technical friend, make a clean break for it, and finally get out into the fresh air of freedom. "Okay, Dave," I said to Strawson, in a friendly bid of farewell. "I'll polish this one up for you in no time. It's a work of art as well as of science." "Thanks, Rich," came the gracious reply.

But there was no help for it any longer. The jig was up. As I extricated my sinister foot, it swung out wide enough, despite or because of my gyrations, to fall into full view, basketball toe stubbing ignobly on the linoleum-tile floor. All too obvious. Dave's eyes bugged out a bit, as if in disbelief. He said nothing but I could sense bewilderment in him. I was exposed. In this abject moment I felt I had become a fraud akin to my nemesis as an object worthy of ridicule. Nothing mattered further. Just time enough left to move on and be done with it.

I did find another job within the year, System Sciences Corporation (now Computer Science Corporation), Falls Church, Virginia. Its duties were in fact similar: Technical Editor but with production oversight for the job from drafting to artwork to print shop, substantially more responsibility, and a nice guy for a boss, with the unlikely name of Gene Rasp, a grating name but a deep soothing voice profoundly mellow and kindly, a surrogate father figure for me, a true gentleman who let you do your work and trusted in the goodness of it. I loved him for it. He had a stash of *Playboy* magazines in his desk too, as yet allowable within the double-standard of the time, which my new office mate, also named Jim, used to pull out and peek at during lunch hour.

But at this stage I didn't need cheap thrills. I had been saved. All I had to do now was pick up the pieces, rebuild my public life, solve the jigsaw puzzle that the shattering of my dreams presented to me, begird myself anew, walk the next extra mile in other shoes--those of my regenerated self--then begin to go for it all, at a run.

7

Rebel's Grave

WHEN A DOG CHEWS ON a bone, it is a savory experience, not an occasion for thought. The dog is untroubled by any speculation that its own bones will somehow, someday, meet a similar fate. Indeed, dogs are known to bury chosen bones in anticipation of their own personal resurrection of them. We stopped giving Rebel real bones because the vet advised they might splinter and possibly choke her. We settled for biscuit bones: atomized, metamorphosed bone meal. Better safe than sorry, though Rebel never seemed to suffer from real bones in any way and easily reduced any animal bone quickly not just to splinters but to smithereens. Despite the mortality that dogs everywhere enforce and relish in feasting upon the bones of other creatures, they live free of care from their own inevitable grinding up. Humans can live or pretend to live with the same gusto, but it's with the awareness that we have to make the most of our little space of time. Rebel's death in a curious way intensified my own musing and chewing on this matter of spirit versus flesh and bone.

Rebel died in April 1995. My mother died in December 1978. I visit Rebel's grave from time to time, and attentively. In the more than two decades since my mother died, I haven't ever visited her grave. I didn't realize this disparity of justice until my last visit to Rebel's grave while I was walking Buddy a couple of weeks ago, and it set me to thinking. Did Rebel mean so much more to me than my mother did? Of course not. I revere and honor my mother and her memory. I merely respect Rebel's memory. That's what I think and feel, even if it's not what my action or inaction would imply. My mother and I were deeply kindred souls. Rebel just had "spirit." As imperfect creatures, my mother and I had much more in common. Our loads were internal and largely hidden. Rebel was messy more up front, so to speak.

I live near Rebel's grave and not my mother's. I held Rebel as she was dying, and then I buried her with my own hands. And I built Rebel's tomb and monument--a cairn of rocks carefully laid next to a nurse log, deliberately set under the grandest tree of the neighborhood woods just a few meters off the walking trail that goes through it, and several rods down from the path's entry into the sylvan refuge that the woods represents even in this small, mountain town. When I walk Buddy, it's easy for me to check on how Rebel's grave is doing, and so I routinely look in upon where Rebel is.

With my mother's grave, the situation is not naturally easy, routine, or ritualized. I live three hours' drive from D.C., where she is buried in Rock Creek Cemetery, next to my grandmother, who outlived her by fourteen years, and to my father, who died a year before my mother. So I could get three visits in for the pain of one, and still I don't go out of my way to do it. I wouldn't mind it, but it never seems to occur to me as being important. It would mean nothing to them. On the other hand, which is what I have to ask, what would it mean to me? Visiting Rebel's grave is significant to me and I have little trouble appreciating that. Why are my parents and my closest grandparent ignored in this way? I ponder whether this neglect is subconsciously wilful or simply happenstance, without any symbolic meaning. Tentatively, I tried to assume the latter, because I don't avoid visiting the cemetery, I just don't get around to it and nobody knows the difference, even though I go to D.C. many times a year. But I want to make a visit, and soon.

I was at my mother's side when she died in the nursing home, and with my grandmother when she died in the hospital. I saw my mother and then my grandmother each take their last breath and hold it forever. And I was moved to tears for Eleanor and for Elsie. I held their hands and kissed their faces in life and death. And a lot of me went up with both of them.

Rebel was a matriarch too, in her own way. My family was rich with female role models, as if to make up for something missing on the other side in the older generation. My mother, grandmother, and father do not fit together as a threesome. Though they now lie side by side, that is not particularly fitting, for they had nothing in common as human characters and they were not family as a working unit. The death moment of each of the four whose memory I ponder was befitting of their life. My closeness to them at their passing bespoke their bond to me--and by extension to family--frozen in time and eternity as it was in all the years that their lives and mine touched. My father died without warning in his sleep at home, alone.

Rebel died in my arms. I put her in a blanket and carried her into the woods. I found the one suitable tree to put her by--an oak, I guess, old-growth, prime condition, eighty feet high, gigantic trunk, a natural clearing around its base and root system--the landmark of the forest, tree of trees, proud and flourishing. Its main branches were high and full, like smooth muscled existential arms, a primitive confluence of Mother Nature and Father Time uplifting from ages ago. This was one heaven of a tree. I dug out a hollow with the shovel I brought with me. The ground there sloped gradually and gracefully up. I put Rebel, still in the blanket--a soft, Indian blanket--on her side with her head on the high part of the incline. Around her neck was a small tag, a thin tin-wire circle housing a coin-sized piece of paper on which I wrote, on the spot with a Bic pen, *REBEL, 1977-1995, age 108 years. Love, The Trasks.*

I nestled her in place and covered her blanketed body over with the fresh moss and dirt I had just unearthed. I smoothed it down and made everything straight and even, on this gentle slope under the green cover of the guardian oak. And then I built her monument. It was one hundred percent rock, quarried from the surface of that garden plot. Cream and tan colored stone, naturally chiseled to fit together as if by design of the wood-spirit. One solid tier of hard, heavy roof, jammed tight in, each neighbor rock supporting the one above it on the incline and held fast on the side by its companion piece. This grave was a preserve. I stepped back and looked down at it, and I saw that it was good.

Perhaps something more than a year after Rebel died, a fierce thunder and lightning storm hit town. A tremendous bolt struck the tree dead center and sheared off one of its main massive branching arms to the three-quarter point and peeled it over in a long curving arch so that its leaving stems now stick, root-like, into the ground. This accident was an ostensible calamity to me as a lover of our dwindling store of ancient trees and as the creator of this special shrine. But it has not diminished the integrity of the place one whit. The tree lives still, and now the fallen-branch bridge bends over above and just to the side and behind of Rebel's grave, making the place an arbor and a bower. Rebel's grave endures as poignant as ever, even more so with the fall and survival of its woodland sentinel. For me, it is all an eternal wonder as great as any Pyramid.

And were an earthquake to scatter the stones, and toss Rebel's bones asunder, I would pick up, gather, sort, and build it all over again, as long as I'm walking around in the neighborhood.

8

The Road Runner

I LIKE TO THINK OF myself as a sensitive soul, in tune to the concerns and needs of others as well as to my own deep, almost unfathomable wants and desires. Yet I wear my macho gringo imprinting etched deep in my skin, as intractably calloused over as the sundry scars and chafings of my earliest childhood. I am in my deepest heart an arch-romantic, in love with the sky that arcs over my head and blows and snows around me, and enamored of Nature's grandiose manifestations of earth, air, fire, and water--Yosemite Falls, Glacier Point, Devil's Tower, the Mississippi, Joyce Kilmer Forest, the Shenandoah, Topsail Beach. I love these and countless other prominences on the face of the natural world, and also the nameless, numberless spaces between that are still open and breezy, free from too clammy a human hand--the cornfields of the Midwest, the waving highgrass plains farther on, and the hillocks and rivulets everywhere both in the heart and the extremities of the land.

But I carry old-time religion in my brain. It tells me that "perfect love casts out fear." By this creed I love my natural world all too imperfectly. I fear heights, thunder, sleet and hail in a way that, I have read, my American Indian brothers and sisters did not. Overall, I respond to Nature often glibly and shallowly rather than imbibing it into my very being or making the river my own lifeblood or the lightning the fire in my eye. I have become more aware that I've as yet only wet my feet in Nature's inexhaustible fountain. A little glimpse of glory opened up to me when I got my feet wet during a day in a week's sojourn on the desert rim of Ghost Ranch, New Mexico.

Late in the afternoon there was a mushroom cloud shrouding Mesa Montosa. It was gigantic, miles high and wide, exponentially thicker and more vast than the stringy and teetering primitive atomic plume clouds that were manmade nearby six fleeting decades ago. Above me right now was the goddess of all skyfoam, Mother Nature nude and rude. The grayblack bloated mass covered half of the right horizon symmetrically like an oversized cupful of heavy heaven hung upside down, overspreading the long, prone spiny uplift of the mesa yonder. The mega-cloud's roots of rain dangled in a filmy dark curtain, a dank translucent skirt swaying in slow motion below the hugeness above it which roiled like a primeval tornado or a hundred tornado tops jammed tight into each other in an epic bulge, charcoal colored, spectacularly horrific. I was witnessing Nature's H-Bomb, a gigamegaton desert thunderstorm.

It coincided exactly with my afternoon run in the desert, with me having prepared myself by being all sunblocked up and longsleeve shirted as is my usual practice, like I had read how to do in *Outside* magazine. There was about ten miles between me and the rain. Just right for a cosmic game of chicken, my inner *Sports Illustrated* persona told me. The *Sports Illustrated* interviewer inside me said, editorially, don't play games with Mother Nature. She'll screw you rather than the other way around just about every time. But I said to myself in my philosophical existential mode, all life is a calculated risk, right? It's a gamble running into the teeth of the storm. These are the wide open spaces I love so well. I'm betting it all that this apparition will miss me here and now, pass by on the other side in unconcern. I think I can measure a storm if not measure up to one. I'm beginning to learn how things work around here. I can even name some of the places I'm running up against--Chimney Rock, Kitchen Mesa, Box Canyon. Such homey, even homely names for infinite, unmitigated beauty, comfortable but inept epithets for ineffable grandeur. Our puny human race is to these phenomena as these household names are to the unutterable Holy of Holies.

My mind was muddling, meandering, wandering. Time to focus in on the task, the goal. Ahead was a mountain of rain. I was running toward it, hoping now, in my *Playboy* persona, that Mr. Mesa would keep Miss Maelstrom occupied on top of him just for the next forty minutes, while I would run two miles out and two miles back in my little world on this not entirely level playing field of the valley floor. This teasing reverie abruptly became violently shattered. The lightning hit, seemingly all at once. Not the thin veined, twig branched, filigree, decorative pattern. It was an albino Paul Bunyan Rocky Mountain rattler, Anaconda model, an instantaneous snapping menace, head-high at eye level, shooting direct and straight to the point. Bang! A hundred critters smoked in a microsecond. Crack! Two hundred more, all goners. Bam! Another jolt, a close, long channel shot straight down. Zeus's juice at the speed of light, to the beat of Thor's drums. Bolt after bolt, violence like a Western gone amok, making Clint Eastwood's day. Magnum Force after me! The most powerful fireblast in the world, and it'll blow your head clean off. So in my Eastwood persona, you gotta ask yourself one question: Do I feel lucky? Well, do ya, Punk? Or is it, Do I feel punk? Well, do ya, Lucky?

While I had been playing games with the naming of Mother Nature's public and private parts, was the Eye in the Sky aiming a personal missile with my name on it? My gutter-bound Lilliputian mind joked to itself in its *One Hundred Truly Tasteless Jokes* mode, spitting back in the face of the awesome unthinkable: To be stricken by a thunderbolt? Obscene! A fatal dose of clap from those fornicating pagan Titans!

I jumped the chain of the private road fencing off the desert against pigheaded bastards like me. "I have promises to keep," my *Snowy Woods* persona said to me, "and four miles to go before I sleep." I jogged at my usual plodding pace, nothing under a ten minute mile. How casually we appropriate Nature's power to ourselves by way of metaphor: a fast runner has "lightning speed"--what a joke! And now me, I want to get in a race against lightning? Not that I wanted to. The luck of the draw, or, in this case, of the arroyo. My little habitual ritual had put me in harm's way. What a rush!

Earlier that afternoon, I had been to Chimney Rock, seven hundred feet above the valley floor, watching this very storm build in the distance and surveying my running route of yesterday and today. Such a long way my road running seemed, even from that vantage point actually encompassing a turning of the head from left to right--a two mile stretch of open sand and low scrub, a lot of territory for two scrawny legs to conquer in a few measly minutes, but the merest nothingness to the wide expanses that surrounded it on every side for unseen hundreds of miles, an ocean of the ages, an almost eternal tapestry that, for human contemplation, had frozen into the still life of a snapshot view. And now I was running perhaps literally for my life across the merest few meters of it.

The wind was picking up. The storm was moving, though slowly, in my direction. Perhaps now only eight or nine miles between me and it. And still at least three miles between me and either safety or eternity. I looked up at Chimney Rock. Its left side was facing me, a long way off it seemed. I pondered my legs, in my David Attenborough mode.

"You know," I mused, "these legs used to be slime, crab claws or the equivalent, maybe when these rocks or their ilk were themselves crustaceans underwater in the Inland Sea of Laurentia. The local velociraptors have come and gone, seventy million years ago, give or take ten million, even the precocious two-legged chicken size *Coelophysis* they boast about around here--what a turkey! I'm way above and beyond all that now. I can get past Chimney Rock in much less than eons. I'm one of Nature's supremely arrogant beings."

Thereupon I bolted past two medium-tall trees, sentinels on each side of the dirt road at a little rise. I was now dead-center at the axis over from Chimney Rock. I was, I vowed in my andro mode, going to beat Mother Nature if it killed me, meanwhile chuckling at that casually used dire metaphor by which we automatically mock our little capsule of time. Eventually I charged way beyond the other side of Chimney Rock, on *The Far Side* as I said to myself in my Gary Larson mode.

I pondered the fictive beings inside the cloud, guiding it at the microcontrols. They knew what they were doing. I could hear them cracking their sick jokes, like "Now we got the sucker right where we wanted. Hung back just long enough to entice him into the open without cover. Now watch him scramble when we fire one over his head, then aim low to give him a hotfoot before we finish him off. What a simpleton."

Flashing back to my reality mode, I came to the fork in the road, the left tine of which goes to the Ranch Director's House. Not being the Director, I veered right, then along this stretch to the densest patch of yellow flowers (my David Attenborough mode in its meagerest nomenclature). And there the turnaround toward home. How quickly I have appropriated Ghost Ranch as my home, my shelter from Nature! The dark storm seemed to pause in its approach, still a few miles off. Okay to turn my back on it--even for twenty minutes? It was crunch time now, *Sports Illustrated* mode--do or die, a phrase which began to transcend cliche in this arena, just as for Robert Burns who coined it. I found inner energy I hadn't tapped in some decades of my eternity on earth. I was smoking like steam and buzzing like diesel combined. An eight minute mile, maybe even a seven minute one. I felt a preternaturally divine power in me. I'm not this fast a runner. Haven't been for fifteen years. I knew about adrenaline, in my Dr. Gott mode. But I wasn't panting or gasping for breath! Usually I hit the wall early and often. The barrier had come down. I was loosed from the corrosive force of lactic acid!

In good order I passed again into the compound and from there to the complex of its innards, some minutes before the deluge which lumbered behind me and shortly drenched the place. I had encountered the simple, primal forces and survived. I had engaged Nature and emerged in one piece. I was becoming a cloudburst baptised whole person. Could I in time be born again as Nature's unspoiled child, like the true red-blood man or woman? Nature's forces had given me in this instance not only a second wind but a fresh breath of life, a natural high in a race with the wind. I came back from this encounter in better shape than ever before.

I got lucky. It might not have happened that way--unless I raced the clouds daily and came to worship the storm rather than myself for escaping it. Unlike the American Indian, I and Mother Nature are kin but estranged ancestrally. We don't always, in my and her native mode, respect each other, and thus we continue essentially as antagonists. Nature's bones remain in me, but her elusive ghost having passed up, up, and away some millennia ago, we are to each other reckless, unpredictable, and ominous face to face, Road Runner fleeing Coyote. Beep Beep!

9

Lyric Love

Sir Philip Sidney was a fine Elizabethan poet, one of the first and best writers of English sonnets and a good romancer both in story and in life. And not only could he do all that, he could also teach. He was a literary critic, one of the first and best of those. He captured in one succinct concept the secret of all good literature. It must do two things: teach and delight. He wasn't the first to say that. Chaucer, for example, said so too. His criteria for tale telling were the same: to edify and entertain, or in his own words, provide "tales of best sentence and most solace."

Sir Philip Sidney also was one of the first to complain of the malady today known as writer's block. Like staring at a blank sheet of paper hours on end, distracted by hopeless love. In Hollywood, no scriptwriter would ever choose to reside on writer's block. Sir Philip found, at the point of committing quill abuse, the answer, the breakthrough:

> Biting my truant pen, beating myself for spite,
> Fool, said my muse to me, look in thy heart and
> > write.

The deeper the wounds of love, the more blood to spill out onto the page. Shelley knew the pain of love: "I fall upon the thorns of life, I bleed." And so did I. So does everybody. Could I write about it from my heart? Would it be in a form to teach and delight? I knew how entertaining the dark side can be. I learned it from Poe. He was my favorite writer from my early teenhood on. In late middle age I read his secret, his heartfelt confession, his own wellspring:

> From childhood's hour I have not been
> As others were. I have not seen
> As others saw. I could not bring
> My passions from a common spring.
> From the same source I have not taken
> My sorrow. I could not awaken
> My heart to joy at the same tone.
> And all I loved, I loved alone.
> Then, in my childhood, at the dawn
> Of a most stormy life was drawn
> From every source of good and ill
> The mystery which binds me still.
> From the torrent or the fountain,
> From the red cliff of the mountain,
> From the sun that round me rolled
> With its autumn tint of gold,
> From the lightning in the sky
> As it passed me flying by,
> From the thunder, and the storm,
> And a cloud that took the form,
> When the rest of heaven was blue,
> Of a demon in my view.

Sad and scary, this revelation. Inspirational too. It helped me count my blessings. By the time I read Poe's lament, *Alone*, I had exorcised some of my own demons. So I determined to write a sequel to *Alone* in honor of Poe, letting my own latterday joy transmute his woe by taking shape from his sorrow. My poem would exploit Poe's poem's images and form to express the flip side of life. I would write a love poem from the seeds of despair in Poe's lyric. The year was 1988. I had been married to my wife of that era for twenty-four years. We were still in love, it seemed to me. We had a nice life on Grandview

Drive, four happy, successful, cute, bright kids. No major problems. We had it made, back then. I wanted to tell her so in a special way, poetically.

We were separated at the time. Not a legal thing or a fighting thing or a disputing thing. I was in France for six months on a teaching exchange, at the Universite du Maine, in LeMans. Barbara was back home, in the midst of a job search after completing an internship and degree work which she had put aside at the time we had gotten married more than two decades prior.

I missed her. I had wanted her to accompany me during this exchange but we both had agreed that getting a job at this juncture could accelerate her career progress. She was excited about it. I would rough it on my own in the Old World, in a part of it new to me. It would keep me occupied though alone. I had a big apartment reserved for visiting faculty, right on the edge of campus—living room, dining room, two bedrooms, kitchen, just for me. All that empty space made me the lonelier, naturally.

I knew mostly tourist French, did my teaching in English, so I was at least initially pretty much cast adrift. I had vowed to speak only French to strangers and not to resort to English until a more than short-term relationship with any person met was in the offing. I would muddle through, making a fool of myself in the process until I sank or swam. That was my vow to myself, which I steadfastly remained true to. And I both sank and swam. I didn't ask for a shoe with cheese on it (*fromage sur chaussure*) like Steve Martin did, but I did get short-changed at the neighborhood vintner's, I discovered after the fact.

While I was settling in, I had a lot of time alone. Homesickness hit early and hard. I had to write a love letter quick or else start singing the blues. If I had been Robert Burns or a clone of his, it would have been easy. Burns had been perhaps my favorite poet in high school. He was so famous, and so good. "A precursor of the Romantic Movement," the professor at Sewanee my freshman year termed him. "Precursor," my eye! Burns was "love" shot through. Sure, he loved the lassies, oh! And moreover he was in love with love *per se*. God gave him "passions wild and strong," he proclaimed. Not till the precursing of my own dotage did I come to realize that Burns's pledges of undying love ring hollow against the long, vacuous roll of lady loves that he charmed in his short zappy life. One of his most famous love lyrics is, it turns out, so generic that it has the depth of your daily horoscope entry:

> Oh my love is like a red, red rose
> That's newly sprung in June.
> My love is like the melody
> That's sweetly played in tune.
>
> So fair thou art, my bonny lass,
> So deep in love am I,
> And I will love thee still, my dear,
> Till all the seas gang dry.
>
> Till all the seas gang dry, my dear,
> And the rocks melt with the sun.
> And I will love thee still, my dear,
> While the sands of life shall run.
>
> So fare thee well, my bonny lass,
> And fare thee well awhile.
> And I will come again, my dear,
> Though it were ten thousand mile!

Beautiful, true. I like it. If Burns lived today, he could xerox a thousand copies of this one and give the dittos to each lassie he wanted to charm the panties off of for that day or night. One poem applies to all. I dearly love Burns, to this day, yet he was not the apostle of love for a "one and only." My poem would have to do more than Burns's concept of love. Mine might be generic, but it would be unique, special: Inspired by Poe, transcending Burns, from the nostalgic loneliness of my cavernous abode in LeMans, home of the twenty-four hour auto race to nowhere.

Poe's poem, "Alone," is grounded in Nature, as befits a full-blown romantic. I'm a romantic too in this tradition. My love must encompass Nature. I had a true love, my wife, Barbara. She perforce was my all in all. Where Poe looked at the sky and beheld the cloud of a demon, I would look and see my angel, but in a more expansive metaphor. Despite earthly limitation that constrained and finally, ironically, doomed our love, this poem managed to soar above all that, then and abstractly even now.

You Are My Sky

> You are my sky,
> True blue as your eyes.
> I look in them and see
> My life's dream, you and me
> Each one another's truly.
> Can we guess what we may be
> When our two souls are one up at this height?
> The sun is not so bright
> As our love's growing light.
> Open to me your soul
> Redemptive of my being,
> Whole within your truest essence.
> I want none other being
> But the feeling of your glowing,
> Heating my rocket's flight
> Far out of sight of the world's eye.
> You are my sky.

This piece taught and delighted an audience of two, myself and Barbara. Subsequently I shared it with a gathering of faculty at an informal talk in the Faculty Lounge recounting my academic sojourn in France. I was making the point to them that journeys afar help you appreciate the near when you're not there. Several years later, when Barbara and I were separating for good (what a nice double-edged phrase), she often alluded to the poem and tried to hold me to it.

At that point it was working for her but not for me. Nevertheless, I stopped short of xeroxing it off and passing it around to any other true loves of the newer time. That one was for Barbara and will remain so.

This heartfelt poem was not my first foray into verse. I got into poetry as a do-it-yourself endeavor during my freshman year at college (1959-60). It was a time of dislocation. All in all, I ended up having a miserable freshman experience, exiled it seemed on a monastic mountain—six hundred elite Southern gentlemen constituting the student body. I was not elite, Southern, nor a gentleman in the sense of breeding. In brief, I was a teenage slob. I chronically skipped dining hall breakfast and made do with a late morning sweet roll and milkshake. Didn't know about the dangers of noncomplex carbohydrate overloading and suffered accordingly, the vicious high/low cycle of a sugar junkie.

My mother wanted me to go to Sewanee because it had a neighboring Episcopal seminary. She wanted me to be a priest. Alas, I hadn't got the call, and didn't get it. Sewanee and me didn't get along. It was six hundred or more miles from home, preventing me from dating any of my incipient girlfriends. And there were no girls within miles of Sewanee. It was like the monastery on top of Mont Saint-Michel, only without the view.

The winter was cold and dark. An ice storm froze the pipes for two weeks, no flushing of toilets within that span. Six hundred elite Southern gentlemen's poo smells no better than that of six hundred swine.

I was all thumbs and tongues in chemistry lab. There was a device like a metal straw with a bulb-like bulge halfway up it. You were supposed to suck acid into the bulb with your mouth, like it was a soda, but just so far. I sucked too hard and sucked it up, into my mouth. Luckily, that draw was not acid but a base, sodium hydroxide. It felt slippery and greasy in my mouth, like I imagined antifreeze might feel though never having tasted any. Or like melted silly putty, really melted. I spat it out and reached quick for the antidote, a white pasty compound in a nearby dish. Plastered it all over my tongue and the inside and outside of my mouth. Looked and felt like a clown. If the sucked substance had been sulfuric or nitric acid I would have gotten dangerously corroded. Nitric acid turns flesh necrotic—orange and spongy like leprosy. I knew about that because I routinely splattered nitric acid on my fingers and hands, not deliberately but accidentally. Chemistry lab was to me bodily what Sewanee overall was to me emotionally—an assault to my senses and sensibilities. I didn't fit in.

One of the few concrete details I remember with nostalgia from that lost year was that a Coke, from the machine at the end of the dorm corridor, still cost just a nickel, still had the blue-green glass glaze, the classic hourglass shape, unlike elsewhere.

But I did begin to find a poetic voice there, my own muse. I wrote my first poem on the blank end-pages of my English lit book. It wasn't a love poem but an abstract, generic item of juvenilia about everything, and nothing. It was an attempt to work out of the depression induced by this mountain-malaise:

On Attempts to Alter Joy

How few the times of joy serenely stand
Unhampered, unmolested by the mind,
Which strives so fearful, like each grain of sand
Directed in a flood of air to find
Some structure having mellowed, grayed with age
Though through the years it stood the test of time.
Indeed, Time's aged fingers, skilful, sage,
With weathered brush, with reason, rhyme
Had crafted, tinted, tested with such skill
The outward parts that stand displayed to view,
Installed an ancient beauty, now what Will
Could have the gall to ill, try to renew
What perfected, proved, improved, distilled by Time
Now stands fulfilled, indeed now in its prime.
A mind with thought to alter joy as now its struc-
    tures stand
Must be for sure not worth a grain of sand.

I quoted it to an old high-school friend during one of the few breaks in the school year. He liked it even better than I did. Don't know if he understood it. Don't know if I did either.

I also wrote my first poem under the throes of love. Not much of a poem, not much of a love. It hadn't had time to germinate or jell. It was puppy love, infatuation. But it was more of a real thing to me then than Coca-Cola ever was. And I built it up in my mind to a phantasm that would haunt me for years—the Idea of Love, represented by a person in real time and touch.

I met her on a bus in the summer upon my graduation from Woodrow Wilson High School, 1959. I was en route to my summer job, which was scotch taping paper book-covers into plastic binders, cutting the binders to size, gluing checkout card envelopes onto inside back covers, and rubber stamping it all with the logo *AAAS Traveling High School Science Library*. It was for the American Association for the Advancement of Science, on Massachusetts Avenue, downtown D.C. An assembly line operation. I and my fellow summer vacation high school and college-bound students took turns cutting, taping, gluing, and stamping forty books to a stack, an infinitude of stacks, for eight hours a day. Early morning glue shift for me, then mid-morning tape shift, early afternoon stamping shift, late afternoon cutting shift. The kind of work, actually, that you went to school and college to get out of doing long-term. But good camaraderie and an educational hands-on experiential introduction to the horrors of the machine age. One can put up with almost anything for three months, each year for four years or so.

And as far as assembly line jobs go, this one was a piece of cake compared to those I read about in an unintentionally fascinating U.S. Government publication, a massive tome labeled *A Dictionary of Occupational Titles*. All the following job titles from the workplace are true and indeed sound stranger than fiction. Worst were the slaughterhouse jobs of that era, like Snout and Lips Cleaner, Sticker, Head Choker, Head Chopper, etc.

Not much better were jobs like Chickle Grinder Feeder, Coiled Coil Inspector, Oyster Floater, Nose Crimper, Chlorinator Operator, Hand Chewing Packer, Chewing Twist Prizer, Chocolate Dipping

Machine Feeder, Cigarette Book Folder, Cold Water Lapper, Mop Comber, Convolute Tube Winder, Cornflakes Man, Crackoff Man, Cranberry Snapper, Cyanide Man, Decal Applier, Defective Work Carrier, Defective Work Returner, Odds and Ends Seamer, Doped Leather Baker, Germ Drier, Edge Gluer, Egg Smeller, Pretzel Dipper, Nose Forming Helper, Mud Man, Muck Boss, Noodle Man, Negative Worker, Continuous Towel Roller, Odd Piece Checker, Oil Boiler, Opener Feeder, Ox Feeder, Defective Cigarette Ripper Picker.

But a few jobs listed in the compilation exuded a certain appeal though it wasn't clear quite what to make of them, like Chicken Fancier, Donkey Doctor, Donkey Puncher, Doodler, Christmas Character, Flower Clipper, Moocher, Knuckle Man, Kiss Machine Operator, Leg Examiner. Yes, some daily grinds had their charms, literal or implied. But I was ready for a new, truly human encounter.

So she got on the bus, my short-blond-haired vision of delight. I was in the front seat behind the driver, one of those old double-seats parallel to the aisle. As she turned from the coin-drop box, her eyes met mine. "Robert?" she said. "Hi," said I. "I'm Richard." "My name is Margeaux," she continued. "I know I've seen you at school. Sorry for the mistake."

She sat down across the aisle in the other parallel double-seat, facing me. I was smitten already. She was elegant. White sweater. Don't remember the conversation. She talked about her summer job. I laughed about mine. We made a date. It was only a week or so before I was due to leave for college, my freshman year at the University of the South. She was to enter American University, the School of Advanced International Studies. Her dad was a Marine colonel. She had transferred from Japan to Wilson High just for her senior year.

We went to dinner at Mary K.'s Toll House in Silver Spring. Bill was $7.50. I tossed down a ten dollar bill and didn't wait for change. I wanted her to brush up against me again in the parking lot as had happened on our way in. Could feel her bosom against my side that way, once again.

We drove around and got out in the dark at a park by Sligo Creek. Swung together in the kiddy swings, which were painted with red and white stripes like candy canes. Took her home to a polite goodnight. Promised to write.

Cursed my fate that I had to leave town so soon and for so long. Saw her again on a quick break Thanksgiving Weekend. Took her on a walk along the C&O Canal. Had bought and hid away an orchid for her. Whipped it out on the sunny bankside of the canal. She beamed. Then, smack, a juicy full kiss on and within the lips, her the initiator. Boing! That was it for me. She's my one and only, thought I.

Back at Sewanee, I wrote a poem to her. It was pitiful, not even a love poem. I was testing the waters. Don't move too quick, I strategized. This is for the long term. Better show her the inner depth of my soul before I undertake anything easy or cheap. It was courtly love on my part.

The trouble with courtly love, in the traditional sense from medieval times, is that it's not a two-way thing. It is a formula for disaster. Its main ingredients remain more or less intact to this very day and embody the clichés of most of the love songs from the past several centuries. First is the concept that there is a one and only one true love for you in all the world. Funny how an idea so absurd could last so long. If the idea were true, there would be almost no chance of anyone finding in all the world the one and only person who was their needle in the haystack. A person can by exertion of the will try to make it come true, of course. Like when you get married your spouse is your one and only true love in all the world. But that's only because both partners in the marriage agree to make it so and somehow pull it off throughout life.

With courtly love it's a bit different. Your one and only true love is the love in your own head for the beloved object, not considering that it takes two to tango. Because your one and only became your true love through the other medieval condition of courtly love, love at first sight. "Just one look," the song says. That's all it takes. True love at a glance. Actually, this can happen and end happily, that is, in a loving, durable marriage.

For example, Terri Irwin fell in love at first sight with the Crocodile Hunter, Steve Irwin, when she visited the Australia Zoo and saw him charm crocodiles. They lived and worked together in true wedded bliss for fourteen years until his untimely death from the barb of a stingray to the heart.

There must be many other examples of fully fulfilled love at first sight relationships and marriages, though I do not know of any others myself offhand. I do know of other, maybe many other, cases of love at first sight getting nowhere. The odds overwhelmingly favor this second outcome, no doubt about it. I suppose I've fallen in love at first sight many times on my own, and almost all of those plunges went nowhere but over the cliff. All but two in my case. Brigitte Bardot didn't know I existed.

I had that first glimpse of Margeaux on the bus and quickly took the plunge. My search was over even before it had begun, if all went well. The third condition of courtly love also applied to me. There must be an impediment to the love, so as to make it excruciating and to enhance the longing in nonfulfillment. The initial impediment was distance. Sewanee was seven hundred mountainous miles from D.C., and our romance consisted mainly of that first look and one subsequent kiss. Not much to go on, was it.

At that time, I didn't know about the hopeless history of medieval conventional courtly love. I thought it was the real thing happening to me. Didn't know the odds, or about the excruciation and lasting torment I was setting myself up for because of all the clichés we have swallowed and taken to heart in this romantic convention.

The poem I wrote to Margeaux upon my return to exile in Sewanee from that brief Thanksgiving vacation back home in Washington was a philosophical rather than romantic lyric, strange to say. I was taking the advice of that second great precursor of the Romantic Movement, William Blake:

> Never seek to tell thy love,
> Love that never told can be.
> For the gentle wind doth move
> Silently, invisibly.
>
> I told my love, I told my love,
> I told her all my heart.

> Silently, invisibly,
> Ah, she did depart.
>
> The day that she was gone from me
> A stranger traveled by.
> Silently, invisibly,
> He took her with a sigh.

Well, I wasn't going to give her up that easy to a passing stranger by blurting all my love out at once to be shot down so quick.

Win her mind, then her heart, then her body, I fantasized. Probably I wanted her in reverse order to that list, like any healthy late teenager. Just as Lord Byron had written:

> She was a phantom of delight
> When first she came into my sight.

And the Sewanee underground literary rag parodied:

> She was a vision of delight
> When she first fell upon his retina.
> But she soon faded far from sight
> Because he couldn't getina.

I of necessity had to bide my time because of the requisite medieval impediment, the physical distance between us. My poem would explain everything that all the philosophers from ancient to modern times had speculated about, and it would do it in a nutshell. If she would see the light and take me, she would have all the world as well, in the person of yours truly. I put it to her this way:

> O Ultimate Reality
> Is not the triviality
> The name may seem.
> In its final embodiment
> Is surely found unreal content

That is a dream—hence
Not to be attained here,
But at the end of life,
Which surely is a recompense
For worldly strife.

I dropped it in the mailbox and waited for the effect and the reply. The reply came but not the effect. I wanted to hear love from *her* lips, or from the words transferred from heart to head to pen and paper. She sent back during December a brief-seeming letter saying that she thought I had poetic talent. Though gratifying to me intellectually, that wasn't what I needed to hear. I wanted her to confess undying eternal love for me. In short, I wanted her to be hot for me. It seemed she was not, not yet. But she herself was a hot item, or just "hot" as they say today. I had better move fast or she might burn soon for somebody else, with me *in absentia*. I had maybe just one last shot, coming up soon—Christmas vacation.

Christmas came and went. Nothing under the tree for me that would last beyond the season. She worked through the vacation, at the Library of Congress. She was mostly too busy for me. I sometimes took her to work but didn't get many evenings with her. We went to see *Ben-Hur* on one of our few dates. She was impressed by the chariot race.

I was unable to communicate to her by any means that she was my one and only true love forever from first sight as excruciatingly confirmed by the impediment of the long distance between us. Throughout my spring semester at Sewanee her notes to me became briefer and more infrequent regardless of the frequency or fervor of my letters. It devolved to a postcard from her every three or four weeks. By summer she was involved with one or more other young men, and I and my imperishable work that I had dared to share with her were both dumped as if of no account to her.

That is the tragedy of courtly love, but just the first chapter of its miserable saga, rendered in umpteen thousand lyrics, poems, stories, and lives. The continuation of the story is the broken heart, another legacy of the twelfth century troubadours.

Yes, I was heartbroken. The image of my lost non-love stayed with me, and though I got over it in a practical sense, fell in love twice again and got married to both of my latterday true loves, I never forgot the heartache that lingered for a matter of years. Despite the indispensable boon that an idealized love is for the arts and literature, the suffering it causes in real lives is a heavy price to pay for that entertainment in the fictive world.

My daughter Mary likewise, to take another case close to home, suffered from exalted images of a one and only true love. Her junior prom date was an athlete, poster-boy handsome, and she took her idealized image of him to college and beyond. Her true love must be an All-American athlete, Hollywood handsome, and both hunk and comedian. The scores of men she dated in her twenties all failed to meet one or more of those criteria. The closest man to that image that she found, and finally married, endured a courtship of a decade before she finally caved in to a real person rather than an idealized figment of her own imagination concocted from the idylls of romance, to wit, the beloved one is perfect in every aspect—physical, mental, spiritual. No blemish is to be found on such a one, on my one and only true love.

The great seventeenth century poet John Donne tellingly spouted all the medieval clichés anew from his gut in his own love-sickness, the tortured outcry of *The Broken Heart*:

> Ah, what trifle is a heart
> If once into love's hands it come!
>
> . . .
>
> If 'twere not so, what did become
> Of my heart, when I first saw thee?
> . . . Love, alas,
> At one first blow did shiver it as glass.
>
> . . .
>
> And now as broken glasses show
> A hundred lesser faces, so
> My rags of heart can like, wish, and adore,
> But after one such love, can love no more.

The nineteenth century poets of the Romantic Movement reinforced this tradition of the love object being all in all. In an elaborate metaphor of the idea that your ship has come in, Poe wrote, in *To Helen*:

> Helen, thy beauty is to me
> Like those Nicaean barks of yore
> That gently, o'er a perfumed sea,
> The weary wayworn wanderer bore
> To his own native shore.

The beloved embodies all the beautiful aspects of the natural world, as did "Annabel Lee" to Poe:

> For the moon never beams without bringing me
>   dreams
> Of the beautiful Annabel Lee,
> And the stars never rise but I see the bright eyes
> Of the beautiful Annabel Lee.

As for Margeaux, she showed up forty years later, in the year 1999, at the Woodrow Wilson High School reunion, class of 1959. She looked then like a woman in her late fifties, true to what she was. Nice enough but not love at first sight anymore. I, likewise, no doubt looked like a man in his late fifties. But by then my angel had flown, my demon had been exorcized, many a year prior. I suffered no more over that first fling, only with its latterday incarnation in the form of another person, my second one and only true love, my first wife Barbara.

Once again it was love at first sight. We were both undergraduates at George Washington University. It was fall semester, November 1962. I had found an empty classroom to study in before my next class. A sprightly, fluffily coifed amber-haired coed bounced in by the front set of doors on the right. I sized her up. Nice tight-fitting tan sweater, full bosom. She was hot and so was I. I had cozied up in the back row, sporting a three-day beard, that is, unshaven, unkempt.

She bustled over to the row of windows on the left side of the class-room and proceeded to open one or more of them to let in some fresh autumn air.

"I never obey signs," she remarked to me, with reference to a block-letter warning posted above the all-green blackboard behind the front desk: KEEP WINDOWS CLOSED.

That was charm enough for me, on top of her bright shining face with evident disposition to match. She had made an overture to me! I had to pick up on this once in a lifetime opportunity. My one and only? I would give it a shot, fling back a Cupid bolt myself. Somehow I wangled a date out of her, for a concert at the Library of Congress, one of the scenes of my former floundering in love. It was an event on November 22, the day of St. Cecelia, patron saint of music. Alfred Deller, noted countertenor, would sing, probably some songs of courtly love. To these I would eventually add my own. At the concert that evening, Barbara took my hand in her own, and fourteen months later I gave her my hand in marriage.

This being a courtly love, however, there was an impedi-ment. I was Episcopalian, she was Roman Catholic. But I had been tutored that way myself in the ultra-high Anglo-Catholic parish of St. James, C Street, Northeast. Catechisms, rosaries, the whole bit. I went to church with Barbara during our engagement, got to like the mumbo-jumbo of the Latin mass, its mystery and holy smoke. Got inducted into the Roman church before our marriage and was con-tent. We had both saved ourselves for marriage, as the saying goes, and were ignorantly blissful. Since I knew nothing about sex up to that time, I didn't have a sense of missing anything other than what I would now get to know in full legitimacy imminently. No impedi-ment seemed then to loom at all. Barbara was to be my one and only Playmate.

We married January 28, 1964, just after my graduation. Barbara had a semester to go but could put that on hold for the moment. My first poem to her was for Valentine's Day, less than three weeks after the wedding. It alluded mainly to sex but also to a bout with the flu that Barbara had had during our courtship:

This is bliss: a kiss
From you, or maybe two,
Or four, or many more, aha!
A mess o' greenery,
High and dryness tongue
On limbtree thistle-willow
Humming oozy music,
Strumming green-filled extrasy,
Hula-hooping it up for
Funny Bunny madfling Annie.
How now, green gal!
Good for using tool-feet squirming!
A Valentine, a repining ripening vine
Of eglantine in the shadow of Time
Betwixt and mixed within the sands
Of voluminous strands
And withal the fall of leaves in sheaves
Of frightening brightening rain
No stain of pain will blot,
No spot of rue,
Except for foreign Asian flu
Which we pooh-pooh
When later on it will have flew.
O you won't catch me,
You old Asian flu,
Though I may catch-yew!

Throughout the first part of our marriage, through the birth of our third child within four years, I swallowed the bitter pill of no birth control beyond the so-called rhythm method of enforced abstinence around fertile days, up to about two weeks out of every month, accounting for variables. Obviously it proved entirely ineffectual as birth control for us as a couple. I came to bemoan this fruitless, ironically fruitful ritual as a ridiculous exercise in self-deprivation. Notwithstanding, as I shared with Barbara, that I had written a poem during my college days at GWU which I came to interpret, after meeting and wooing Barbara, as a paean to unfettered sex in marriage, naked love, unshod genitalia, that is to say bouncy without rubbers, breathless and panting without diaphragms.

I hadn't known how to interpret it when I wrote it except that I knew it was about sex and its proper consequences of childbearing, both of which I had been eagerly anticipating without having experienced either of them. Its theme apparently, as I preached to Barbara, was that protected sex (the "painted rabbits' feet" in the first line of the poem below) was, incredible to say, irresponsible and that many children are the unbounded destiny ("flowering of the bower") of those daring enough to go for it all in love and life:

On Without Delivery

Painted rabbits' feet
Running hilly landslides
Palely impaled in fits and starts
Of sweaty succulence,
Breathless ecstasy!
Altering breathing in following feculence,
Altercation with calumnious callous calibrating
And withal ultimate driving decadence,
Foolproof fortune, pleasing placating in charging,
Endless coming and foaming,
Culmination for garrulous slipshod surrealism,
Inundating diminuendo for endless upcharging!
Oh, the surety of future fortuity
If where is known the blown and pale
Flowering of the bower!
To hell with the knell of the bell
Of Fortune's fitful fate,
The date of which is known to few
Save those in view
Of that which came into
The Persian fields of fallacy!

In the event, four children in less than five years, I learned to change my tune. Barbara and I consulted with the local parish priest where we lived at that time, Falls Church, Virginia, about our fertility and our increasingly burdened and barren future prospects financially if the trend were to continue. His best advice seemed more like the uttering of a curse: "You may have fourteen or fifteen children in your household." That jarring incantation was the extent of his solace, the fruit of his wisdom. We took our leave of him. "Unreasonable," "out of touch," "uncompassionate," were some of the epithets we hurled his way, out of earshot, upon our departure.

So we undertook to practice birth control. We practiced for a while, with a diaphragm and phenoxypolyethoxyethanol, as well as nonoxynol, and eventually practice made perfect in this regard. No more after four. Except a cat, Tigger, and a dog, Rebel.

For another twenty years we lived in domestic tranquility, as much as is possible with four screaming and fighting kids around, but with them laughing and singing too, all the while. We had overcome the impediment of overly religious rigor and accommodated ourselves to the inevitable imperfection of things human, accepting the less than perfect accomplished fact in lieu of the unachievable ideal. Our accomplished facts were Tom, Dick and Mary, and Danny, or in birth order Dickie, Tommy, Mary, Danny, all blue-eyed tow-headed bundles of joy like their Mom and balls of fire like their Dad, figuratively speaking.

I remained in love with Barbara throughout this time and sexually infatuated. For Christmas 1974 I gave her a historically annotated and sumptuously illustrated book *Astrology* by the famous British poet Louis MacNeice. Inside of it, I tucked a small bright red card with a picture of an elf, and wrote on it a courtly love and sex poem about her as the star of my eye and sky in my own Astrological book:

To Angel Face, From a Horny Devil

Here's how I want to say
You're my glow and gold
And Ho Ho Ho for joys and

> Jollies and Christmas follies.
> Look to the sky, above the tree.
> Do you see an angel with little
> Gold hair right where a star
> Is often set? You are my
> Angel sweet, the star of my
> See and look and sweat and
> Book, and the star of my
> Dream is you and you and
> You. So this book will tell you
> That in the sky of my eye
> You are my morning light and
> Evening star inside my heart. Look
> There and you will find only just you,
> And me too.

It was a love for life. But life also encompasses death within it, several kinds of deaths before the big sleep. Our love was a casualty of one of those deaths within life that in itself had nothing to do with us. It was a freak accident, one neither of us was able to cope with, and it ruined us.

My hearing was traumatized by excessive noise from a too-close loudspeaker. In May 1990 I was seated in the front row of faculty at a university graduation ceremony. The next morning I awoke to a rattling sound in my ears, which altered in tone and intensity but did not abate. It was diagnosed as acoustic trauma with resulting tinnitus. Depression set in, a clinical depression as diagnosed in August of that summer.

I lost fifteen pounds and could do little but try to exercise—jogging or tennis. That fall Barbara took a job in Arlington, Virginia, 150 miles from our home in Frostburg, Maryland, returning on weekends. Still enervated and anxious in fall semester, I went through the motions of work minus the joy of life.

I turned for solace to a tennis compatriot and professional colleague, Karen, not without telling Barbara about it from the first inappropriate overture to Karen on my part. Barbara could deal neither with my injury nor my pulling away from her, and I struggled likewise. We separated fully within a year and were divorced finally in 1995. It broke my heart, much more so than the first little heartbreak I had had back when.

Karen became my third one-and-only love. I started to write poems to her instead of to Barbara, as if I were Robert Burns or somebody. I now write poems to Karen regularly, like clockwork on the anniversary of certain occasions: our first date (October 2), her birthday (December 1), Valentine's Day, and our wedding anniversary (May 5). Was it love at first sight? It was look at first sight, that is, look there, nice new lady, eh? Recently widowed, I was to learn. Short blond hair, fair skin, narrow shoulders, narrower waist, friendly eyes, fine soft features, bosomy. Could have been my type. She was a new hire, September 1983. It was a committee meeting. Didn't have much better to do at such things than admire the new hire. But not love. I wasn't free to fall in love then, anyway. My peace of mind had to die first, which it did on May 12, 1990, at a graduation, electrocuted by the sonic jolts of a loudspeaker.

Luck was a goddess to the ancient Romans. The name was Fortuna, the prototype of Lady Luck for us. *Fortune, fortunate* came to be associated with good luck. But Fortuna was also mistress of Bad Luck. When you go to a fortune teller, your luck may be either good or bad. The Wheel of Fortune goes spinning round. What goes up must come down. Fortune doles out equal measures of tears and laughter. It's why the ancient Greeks had only two kinds of drama: comedy and tragedy. Personifying the good and bad of life, the accidents and lucky breaks, at least puts a measure onto this chaos. If you don't like the weather, just wait a bit, etc. Things will turn up. These are clichés because they are true to experience. Even though, if one takes time to analyze, much of the up and down cycle of life seems random rather than ordered.

But since we are, in our best form, rational creatures, we are more comfortable with a sense of order rather than disarray in our cosmos. So we look for patterns, and those who seek will find something or other to make sense out of any calamity. After all, there are laws in Nature—gravity, thermodynamics, etc. Nothing much could happen without such laws.

There are also principles of disorder: the law of entropy, for example, the tendency of a system to disperse and lose form. In this regard—limits to motion, limits to chaos—science seems compatible to mythology, also to religion. Atomic theory makes sense of matter. Mythology and religion make sense to the imagination.

Nevertheless, I'll be damned if I can explain how the universe turns on a dime, how mighty effects proceed from the merest of nothings. A straw broke the camel's back. Helen's face launched a thousand ships. The sun and moon appear to us the same size only because the sun is four hundred times the moon's diameter and also, coincidentally, four hundred times more distant than the moon; and so on. There is much more mystery than there is history, and there seems to be more nonsense than science.

Take me and Karen, for example. Our courtship and marriage of many years duration was, to my mind, set in motion at a critical juncture of random forces over a space of less than five minutes.

On October 2, 1990, I was sitting in my little Dodge Colt in a parking lot of the city recreational park of Frostburg, waiting to do one of the two things that enabled me to endure life after the acoustic trauma accident four months prior at May graduation. I anticipated a game of tennis that afternoon. Maybe I would go for a long jog in the early evening. Tennis and running were my two lifelines to grasp onto as my head vibrated from ear to ear with random-seeming hisses, pings, and whines emanating from deep within the inner ear and the ruptured and wavering cilial membranes of the percussed auditory nerves. It was as if I had my own relic echo of a prior Big Bang, like the universe does in its background microwave radiation.

So I sat there listening to myself in the little cab of my little car, awaiting the appointed time for my little game of hitting a little ball back and forth with some marginally less bothered human being than myself. That would be Karen.

She was a psychologist, the teaching kind. I was a professor of English, she was a professor of psychology. She didn't exactly know what was eating me at the time, but I may have sensed a capacity in her to understand some of that, given her profession and her empathetic disposition.

Our little tennis group consisted of up to half a dozen colleagues and acquaintances. We would often meet at the park at four o'clock, by prearrangement, so that a given four of us, or rarely at least two of us, would have a workable game set up. On this day, Karen and I were the only prearranged players for rendezvous at 4 p.m. I would have to play singles. Okay by me. That was even better exercise than doubles and might exhaust me enough that I could try to get some sleep that night despite the whistle blowing from my ears in the darkening world.

Four o'clock came and went; 4:05; 4:10; 4:15. Did she forget? Had some other last-minute obligation obtruded, such as an emergency meeting of Change Agent Coordinators? I wasn't having much fun sitting by myself listening to Loony Tunes in my queered ears.

An inner monologue took over. I'd better leave and go for a long run, six to ten miles at least to choke off my sorrows in road dust. Looks like I'm being stood up, but innocently so. She can be flaky about tennis time, I guess. Who wants to play with a mess of a guy like me, anyway? I'll wait five more minutes. Nobody's ever this late, not even me. Gersham Nelson, of Jamaica, my history professor tennis buddy, often keeps me waiting ten minutes (Jamaicans may have a different sense of time, I rationalize), but nobody waits more than fifteen minutes or so that I know. Now it's 4:20 p.m. Oh well, today was already a lousy day. This just tops it off in the same mode. A wretched end to a wretched day. It's fitting. What more should I expect of my miserable current existence? Time to leave. No hope now.

I fumbled for the ignition key. Cranked the motor, got it to idle. Fiddled with the radio out of habit, but that was no good either. I got no enjoyment from music anymore because my ears clashed with it. Had to protect my ears from further trauma by inserting foam earplugs into them, which however intensified the internal noise. So I compulsively pushed and pulled them in and out according to the level of external noise or potential noise. The park was quiet so I had pulled them out. But driving in street traffic was often noisy so

I had to put them in. A total pain all the way around. I twisted the plugs into the required golf-tee shape and pushed them into both ear canals. I was ready at last to motor across town and forgo hope, of tennis and of most everything else worthwhile.

Time, 4:22 p.m. As I was shifting into first gear, a VW wagon pulled into the lot. It was Karen. She had been kept late in conference with students. So we played singles after all. She had rescued me from the oblivion of another dark night of the soul.

We quit about six o'clock. As she was about to leave I invited her out to dinner at Gehauf's Restaurant in LaVale, five miles down the road. It was mid-week. My wife Barbara was working in public relations at Holiday Inn, Ballston, Virginia. She would come back for the weekend. No dinner ready for me in my empty house. Karen said okay. It was in effect our first date, Platonic mode.

I told Barbara about it later that evening when she called me at home. She came back early, before the weekend. We undertook counseling on an emergency basis, by mutual decision. But it was already too late. I was in courtly love with Karen. There was an impediment, as required by convention. I was married. Counseling took two years and more. But eventually Barbara and I separated and divorced. I had ended a second courtly love to begin a third. Not exactly according to Hoyle but by collusion of the lower and higher powers that be. It broke Barbara's heart and also my own. I never thought myself capable of doing that. Sometimes I had lusted in my mind but never in my heart.

Earlier that semester I had befriended one of my senior honor students when she was temporarily short of funds. A kindred spirit. Fresh Nordic look. Viking blood maybe. I treated her to a dinner at The Stray Cat restaurant, aptly named if I might take the hint. Even shared with her on that occasion some of the troubles of that distracted time of my life. The Stray Cat was in Keyser, West Virginia, just across the Potomac River from nearby Cumberland. I was close to another border crossing as well. I knew that Mira had a soft spot for me. She took all of my courses, History of the English Language, Chaucer, and most recently a special topics course, Madness in Literature. Indeed, she had a kookiness compatible to my own. She was a brilliant writer and a deeply thoughtful humanist. But she was more occult than I ever was, believed in the stars, astrologically. That lore, its multilayered interconnected fatalism, outshone the self-abnegating Augustinian Catholicism of her upbringing, I sensed.

Unprompted, she professed a longstanding spirit of "connection" with me, as she put it that evening at The Stray Cat. It was all in the charts and the cards, Tarot style, she indicated.

I confess that in earthly terms, moreover, she was totally hot, and less than half my age to boot. Maybe I could have tried a furtive move that evening, but I was able to figure out it wouldn't be in her best interest, nor my own even. Considered myself scrupulous. Hooray for me.

I convinced myself after the fact that if Karen had showed up at 4:25 instead of 4:22 p.m. I would have been long gone and that pivotal desperate moment in my life would not have been replicated, guilt-ridden bastard that I am. All in all, I owe my third courtly love to one moping but magic minute of time, the sixty seconds of stalling ignition between 4:21 and 4:22 p.m. that day.

So Karen in that brief few seconds of time came into my private life, or was drawn into it by me. It was a strangely ironic juncture, a trusting leap of faith by way of incipient infidelity. I was putting a lot of people at risk besides myself. It was untrodden territory for me, an existential battleground and a minefield in practical terms. But it got my mind off my ears, which I had been obsessing and compulsing on interminably. I had of my own volition entered the Twilight Zone between heaven and hell, in an ethical sense. That uneasy locus, however, was also the traditional habitation of the courtly lover, tormented in the beatitude of idealized romance. I smashed the impediment barrier. And then I went about the business of making alien territory a home away from the old familiar, comfortable, and cherished albeit empty-nested homestead. It was simultaneously an act of deliberate direction and a flight of fancy. Maybe writing about it would help.

So I began a reflection journal and simultaneously a dream journal. I also started a joke diary. My quota was three jokes of my own devising per day. I eventually discontinued the two journals, after a couple of years or so, but maintained the joke book while letting the quota lapse. Ten jokes or one joke per day would do, even no jokes sometimes. But life is too strange not to also be strangely funny on a daily basis. When the unexpected occurs, we say "That's funny," meaning odd. If you tell it like it is, something both funny-strange and funny ha-ha is sure to pop up before long. Courtly love, for example, is funny enough in itself. Even Randy Travis knows that: "Since my phone still ain't ringin,' I assume it still ain't you," etc.

Most therapeutic of all, though, was my return to writing poems. Not only did the feelings find expression thereby, they took a form pleasing to the mind's eye and ear, transcending the cacophony of the tinnitus still ringing in my physical ears and rattling my cage. I started writing poems for Karen on occasion—her birthday, Valentine's Day, and as years began to pass and the thing would last, on the anniversary of our courtly fall, October the second. It was earnest stuff at first, becoming more and more droll as surprise succeeded surprise. The experience seemed unreal initially because of the accidental, incidental nature of its inception. A conjunction of unforeseen elements had brought us together. The flight from former life was hard but the landing soft. Waiting and wishing is a main theme, and an old courtly one. From the next Valentine's Day:

> You are in me
> And I in you
> In the dark winter of waiting
> Love rains its tears
> Moistening the new earth
> Of the secret garden.

As my mother would have said, had she lived to witness it (praise the Lord she didn't, it would have killed her a thousand times over), Karen and I lived in sin, sharing a household from New Year's Day 1992, till we had a quiet wedding on May 5, 2005 (Cinco de Mayo), at my ancestral low Episcopal church, St. Columba's, Albemarle and Forty Second Streets, Northwest D.C., one block from my parents' former house. My mother could not have dealt with this second marriage and would have acknowledged it with greatest difficulty. She had bit the bullet, why couldn't I? She would have thought, though not have said so, that we were still living in sin nevertheless. For there are no second marriages in heaven, neither on earth if the first spouse is living. In my heart I do not believe that my mother, wher'e'er she be, looks down on me now in disapproval. I don't think she looks down on me at all. Even in her time on earth she always looked up. And that's what she must still be doing now.

In the courtly love tradition from medieval times, the lover was expected to pine away for a period of seven years at least, longing from a distance for his lady love who might not even know of his existence (that's *really* loving from afar!). While suffering sleepless nights and meatless or even eatless days (can't sleep, can't eat, can't think, can only sing and suffer over my lady that I love so well), he might perform acts of derring-do and deeds of charity to be enabled to win his lady by dint of proving his love chastely and proving himself worthy of her love through nobility of character. That was in the good old days.

Karen and I took a lower road, a shortcut. So we leap ahead. From Valentine's Day 2006:

> My muse you are,
> You amuse me, you do.
> You're cleverer than words can say, even Jumbles.
> Let me try to count the ways I love you,
> 'Cause I'm better in numbers than you
> Sometimes. But it's impossible to number
> Because you're not only number one to me,
> You're number "un," like
> You're the *un* to my *cola*,
> The *vic* to my *trola*, the *gran* to my *ola*,
> And et cetera.

We were singing an old song. All the clichés were coming true. I don't think I left any out. But it was new to us, in our fashion. Cliché with a personal twist, musty rhyme in re-verse. Somehow it seemed to work in a goofy way, this unlooked for Garden of Eden of our own genesis and cultivation. Karen actually does have a green thumb—unlike Eve, who didn't need one. On my part I planted a fig tree for the figs, not the leaves. Anyway, having dawdled long enough and gotten married, we had a wedding anniversary, another occasion for a poem:

> I want to celebrate a year
> of wedded bliss with you
> With a kiss with you.
> And with another ring,
> Like, an ear ring.
> My ear, too, rings for you.
> But these here ear rings I've got for you
> Are solid gold underneath
> With lots of karats
> Since karats are good for you,
> And vice-versa too,
> My gardener-angel.
> You're my Garden of Hedon-
> Ism in a down to earth sense.

I discovered, by doing, that love poems from me are extremely light verse. Why do I in effect make fun in rhyme of this august subject? The medieval courtly troubadour-type poets weren't on the whole humorists. Most love poems that I know aren't funny, if they're about real-life love. Why is my love life funny to me? The simple answer is that it's funny because it's fun. Overall, for me, fun also means funny, both funny-strange and funny-ha ha. We laugh at things that are incongruent, novel, surprisingly interesting and therefore pleasant to contemplate, refreshingly different. We require routine to put order into life and yet we crave a break from that as well. I thought I was happily married the first time. I got injured in a freak accident, unexpected but in an unpleasant and debilitating way, ironic but not funny. The result was grotesque. It lacked the solace of humor, which is spice. Barbara knew not how to console me or lift me up, through no fault of her own. She was baffled and stymied by my incapacitation. I sought to survive through physical exercise, and to maintain a holding pattern. I let the pattern slip. What intruded was intriguing, pleasing to behold though painful to grasp. It took a while for the new scenario to unfold in its manifold panorama.

A paradox emerged, joy piercing through pain--an earthly salvation of the prodigal, the stricken, the dumbfounded. Funny how it came to pass. Notwithstanding the dark side, in the right light it's pretty as a picture: polychromatic, sort of like a poem.

10

The Mind of a Terrorist

EVERYONE'S BRAIN IS A COMBINATION of smart spots and dumb spots. I, for example, have a great memory for trivia, useless facts. I know that the first thirty-five U.S. presidents' last names, in chronological sequence, begin with the respective letter *W A J M M A J V H T P T F P B L J G H G A C H C M R T W H C H R T E K = Washington Adams Jefferson Madison Monroe Adams Jackson Van Buren Harrison Taylor Polk Tyler Fillmore Pierce Buchanan Lincoln Johnson Grant Hayes Garfield Arthur Cleveland Harrison Cleveland McKinley Roosevelt Taft Wilson Harding Coolidge Hoover Roosevelt Truman Eisenhower Kennedy.* I could never remember all their names or initial letters until I read how to do it in Peg Bracken's *The I Hate to Housekeep Book*, using a mnemonic device.

I could have made up such a mnemonic device myself but never got around to doing it before. Anybody can do it, such as in newly contrived nonsense sentences for the *WAJMMAJ* sequence where: "Well, All Jerks May Make A Jolly Vow Healthily Till Perhaps Their Freaking Pill Box Locks Jewels. Gosh, How Ghoulish All Chaps Heave Cold Martinis Regularly. Ticking War Horses Have Races Timed Elsewhere Keenly." I can also recite the eons of geological time down from the Cambrian period using the same technique, and I'm murder on dates (I mean calendar-type, not "human factors").

Trouble is, I have a devil of a time connecting names with faces. Names of real people in realtime life hit a dumb spot in my brain. Like, I would mistakenly call a student in my linguistics class, whose name was Mitch Raful, *Ray* instead of *Mitch*, I freely substitute *Robert* for *Richard*, etc., and I called a cop I knew named Brian Shanley *Gary* (as in Gary Shandling, the comedian), which he didn't think was funny, and it wasn't meant to be.

What all this means, to me, extrapolating from these examples out to infinity, is that we are all simultaneously geniuses and idiots in different ways and degrees. When we witness and ponder human creatures toppling the Twin Towers in New York City, wilfully killing their guilty selves and thousands of innocents for the sake of calculated mayhem, we see this genius/idiot syndrome at work in an ultimate extension of the paradox. It is disquieting to realize that the prodigious powers that lie in each of us are everywhere subject to distortion, misapplication, and, what is worst of all, to sincere focus on a mistaken target.

The lessons of daily life are instructive. Locally, for example, a ferry goes from Southport to Bald Head Island, North Carolina. Not too tempting a target for terrorists: a few tourists, some commuting residents, a seagull or two. But this time there was a terrorist onboard, unbeknownst to anyone.

The trip is twenty-five minutes, less than five miles. At 9:30 a.m. the *Sans Souci* slipped quietly, after a shrill microsecond toot of the horn, from Southport Harbor into the Cape Fear River, bypassing a sister ship, *The Revenge*, still at anchor. It sluiced through the pylons into midstream, barely ruffling the marsh grass on either side. White ghosts of sailboats and private pleasure-craft, neatly tied and ready side by side, to landward, framed a picture perfect, cool September scene. Fishers, human and avian, tried their luck off the docks, plunging lines or necks into the soft half-surf. (I recoiled only slightly at the sight of a hooked fish in its death throes, gasping in pain, shaking in vain.)

The *Sans Souci* rounded the neck of the inlet into the open water of the mouth of the River and plied toward its confluence with the Atlantic. On the left was Battery Island, a bird haven forbidden to human traffic. On the right, Frying Pan Shoals, where sixteenth century buccaneers had come to grief. Old Baldy, the brick lighthouse of 1812, loomed its 108 feet of altitude dead ahead. This trip was costing thirty-six dollars apiece, and worth every penny. A ferry trip alone would cost sixteen dollars, but our deal included a full-island historic tour and restaurant lunch as a package.

First stop was Old Baldy itself. You had to work your way up to the top, round and round, past several landings, a repetitive sequence of old wooden steps but too many steps to count. The penultimate circular-floor rest stop funneled into a creaky ladder, poking through a dwarf-size hole, up to the lantern outlook. You had to thrust first your head upward to daylight and then scramble, with your legs alongside your torso, up into the sentinel chamber. There was room for four or five in this glass-encased turret. The view was stunning. The island fanned out below, maritime forest stretching from lighthouse foot to the southern pointing tip of Bald Head's triangular shore, where the beach sands of the famous Cape Fear itself obtruded, the southernmost landfall of the state of North Carolina. To the north, an expanse of marsh grass, broken by some meandering streams. The houses and cottages of the rich but not necessarily famous nestled neatly on the southern half, some half-hidden amid shrubbery, in discreetly laid out rows hugging portions of the shoreline.

After Old Baldy, the oversized go-cart conforming to the no-automobiles-allowed policy of the Island putt-putted straight down the old three-mile right of way of the original 1903 railroad that had pioneered the first settlement. We were in the midst of a beach forest primeval. A six-hundred-year-old live oak, spreading several score feet above its ten-foot-wide gnarly trunk, anchored the greenery all around. Lingering here, you could not know, from ground view, that you stood on a mere slip of a sandbar three-by-three miles in dimension.

Lunchtime rolled around. The four of us in our party were by now famished and anticipating our twenty-dollar gourmet lunch, calculating that thirty-six dollars minus the sixteen dollar ferry ride equals a twenty-dollars'-worth lunch. What a feast that must be, in store for us.

At the door of the restaurant, our go-cart guide handed us each a restaurant-ticket and explained: "This is good for eight dollars, not including drinks, taxes, and tip."

What? We all thought, How did a twenty dollar lunch get cut to eight not including taxes and tip, etc.? We might just as well have paid the sixteen-dollar ferry fee and paid eight dollars of our own. Would have saved us twelve dollars apiece. This package is a "deal"? I was the one who had worked out the math of this deal and set our little group to griping inwardly about it.

Being a captive audience, we went into the nice little restaurant with the large glass windows overlooking the harbor and shore. Very scenic, pretty as a picture, so much better than just looking at pictures of scenes on restaurant walls every other place one goes. The server hovered over us at the table ready to receive our eight-dollar order. I, however, wasn't in the mood for an eight-dollar lunch. I wanted my twenty-dollar lunch, and if I didn't get it I would let them have it. I decided not to take this economic insult sitting down, and so I spoke up about it.

I came up with, for starters, "How come this ticket's only worth eight dollars when we paid twenty dollars on shore for the lunch?"

The serving person said, "We don't sell those tickets. You'll have to speak with those people about that."

I continued, heated up for battle, "Well, look, I paid twenty dollars for lunch, and now I'm given a ticket worth eight dollars not including taxes, tip, and drinks. That doesn't seem fair for you to be party to such an arrangement." At this point, the serving person excused herself to appeal to higher authority. The restaurant manager duly came over to our table.

"Yes, sir, what seems to be the trouble?" Challenged by this new foe, I let the manager have it with both barrels.

"We got this deal, see. Thirty-six dollars for ferry and lunch, you know? The ferry is worth sixteen dollars. That makes lunch worth twenty dollars. You're serving lunch, right? I want my twenty-dollar lunch."

Actually, it wasn't a matter of lunch. It was a matter of justice. Somebody was making off with too much of my money for service provided. Somebody would have to pay for that, I would see to it. If this manager didn't see the light, too bad for the manager. The manager was in the way and would have to pay.

I would stick to my guns. I had the right on my side. I was standing up for law and order. Crime would not pay. I would get my due. I would be heard, seen, and felt. I was a mean, fighting machine for truth, justice, and the American way. I'm not going to pay your damn tax. Take a tip from me! And as for drinks, you can throw all your tea in the harbor, for all I care! The reflex muscles of my subconscious were into high gear by now. No one could stop this righteous crusade. God and the Right are with me. Cursed be the one who thinks evil. Give me Liberty or give me Debt. But give me my due.

"Sir," the manager intruded into my interior monologue and exterior harangue. "Perhaps you have miscalculated. We do not control those tickets, in any case. We will be happy to serve you on the terms of your agreed-upon contract."

"The terms are a ripoff," I maintained. "How can we be happy under such terms?" I would not cease and desist. I was committed, or might have been committed if this scene continued much longer along those lines.

At this point, God be praised, an intercessor came to the rescue. "Honey, you know, there were two deals on the brochure. You may be confusing the 'west-east-west way' deal with the 'east-west-east way' deal."

"Oh?" said I, to my guardian-angel wife. "No way. I memorized that brochure and I'm quoting it verbatim to myself and everyone around. A deal is a deal, period." Awkward pause, allowing Karen to have the last word.

"Okay, you've had your say. So now let's just eat, okay?"

Mercifully, I reverted to plan B which in my book was, Just shut up, everybody, and eat. So that's what we did, an eight-dollar lunch instead of a twenty-dollar lunch.

Back on shore, in Southport, I checked the brochure at the terminal, the brochure that I had memorized and neglected to pack along (no need for it, since I knew it by rote). In a nutshell, it said, *Excursion: Southport to Baldhead to Southport, $36 including historic tour and lunch. Baldhead to Southport to Baldhead, $16.* Plus much other irrelevant information. Bottom line: the historic guide-tour was the missing twelve dollars.

So, instead of a twenty-dollar lunch, I ended up eating crow. And (operating impromptu in mammalian rather than reptilian "blood heat") I had done violence, fortunately constrained in this instance to verbal violence, to several innocent parties through direct salvo or aftershock: the server, the manager, and my lunch companions. All in the name of justice, principle, a righteous cause, honesty and decency.

I was the terrorist of the day, on the Bald Head Island ferry. If I had taken *The Revenge* instead of the *Sans Souci*, it might have turned out differently. We're always in a state of war, against them, and in ourselves.

11

Piranhas at the Pond

I'M A NATURE LOVER. I also like dogs. Maybe that's why I still revere the outdoors despite its random violence, periodic fits, and cruel annihilations. Indeed, we can say that Mother Nature is a Bitch. Every placid place, wide vista, arboreal retreat is a monster's den. The quiet sand of a deserted beach harbors a million mouths. Every smooth place is a façade, like the rubbery white closed lips of Jaws. This reality is functional. It is Nature's garbage disposal.

I live on a pond just east of the Great Green Swamp in the southeast corner of North Carolina. This pond took shape a few years ago from the digging out of the local swamp for residential purposes to create a place called Arbor Creek, mostly for middle-age fugitives from the north. This pond acquired the monicker of Willow Lake, though ringed by paper-pine timber, not willows.

Our house is on Waterlily Lane, though there's nary a water lily on Willow Lake. This pond-lake is dumbbell shaped, about two hundred yards long and a hundred wide at its two ends, fifty yards wide down its long middle. It seems lifeless most of the time. However, in February up to twenty hooded mergansers settle in for a couple of weeks on a sojourn during their winter migration northward. They feast on the dozens of minnows and sundry small fry flitting about just under the surface of Willow Lake. Mergansers are a spectacular black and white with luxuriant streamlined jet crests that flash in the southern sun as they duck and dive again and again in fishing to fortify themselves for their inevitable takeoff too soon in early March.

The other notable sign of life in Willow Lake is the occasional alligator, six to eight feet long. There have been three of these on separate occasions in the last two years. Two were removed by authorities using marshmallows on a stick as bait, then expertly gaffed and relocated. One, a smallish one, is still there, I think, somewhere over in the corner neck of the dumbbell end, not attracting much notice anymore.

In early summer I was made aware of a much larger than usual fish that dwelt in our pond, sort of like the Loch Ness monster, hitherto always there though never seen or even believed in by many. My wife told me about it, almost as an afterthought one day.

"Honey, there's a huge dead fish in the lake out back. Would you take care of it, please?"

I surmised that the way to take care of a huge dead fish was to get rid of it rather than to mount it on a plaque or save it for some purpose. So I went out to take a look. It was the biggest recently alive fish I had ever seen in the flesh, about two feet long and pudgy, though not yet puffy. It was nondescript ugly, not like any pretty pictures of fish in books. Just a big long, bulky, fishy fish. And it was beginning to reek. It was in the shallows, side or belly up just a foot or two offshore. I went to the garage and got out my biggest shovel.

I returned to our little mud beach and looked around for a suitable gravesite. About twenty feet to the left of our back yard was a somewhat overgrown common area between our house and our neighbor's house at the curve of the lake. Here next to a large long leaf pine I found a somewhat clean area that seemed commodious enough for Mr. or Ms. Fish. I dug a trench two and a half feet long and a foot deep. The soil all around is soft black sand and makes for good digging. I didn't dawdle or bemoan this melancholy task. I just wanted to get it over with. I then went over to the fish and hoisted it, with some hefty leverage effort, onto the broad curvilinear shovel blade. The carcass was not only big, fat, and long, but heavy, seemed like ten pounds or so. I hauled the fish at shovel's length to the trench and tossed it in, a perfect fit, shoveled the dirt over, smoothed it down with a few sharp pats and clangs, and let it be. Job done. I returned to my leisure. The fish would trouble me no more, I believed at the time. Safe even from curious cats.

We don't have a cat but we do have a dog. Two dogs, actually, one a senile yellow Lab (Buddy) and the other a frisky Staffordshire terrier, a.k.a. pit bull (Dixie). Dixie is cute and seemingly diminutive, though strong as a bull, and so we pretend to everyone who doesn't know better that she's a miniature boxer. Dixie sometimes spends time on a long chain in our back yard. She also likes to dig in the dirt. I realized immediately that the fish grave was in range of Dixie's chain. I went outside to check, just in time to prevent Dixie's thorough violation of the shrine. She had just ruffled the dirt at one end of the trench and exposed the fish's tail. I repacked the tail, fish intact, and duly shortened Dixie's range so the fish could be out of harm's way for the eternity to come.

The next day, though, I figured that rather than restrict Dixie's rummaging, I could expediently relocate the fish corpse so that the lingering fishiness wouldn't annoy Dixie and so that I could be rid of these haunting threats of grave visitation and molestation in perpetuity. I resolved to dig another grave at a fuller remove. I scouted out the terrain along the shore in the other direction. There was a wide open, flat expanse of common ground between our house and the neighbor on the other side, away from trees and far beyond Dixie's province.

I got out my shovel and dug out the new site, thirty inches long and twelve inches deep and wide. I congratulated myself for being so proactive and preemptive rather than dwelling on my shortsightedness for not being so in the first place. I went to the big tree and the last remains of the fish, so as to haul it over for redeposition. The carefully handworked grave was smoothly intact, my precautions regarding Dixie proving effectual.

But though the surface was unruffled, I was intrigued that the covered trench had subsided a bit, as if some interior depression within, hid from view, had been activated by my previous day's work. Nevertheless, gratified that the grave had not been violated from without, I began to dig. I marveled at why my undigging was now, however, taking longer than the previous digging. It had been a relatively extended grave (for a fish) but nonetheless a somewhat shallow one. I dug several shovelfuls but initially struck nothing.

At length, a hard small semi-spherical mass clanked the shovel. It was a fish skull, or at least the better part of a fish skull. There were also a spare few seemingly random shards of bone, casual bits of scale or skin in a spotty file along the expanse of the trench.

There was something else, too. Maggot-like creatures, insect life, an almost foaming feeding frenzy of it. By this ravaging, ravenous horde the fish had been penetrated, masticated, consumed, obliterated. The efficiency and rapidity of this immolation almost defied belief, but there I stood in testimony and as witness, in real-time. It was gone.

Mother Nature had had her fill, ten pounds of it, in a single day. The creatures of the night had been at work while I slept. So much for an eternal resting place. The Earth had swallowed, and the fish had gone the way of all fish, and of all flesh, in a moment, in the twinkling of an eye.

So when you tell a story of the fish that got away, remember. No fish gets away. Not away from Mother Nature. Mother Nature is nurturer and devourer. Mother Nature can appropriately be called Maw Nature, with open jaws like a hell mouth. Mother Nature is a Bitch. And of course, in the long run, Father Time is pretty mean too. We are a cosmic family of abused children, in one form or another.

12

Night Run

HE DIDN'T WANT TO GO to Mexico this time. Good time of year, sure, a week in January, and just at the cusp of the New Millennium, 2000 A.D./A.C.E., the alternate abbreviations signifying an old time/new time interface. But the water. That was always a problem. He liked to splash in a tub or shower without worry about micro-organisms. He didn't care for third world water. Nonpotable. So, this time were hauled in extra tanks of U.S. H_2O. Big blue cannisters, to brush teeth and shave face. Still a hassle for the wimpy tenderfoot. Hard to call such an alienating locus home. But he took comfort in cliches about the inevitable imperfection of the temporal, no matter where you hang your hat at any given time. In this case, he recalled a saying edited into memory in the form, "Your Home is Your Hassle." And so he determined to make do, to rough it in comfort as far as he would be able. To open his eyes and mind to the new, and to the old.

The place in question this new year was good old Rocky Point, Puerto Penasco. It's an hour south of Lukeville, Arizona, which is two hours west of Tucson, the (to him) more familiar concept of God's country, the Sonoran Desert, a veritable forest of saguaro. The saguaro was God's cactus, uplifting and everlasting arms, bending in a consonance with the curvature of the cosmos: haven of woodpeckers.

The landscape can get ever so desolate as one meanders southward, but it radiates an eternal vastness that stimulates rather than stultifies the mind, energizes rather than enervates. Yes, he could endure a week and more of this essence, in a car heading toward a condo. South of the border-gate and guardhouse, however, into the upper reaches of what he thought of as Cisco and Pancho country, they encountered the litter. It hung in shreds and tatters festooning the junk on every side from the border town into the circumscribing desert which shared now in its blight.

As mile upon mile of this degraded nothingness emptied its load into the eye, he asked his wife Karen, who was driving, "How is it possible to kill a desert? This part of this one done died, it looks like."

What should be sand had eroded to dust. What should be proud cactuses were droopy-armed burned out carcasses. What should be mountain vistas on either side and in the distance were hazeblurred sour-milky stains in an opaque off-white background, even the disk of the sun itself having been dirtied into a bland vagueness, its bright rays and rim squeezed pale.

The Gulf of California, the Sea of Cortez, was another story and a better one. The haze lifted a couple of miles to the north of it, and as the car skirted its northeast crescent, the blueness of sky meshed into the calm and cool deep purple of the gentle rocking wave-wind ridges. And this water mixed well with alcohol. One quick stop to pack home their own sun of Sol and Corona, the beer to accompany the brandy fit for a president, El Presidente, and a bottle of medium dark rum.

Into the palazzo, unkept and unswept but no matter. A few whisks and fluffs, some scrubbing and buffing, and all was good as new again. "Maid service just missed the boat, apparently!" someone said.

The inlaws and their brood, with him and Karen, settled down on this quiet overlook a couple of miles downwind from the cliff and city of Rocky Point. The beginning of a perfect evening, the eve of a dawning, yawning day and, unaccountably, of a night to remember—an encounter with the depths.

He slept in next morning and all of the afternoon too. First time in his life he could remember doing that. Got up at 6 p.m., just in time for happy hour. Brandy was the candy. Fish was the dish, halibut with marinade ala *Washington Post* by chef Bill. Potage by Padre Kino, a fine enough white wine (any vintner-priest is indeed keeno!) He would have played after-dinner dominoes with the rest of the gang, but his old friend Gersham, from Jamaica, its erstwhile national champion, he supposed, had given him a recent all-night tutelage and drubbing in the sport, which constituted his fill of it for the time being.

He needed a run. Now 9:30 p.m. Dark as pitch. But still, all that was lacking to make a blissfully uneventful evening complete and perfecto was a good workout, an outdoor night-time adventure. He donned his two-piece sweatsuit--charcoal shirt, midnight-blue pants.

Karen cautioned, "Maybe wear something white at night?" So he pulled a T-shirt over top of his top, glad of such a sensible solicitation.

Out the door and into the night, for the quota of a forty minute ramble. He can run all of ten minutes a mile, so he had four miles of new territory to cover with his feet and uncover with his mind.

He recalled the road they drove from Rocky Point to the casa. It was hard and unexpectedly smooth, obstacle-free at first viewing--a fine road for running, he had thought to himself. He would have to trust to memory. Once outside the door of the house he couldn't even see his feet. His watch, however, had a pushbutton glow face. He checked the time: 9:37. Three minutes for a warmup walk. He ambled up the little hill of the seaport's enclave to the crest overlooking the desert interior, now just a blackboard backdrop. Time, 9:40. He bolted off, down the incline's other side and into the void. He sensed a turning off to the left of the abyss, corresponding to what he recalled by the road of entry. He eased over into it, peripherally gleaning an amber-tinted margin of what must be the roadway.

His body felt light and strong with the combination of snooze and booze. He charged along in the dark, alone with his thoughts and his reviving ego. Yes, this was life, he and the dark: chugging Mother Nature's spirit. And in the emptiness, a fulfillment of its existential possibility of becoming something. An *ex nihilo superbo!* A beginning of something from the nothing of his mundane middle ages--a renaissance even, potentially, from this little bit of a nothing run on this infinitesimal speck of planetary dust. He was ready for a revelation. A great expectation for no goddamn reason! What could befall, here in this empty place of space and time? He paced himself. Ten-minute-flat mile gait. No sweat. He knows his limits! Still darkness all around. A quiet emptiness of all things. What will fill the forty minutes of finitude? A look ahead.

Suddenly, as he passes the top of a short embankment, he sees a line of light! It is far in the distance, a long way off, far, far into the future, a destination for another time. It is the town of Puerto Penasco, stretching from dead ahead to the far right horizon, now illuminated by a seeming single row of white light after white light. A linear row of spangles, dotted with a few specks of red or yellow. The lights of life. Something good to gaze at, without prospect of attainment, much too far to achieve in his paltry forty minutes of time allotted to his breath of the moment, his programmed plan. A good view, anyway, something to stare at, to ponder, to occupy his mind's eye. But his eyes now, it seemed so, were getting used to the dark as the saying goes, and he could see even more of the road ahead and to each side--its furrowed grey-blackness offset by an almost orange sideberm against which he could gauge his step. Telephone poles loomed up and at him on both sides like intermittent goalposts of a ghostly game of football.

He could make up the rules of this game as he pranced along. He didn't like to think of running as work, though sometimes it amounts to that--strain, stress, striving to make it, or to finish what one has begun. In a work sense, though, he will concoct current, short-term, intermediate, and long-range goals. He tends to think of such jargon laden thought as a load of crap, and so he tries not to think in jargon. But he likes to think, to ponder, to philosophize, to wonder. He wonders how far he can go tonight. Maybe all the way? Always a pleasant prospect. He listens to his breath. A nice steady wheeze. Old age not yet at its last gasp, rather a crescendo to a smoking climax. Yes, he is in good shape, sort of. Oat meal, green tea, vitamin C, garlicky fish. No wonder there's nobody around for miles in any direction. And no danger from vampire bats either. But this ugly mush mix turns and churns into creative energy, full pockets of fleshy abs, pectoral potency. All this essence spinning in the abyss of night. "Aren't I something, yes, wow! Puny me on this dusty road to infinity. Hot stuff!"

In this delirium of wonderment over nothing much at all, he looks up and out again. Wonder of wonders! The lights ahead are no longer an unbroken string into the disappearing night on the right but are discrete bulbs, each an island, an oasis, one of which is even approaching toward his left shoulder. He is actually progressing and on the way to an imminent encounter with this shiny city on the hill of the cliff of Rocky Point! He will actually reach a destination tonight, at this unremitting pace!

His scenario for the night's entertainment begins to undergo rapid alteration. "I will cool my heels in Rocky Point before this night is out," he now says to himself. "I will reach the unreachable, set foot on the far distant shore, yet within grasp of my stubby toes. The light on the left looms larger with each pulsating bounce of my rubberman shoes. I can check my newfound nightwatch-timetable in the form of my luminous lefthand wristwatch. As soon as I pass the mansion to my left, the time will be noted and my course confirmed. Here it comes, there it is, now just passing by my slimfast waist. The little hand is on the ten and the big hand is on the eleven, perfecto! I have run fifteen minutes, gone a mile and a half, and reached the first sentinel outpost of the town looming ahead. Another half mile, another five minutes, and I will be within its portals, savoring its all-night existential secrets. I have almost got it made."

He pounds the smooth dusted surface of the road ever more fine grained under the vast crunching of his awesome heels. "Rocky, here we come, get the point?" The leading lights are lining up in his sights, one by one.

He hums, "One casa, two casa, three casa, four, and after four are coming lots and plenty more. Little lights, big city. I see its walls, towers, portico, moat and its battlements towering up over me now at the height of my fancy. On the left is the hacienda grande of El Presidente himself." The runner's high, brandy and rum enhanced, has kicked in. He approaches the portico. The internal monologue continues:

"The gendarmes are there in feverish anticipation of my coming. They are getting up out of their emplacements to utter words of welcome, to hand over to me the keys of the city. My Clorox-clean T-shirt flaps and claps in the onrushing wind applauding my advent to this clamoring, cheering crowd. The herald brandishes his clarion. With a wave of my hand I soothe his apprehension. No need for ceremony, my benevolent glance assures him. I have arrived. That is enough. You have acknowledged my being. Bravo to you, sir, *mi amigo!* I will now take my leave, having graced your day with my entity."

He passes the *Alto* sign by the guard station and does an about face, careful not to diminish the velocity of his Keplerian flyby, then comet-like begins his retro phase. City lights no more. But lo! Altogether unexpected, a myriad lanterns suspend themselves in honor to the night and to him. Yes, these are the stars that had heretofore hid, sometime under cloud, off to the north in that haze he had hissed earlier that selfsame day. These now supplant those human-hung imposters, those imitation luminosities, those dim-bulbs all that pop and flop inopportunely when we read or need them. These true celestial spheres fine tuned to points and suffusing the sky's expanse with an all embracing ineffable glow lit his way home.

He could now fully see the road, which assumed its shape as a pointing path. It rose and fell, wave upon wave narrowing to a shaft of needle sharpness in the distance. All senses--sight, sound, touch, were engaged. A fresh wind blew at his back and whistled in the telephone wires, becoming the hum of an Aeolian harp. It resonated to thrill his own heartstrings, pulsing in an echo up the road back into the unseen air that vaulted him along in a vast weightlessness. He charged along in this electric ocean current like Sir Apollo, star shooter.

He had advanced far in these elapsed few minutes of time and fewer miles of distance. One motor car, only, passed his way on his return, the sole fellow traveler he had had to and fro. It bobbed up and down through hill and declivity in its twin-taillight retreat ahead of him, quickly passing beyond into nothingness to his view. But his journey continued, stretching in the wake of that forerunner as if in slow-motion recapitulation of the past, present, and future that unrolls before all of us who run the race of life through light and shadow.

He reached the turning point, now in reverse to the right, that he had encountered at his outset. He slowed into the glow of the light of a single porch at the top of the little hill overlooking his own gate. And then he ambled in, to a quiet, night-hushed house. The family were still up, each and all in a cozy nook or cranny, noses in newspapers or books, befitting the lulling mood of the evening. He was greeted with cordial albeit indifferent deference and felt again at home after being so many light years away. "Did you have a nice run?" was the sentiment spoken by one as if for all. "Yep," said he in microcosmic affirmation of all that he had seen, visible and invisible.

And at that moment he realized he had learned something in this short night: Four miles can take you anywhere you want to go.

Eleanor and Richard, Byrd Park VA

David (7) and Richard (4), Richmond VA

(clockwise) Eleanor, Richard, Marian, David (Quaker Lake PA)

Tom (9), Dan (7), Mary (8), Dickie (11), Washington DC

Rebel (sketch by Karen)

Dixie, 2009

Zoomer, 2017

13

Numb and Numberer

"I've always wanted a puppy," she said. Trouble is, I thought, puppies are a lot of trouble, and then they turn into dogs, which are even more trouble. She should know that. We do have a dog, you know.

She's always had a dog. Karen, you understand, is a dog lover. Bulldogs, mastiffs, golden retrievers, yellow Labs, mutts, all receive equal devotion and attention from her.

I had had dogs too, even when I was a kid. But they all died, usually horrible lingering or shocking bloody deaths. Skippy, a black and white setter, got pneumonia and croaked in the cellar. Tippytale, a little brown mutt, got squashed by a passing car in the back alley. I heard the stifled squeal and saw the immediate aftermath--the neck and one-half of the skull a bloody pulp. It left a lasting impression on me as a ten-year old.

And the last dog of my adolescence, Pal, was a handsome but high-spirited nuisance. Medium height, burnished gold, mostly collie but shorthaired and short-fused. Would run away through any open door or gate left ajar. Loved to play field hockey, during these escapades, with the girls at Woodrow Wilson High School. One time he bit one of the girls attempting to score in his territory, drew blood, got a death sentence and was hauled to the pound without so much as a goodbye. The family resignedly let him go without attempting a reprieve.

In my adulthood, however, there was Rebel. Rebel was a foundling, a foot-long puppy, lost or abandoned, wandering around our block too long, and we took her in. She grew into a mostly golden retriever. Her distinguishing feature, along with her golden locks, looks and disposition, was her tail, always displayed erect, a multi-stranded variegated extravagant plume of shimmering white-auburn. As she walked at any gait, the plume bounced up and down vertically behind and danced like an effervescent fountain spouting above her haunches.

Rebel liked to run away too, but she didn't bite. Liked to party late at night with the college kids two miles across town (I myself had by this time migrated from Washington, D.C., to Eckhart Flats, situated incongruously in the mountains of western Maryland). The students would call us up when the party broke up about 2 a.m., and we would drive over and pick her up.

Once, on her wayward way to such a tryst, she got hit by a car on Main Street. That broke her pelvis, which mended in a couple of weeks. After that, she walked cockeyed, her front legs about three or four inches to the left on a line back to her hind legs, her backbone a diagonal rod obliquely connecting bow and stern. But her tail bounced and bubbled the same as ever.

Rebel died of old age, at eighteen (either 108 or 126 equivalent human years, depending on whether you count one human year as six or seven dog years), the only pet I had ever had among a multitude of dogs, cats, parakeets, fish, and Mexican jumping beans to die "naturally."

I do love animals. I save turtles whenever I see one on the road, even the snapping kind, by getting out of my car and carrying them to a safe pond or ditch. In this manner I have also rescued numerous snakes and even once, strange to tell, an ailing butterfly which I plucked from a road at Yosemite National Park. I set it down among some wild flowers in the adjoining meadow, where, alas, it breathed heaving gasps and may soon have given up the ghost after I had wished it well and taken my leave. As far as domestic pets go, however, I'm more a cat lover than a dog lover. It's a matter of temperament. I like time to myself. So do cats. Dogs are more in your face.

In middle age I became engaged to Karen. She had at that time a mastiff, named Snag (short for Snaggletooth). Snag was big, and black. A canine as big as a man, six feet long from head to hindquarters, took up the whole sofa. And Snag drooled, profusely. Karen liked to dress Snag in a bandanna around his neck, for decoration, not for any practical purpose. It didn't dry or attenuate the drool a whit. Snag died at age eight from a convoluted intestine.

His place was taken by Buddy, a year-old yellow Lab. Buddy was much traveled in search of a home. Karen's sister had adopted him, which lasted a week. He would destroy or break out of any confined habitat, such as a back yard. Karen heeded her sister's distress call and we drove 450 miles to pick up and adopt Buddy ourselves. On the trip back to our house Buddy, big and boisterous as he was, would continually attempt to sit in either my or Karen's lap, regardless of who was driving.

We discovered early that Buddy had an insatiable emotional need, a longing for security, fear of abandonment, and a jealousy of security or closeness observed in others. He did not like Karen and me to hug one another without him. Whenever Karen and I would embrace for any reason, in any room, he would bark like a nut, jump up and place himself between us to intervene.

Though gradually he became weaned from this overbearing intrusiveness, he never overcame his fear of being alone, or left behind. He broke through a dozen or more screens when left in the house on various occasions, once overturning a huge terrarium set between window and floor, scattering mounds of soil, plants, and cacti to the four corners of the room. He more than once broke through mini-slatted wooden shutters plus screen to jump through a window and escape. He bulled down several iterations of our wooden picket fence at any perceived vulnerable point, and when a repaired section was buttressed and elevated, would find a mini-gap to batter through or just jump that extra foot higher to make a getaway.

One of his best but least successful attempted escapes was from a second floor window, fifteen feet above ground, except that upon jumping out he landed on the porch roof rather than going all the way down, lucky for him. The only effective preventive measure was to make sure all windows in the house were securely closed and fastened before our leaving. Wood and metal mesh were no match for

Buddy, but when in effect encased in glass, he didn't so readily whiff the sweet smell of the outdoors to entice him to break away.

We hated all of that while continuing to love Buddy, the more so when we discovered long scars, inflicted by some hard instrument, underneath the fur of his muzzle, which betrayed violent abuse of him at a tender age, probably in an earlier owner's back yard. Buddy still refuses to rest at ease in any back yard, even our own tranquil one.

With Buddy still in tow, though at six years old a bit the worse for wear and partly hobbled by a bad back from jumping through too many screened and shuttered windows and wood-slatted fences, Karen received another distress call, this time from her daughter, a graduate student in library science at Chapel Hill, North Carolina, 350 miles away. Her landlord owned but could not care for a puppy, a baby pit bull. The pup was chained all day in the basement--in effect abused by neglect.

Would Karen be interested in rescuing this puppy, taking it in, her daughter wanted to know? Of course. "But we already have a dog," I noted. I also noted to myself that two dogs are not twice the trouble of one dog, they're four times the trouble. That is a hypothetical but time-tested mathematical axiom. So I vetoed Karen's suggestion that we adopt the poor puppy.

A few days later she repeated the request and again I denied it. Not only is Karen a dog lover, she is a sucker, in the same sense that all Good Samaritans are suckers. They are not able to behold the misery of the world without partaking of it. I'm that kind of a sucker too, but concerning dogs I was hoping to cop out this time, draw the line and limit the mayhem.

Another week or so went by and the situation had not changed. Karen issued another plea, and realizing the sincerity and emotional truth of the need, I acquiesced, even though I haven't always wanted a puppy and moreover I want a cat.

So Dixie came into our household. She indeed was cute, cuter than any pit bull you'll ever see, even any puppy pit bull you'll ever see. She looked like a miniature boxer, and kept that look as she grew into adolescence and beyond. It was half a year before she grew big enough to be able to jump up into our bed, but she wasn't nervous or jealous like Buddy, she was just friendly. Anything bigger than she was, she would love and lick. Anything smaller than she was, she would kill and/or eat. She was terror on a walk. On two memorable, separate occasions, while at the end of a leash she killed, indeed instantaneously shredded, a possum and a skunk, not without consequences in the latter case.

When Dixie was about a year old we moved from western Maryland to southeastern North Carolina, on the coast near Wilmington. Now, on walks, Dixie kills frogs and toads and swallows them whole in a gulp. Whenever I see a frog or toad I pull Dixie away, but often she's quicker of eye and of lurch than I am, and always faster than any frog or toad. I think it's a disgusting habit, but it's part of the price I'm willing to pay to be a pit bull owner and a dog lover's lover.

Dixie continues to look like a small boxer, and to others we pretend that's what she is. We can in fact correctly use the designation Staffordshire terrier rather than pit bull, and that's how I usually refer to her among strangers. We named her Dixie because we knew we were to be moving to the South, and Dixie feels right at home here.

The son of our kennel owner calls her "awesome." On walks or romps in the park, children are attracted to her and like to walk with her, taking the leash from my hand. She is all sweetness and light to humans.

Dixie is also stupid, a bonehead, a numbskull. On walks through the neighborhood, she would try to charge at any oncoming car or truck, until brought up short at the end of the leash. Until recently, she was so untamed that whenever something would rustle or flit within her sight or hearing, she would bolt after it until jolted by the rope or chain. But she is strong as an ox. Her jerking and jolting would often set her free on a roam or chase because no hand could hold fast against a random explosive burst at any given microsecond. On one of these jolts she broke Karen's right leg, the fibula bone above the ankle, when the leash twisted back on Karen.

Because of this boundless energy Dixie has, we liked to let her run free for a half hour or forty-five minutes daily, to get some of this zeal out of her system. There are several parks and open areas available around Southport where we live. Smithville Park is a good one. High fences, spacious fields, some copses and marshy gullies, and a huge sandboxed play area, kind of a nice pit for a pit bull. There's enough vegetation to harbor black snakes that Dixie likes to try to find for the kill, though I have often been able to intervene effectively and save some wildlife. Even birds are fair prey to her despite being able to fly out of her reach, almost all of the time. I was glad to be able to rescue a fledgling on a recent outing, and in general it doesn't bother me that she chases birds since they have the means to escape her. Running after birds is a good workout. Dixie never tires of the chase, seems unaccountably inexhaustible.

Most recently, I took Buddy and Dixie to Smithville Park for an evening romp, an hour or so before dark. After forty-five minutes of sniffing, snorting, playfighting, chasing and dervish-whirling, it seemed to me that Dixie as well as Buddy had had enough fun and it was time to go home. We were at the grove next to the driveway within the park, and I called to Buddy and Dixie to come so we could go to the car and leave. Buddy ambled over to me as usual.

With Dixie things are often more problematic. It takes more cajoling, and Dixie has more whims, but often she will come to me anyway. This time, though, she willfully defied me, looked back to me in the face, turned then and ran in the opposite direction away from me to and through the entrance gate, now her exit to the outside world and all its forbidden fruit. I ran after her. She turned left into the nearby grass margin of Highway 133 that runs alongside the park and raced along outside the fence for about twenty-five yards.

I called to her again. She stopped, looked back at me, and then dashed full tilt into the highway southbound and against the oncoming northbound traffic. A white oversized SUV approached, lights on, at about thirty miles per hour. Dixie made a bull rush into it point blank, being stopped only by the impact of its front bumper against the top of her head. The clank was like a baseball bat against a metal pole.

I had never before witnessed an encounter of flesh and bone upon hardhitting steel, and I tried to absorb the shock of it without myself crumpling inwardly. I was partaking in a mortal accident in real-time as a first-hand eyewitness--an unmitigated, almost intolerable horror to any civilian, much less a squeamish sort such as myself.

My God! That was my dog! (I knew that "was" rather than "is" was now the proper tense to use in my mental scream.) Death by disaster. Close encounter of the worst kind. Oh Hell!

Even now I tried to rationalize. Yes, it's my dog, but only a dog, thank God!

The vehicle stuttered, jolted, then screeched to a halt down the right shoulder of the road.

It was a young woman at the wheel.

"O My God," she said, echoing my own internal monologue.

Meanwhile, incredibly, Dixie, who had been splatted into the pavement, head and belly, by the several-ton hurtling antagonist, struggled up and hurtled off into the neighboring woods. To die, I guess, I said to myself.

"Oh, I'm so sorry," said the SUV driver. "I jammed on my brakes and stopped as soon as I could."

"I know, you did everything you could. I'm sorry. It was Dixie's fault, not yours," said 1.

"Oh, your little boxer? I have a dog named Dixie too! I'm so sorry."

She was at least as shaken as I was, probably more so, having been even more closely involved.

"Well, look, she got up and ran. She might be okay," I offered.

"There's no way she's okay," said Jennifer, whose name I was soon to learn. "I hit her head on and then felt the back wheel run over her."

"Well, anyway, I'll go and look for her," I said.

"Let me help you," said Jennifer.

"All right, sure, thanks."

So I went around on foot and Jennifer went in her SUV searching the vicinity for Dixie. A witness across the road told me she saw her run into the field there, so I looked around back and forth in that area, but to no avail. It was by now getting pretty dark. Jennifer drove back up.

"I didn't see her around the woods either," she said.

"Well," I said, "I'll look around a while longer, but it's dark now so you'd better go on. I'll call you later and let you know what happened."

"Okay, here's my number." She wrote her name and phone number down for me.

"Thanks again, so much," I said. "You've been very helpful. I really appreciate your concern."

"I'm so, so sorry," she said again, sobbing, and drove slowly away.

I walked around all the neighboring woods and fields, in the dark moonlight, for another half hour, and back to the park and looked around there, no sign or sound of anything, no blood, no cry, no nothing. I went home and told the story at length to Karen. We both then and there began to bury Dixie mentally, stiffen our minds, feel the numbness. We tried our best to sleep and put it to rest and move on, as one must.

Karen got up as usual at 6 a.m. to take Buddy for his early walk, this time without Dixie and trying to get used to the idea, hard as it is to so suddenly adjust to shattering events. At 8 a.m. the phone rang. I picked it up.

"Do you have a little boxer dog who's missing? It's here at Smithville Park. It's been hurt. It's bleeding." "I'll be there in ten minutes," I said. I got there in eight.

A gruff middle-aged but kindly woman was there with her own dog, her cell phone, and Dixie. Dixie was bleeding from her forehead and belly but able to walk and seemingly alert. "Thank you so much. You are very kind," I said, packed up Dixie into the car, and took her home.

She had no hair on the top of her head from forehead to crown or on her underside, which was scraped as if by a shearing knife, and she was discolored by dried blood on head and belly but nevertheless seemed intact. She, it turned out, had no broken bones and no serious internal injuries. She apparently suffered no brain damage because there was very little upstairs to damage. She slept around the house for a week or two, grew back her hair except for a dark one-inch needle-width scar on her forehead and is the same dumb dog as ever, only now less aggressive toward cars, though no less ferocious on frogs.

Snakes remain at the top of her list of antagonists. On a romp in the Fish Factory swamp with Karen, Dixie faced off with a five-foot-long two-inch-thick water moccasin. It began with a fencing kind of dance, then became a jabbing entanglement to the death. For a full ten minutes after getting a jaw lock on the cotton-mouth a foot or two behind its head, in a back and forth twisting whip-lash Dixie shook it to and fro in rapid-fire oscillations of concussive jerks. At length, the serpent broke into two halves, one half still fast between Dixie's teeth. A neighboring farmer also witnessed the struggle. "That dog is a force of Nature," he philosophized.

Dixie, it turned out, had got bitten and envenomed during the fight, and her head swelled up afterwards; but she recovered within a day under observation and veterinary counseling (administer Benadryl).

Yesterday she tried to eat a copperhead. It bit her. I saw the encounter occurring by the edge of our front drive. The snake was a diminutive but definitive pit-viper with the distinct triangular markings and beautiful, burnished skin. Pit-viper versus pit bull—good matchup.

I eased toward the reptile and, making as if like Steve Irwin, picked it up by the tail. (Dixie's dumbness is infectious, it would appear.) The rope of reptile whipped back on me and, empty-fanged, "brushed its teeth" on my arm. I felt a graze but no puncture. Apparently it had spent its entire load of venom on Dixie's muzzle. With two sticks I carried the snake over to the neighboring thicket and let it slither off.

Dixie's nose immediately bloated and in a matter of minutes she was markedly swollen and distended all along the throat, rapidly developing a pendulous bulge from mouth to chest. We consulted the vet who observed that our type of dog is more snake-resistant than we, and advised appropriate over-the-counter medication (administer Benadryl). A day later Dixie was strutting around again more or less normally! I guess there's just no getting rid of her, is there!

So I just go on whistling Dixie, interpolating as well some adapted strains of *The Froggie Would A-Wooing Go*:

> As the froggie was crossing a brook,
> A little brown dog came and gobbled him up,
> Uh-huh, uh-huh.

This dog is truly awesome. Dumb, yet awesome just the same.

But I still want a cat. Truly awesome too, a step ahead of the pack. Even have a name already. Zoomer.

14

The Writing Well

THE PRESCRIPTION OF SIR PHILIP Sidney to "Look in thy heart and write" is good advice. But no heart pumps in a vacuum. Our lifeblood goes back through a long stream of creatures. Rich and red though human blood is, chemically it is closely akin to seawater. The distinction between us and the depending chain of life that we head up is our intellectual heritage, the lore that we pass along and recreate from generation to generation. When we write, we pick up from what has gone before. Even the Bible needs to be approached afresh as its eternal truths are taken to apply in varying ways to societal contexts that change. Seven days of Creation in Genesis expand to seven ages of human development in Shakespeare:

> All the world's a stage, and all the men
> And women merely players. They have their exits
> And their entrances, and one man in his time
> Plays many parts, his acts being seven ages.

Shakespeare's writing stands on its own, but we can take a boost off his shoulders whenever we like. Actually, we can apply aspects of his work to suit our own fancy in a different way from his own intent. His sonnets were at the pinnacle of that form of poem, and we needn't be thrown off when we learn that some of the most romantic sounding of them were written for a man. A case in point is the famous "Shall I Compare Thee to a Summer's Day," which can be taken now to apply to anybody, particularly someone of the opposite sex, though to Shakespeare it was a statement of idealized friendship for a young man of his acquaintance:

Shall I compare thee to a summer's day?
Thou art more lovely, and more temperate.
Rough winds do shake the darling buds of May,
And summer's lease hath all too short a date.
Sometime too hot the eye of heaven shines,
And often is his gold complexion dimm'd.
And every fair from fair sometimes declines,
By chance or Nature's changing force untrimm'd.
But thy eternal summer shall not fade,
Nor lose possession of that fair thou owest,
Nor shall death brag thou wanderest in his shade,
When in eternal lines to Time thou growest.
So long as men can breathe or eyes can see,
So long lives this, and this gives life to thee.

Sonnets are one of my favorite modes of verse; they have been a staple off and on for almost half a millennium. I like to write betimes in that form myself. It's still a cogent package for a little love poem or a reflection about almost anything, concrete or abstract. A few years ago a couple in my church were about to celebrate their fiftieth wedding anniversary, so as a present to them I composed a love sonnet taking off from Shakespeare's encomium to a young man.

I exploited, as did Shakespeare, images drawn from the natural world and celestial phenomena, stock material for metaphor. To that storehouse I added modern scientific terms, some idioms of colloquial currency, my own spin to the poetic loom. The theme was ageless love in the form of an elderly, devoted husband and wife whose names were Bob and Carolyn:

Com-pair: Two, One to One
(Easy as CAB, BAC, Carolyn and Bob, Bob and Carolyn)

Shall I compare thee to the break of day?
Thou art my love, the sunrise to my earth,
The dawn of each new morning, come to birth,
Infrared and ultraviolet ray
Both light my fire for you anew, today.
Awakening to the sunshine of your mirth
I feel your warmth, an everburning hearth
Which holds the sun that glows within the grey.
And oh! how my love rises up, surrounded
By your sky, free as the air all new
Which breathes in you and me all interchanged,
And now takes on the ocean's deepening hue,
As looking in each other's eyes, reflected,
Each to each, we see ourselves, perfected.

Although I saw Bob and Carolyn every week in church, and occasionally heard Bob give a talk about a current event or two, and once attended a party at their house, I didn't feel as though I knew them very well. They appeared to be in their late seventies or perhaps even in their eighties: telltale shuffling gaits, moderately stooped posture, hearing aids, canes, the full panoply of age. I had within myself, however, a deep sense of the quality of their relationship. Their mutual love was evident in every shuffle. They shuffled almost in unison. Bob retained the chivalric gestures of a bygone era, one he had partaken of personally. Carolyn was likewise of the old school, and was now a grande dame with an aura like a Queen Mother. As they had aged, they had continued to meld. It's a beautiful thing to behold.

One of the best analogies in Nature, though one I didn't use probably because it didn't come to mind but just now, is that of an old-growth tree. Live oaks and redwoods not only continue to grow with age, they grow better with age. They are higher, stronger, deeper, more grounded than a young adult or middle-age tree. Their foliage is more luxuriant, their canopy more imposing. They have achieved both stature and statuesqueness. They are the glory of any forest in which they reside or any block where they hold sway. They are what every tree would aspire to be, the epitome of success.

The other analogy which I didn't use is wine. When a good wine gets old enough, it becomes too expensive to consume in the ordinary way. It becomes an object to be revered. Such was the reverential stature of Bob and Carolyn which I experienced merely as an observer but was proud to memorialize in literary form, using the model of a Shakespearean sonnet, albeit in the Italian style of rhyme scheme.

Shakespeare called music the "food of love": "If music be the food of love, play on." Music is also the food of poetry. It is what sustains its form, enlivens it, provides its rhythmic breath. Most good poems are melodic. Many are set to song. Sonorous vowels, matching and meshing consonants are arranged intuitively or deliberately by the composer of the poem. It is why the word *lyric* or *lyrics* simultaneously means word and song. In my career as a professor of English I took time avocationally to participate in music activities at the university. I studied voice, sang Renaissance madrigals in the Collegium, enrolled in the opera workshop, played the part of the bat in *Die Fledermaus*.

At Christmas season the Collegium put on a madrigal feast for the public. We dressed in period costumes, paraded out with a fake boar's head, and generally made merry as we sang while the patrons feasted. I was appointed court poet for the occasion. All my poem lacked was a tune to be played on instruments and sung. It was composed to be recited by me as spoken word. My challenge was to make melody in words alone. But that's according to my theory of what a poem, a good poem, does naturally anyway. All I had to do was pull out a few extra stops to let the music of poetry sound out full blast:

Our Music is the Food of Love

December is a festive month for all,
And Musick is the symbol of our feast.
Yes, Musick is their food, our mad regale.

> They stand, they sing, they smell the roasted beast,
> They fill their throats with notes withal, the while.
> With you, our guests, they hail the rich pale rum.
> Their voices lift, and they your ears beguile.
> Their lips and tongues do savor every "umm,"
> Transmuting to ambrosia. They serve it forth,
> Each blissful course, each chorus a repast.
> How merrily they sing! How saucily it poureth!
> A season's spicy blend. Makes pulse go fast,
> Then slow: a rush or hush—your heart's desire's
>   refrain!
> *Your* thrill is ours, *your* happiness *our* gain.

The audience was doing the eating. We were doing the singing. I tried to make the poem sound as if singing was an imbibing and ingesting action, a feast in itself. Indeed, the phrase "a musical feast" is a cliché often invoked to sell or label a festive concert. Music and food feed upon each other. Fancy restaurants feature a pianist, strummer, or string player. Dinner or table music is a longstanding tradition. The engagement of one of the senses is nicely accompanied by stimulation of another. Just as in romance, the more senses we stimulate, the more complete the pull and release of mental, emotional, and physical capacities, yielding an ecstasy or rapture. This constructive play not only builds baby's brain, it is a natural high for anybody. Gets the right and left hemispheres of the brain working in concert, which is also the game of creative writing. When we note that phrases are musical sentences, we see the intertwining even of the terminology of musical and verbal composition. We are composers when we write notes or words, and our constant theme is to make words sing.

Even more fun than food songs are drinking songs. At the low end of the spectrum of these is "A Hundred Bottles of Beer on the Wall." At the high end is Ben Jonson's "Drink to Me Only with Thine Eyes":

Song to Celia

Drink to me only with thine eyes,
And I will pledge with mine,
Or leave a kiss within the cup
And I'll not look for wine.
The thirst that from the soul doth rise
Doth ask a drink divine,
But might I of Jove's nectar sup
I would not change for thine.

I tried rewriting "A Hundred Bottles of Beer on the Wall" for the occasion of my paternal grandfather-in-law's hundredth birthday party celebration a few years ago. The revision got lost in a computer crash after the event, but as I recall there were few distinct words in that song even newly turned. It still boiled down to an old tired refrain:

A hundred years and havin' a ball,
A hundred lotta little years!
Take a frown, turn it upside down
For ninety-nine little years, that's all!
[*Etc., etc.*]

I was in charge of leading and conducting the singing of this itsy bitsy ditty to the large gathering of a hundred or more at the ballroom rented for the event, and I'm sorry to say the attempt fell flat. Didn't get any eggs thrown in my beer but got no cheers either. My aim was to demonstrate at length how long a hundred anything is, by following through on this interminable loop. Thought the crowd would appreciate the survivor theme by mimicking it in little at the expense of a few hundred precious moments of their own time. They either didn't get the point or didn't appreciate my method of presenting it. I had forgotten in this endeavor the second half of Sir Philip Sidney's lesson on literature. It must delight as well as teach. As Chaucer noted, if your audience drifts off, no idea will be heard or heeded. I barely got down to "Eighty-nine lotta little years" when I knew I had lost them, and it. I was by that time singing solo and pleasing no one including myself. So I gave it up. Nothing left to do but reach for a beer and take one down off the wall. Indeed, that little escapade was a tad off the wall, so it appeared to all. I was out of touch with public taste. It should have been obvious to me. It flopped because I had messed with a drinking song. If it ain't broke, don't fix it, even if it's ugly.

So I set out to writing drinking songs from scratch. Being an occasional poet--that is, I write poems for particular occasions--I became inspired by a Guinness ad to write a poem and win ownership of your own real Irish pub, in Ireland of course. The odds were long but at least I would get a poem out of it. Actually, I drink Guinness stout hardly at all. But drinking somewhat rarely is not teetotalling, so at least I knew what I was talking about. I've chugged a bottle of Guinness or two in my time.

And I'm an opportunist. Although I almost never smoke, for example, I entered a Marlboro sweepstakes to try to win a trip on a special smoking excursion train. No poem required, just an entry blank listing your brand of cigarettes. I put down *Erik*, because I had bought a pack years ago to take to a poker game. Liked the Viking logo on it. But I didn't win the train trip. I was willing to sacrifice my lungs breathing three hundred Marlboro Men and Women's smoke for the sake of a cross-country train ride, No Nonsmoking allowed. And I was willing to swear that Guinness was the stout king for the sake of playing the game of words, my game if there ever was one.

I had written a poem about drinking, pagan style, long before. One of my greatest fictive heroes, Beowulf, was its inspiration. Beowulf drank beer, ale, mead, and fermented mare's milk. And in retranslating that great epic poem in my own right, I had demonstrated how to maintain the spirit of Anglo-Saxon Old-English poetry in modern English by retaining the Dark Age epithetic style and by varying the alliterative pattern according to the original rules of Old Germanic poetic composition: "In the feel of froth, foammad forever," etc. This Guinness challenge was my meat, my cup of tea, my bottle of beer. I could pretend for the nonce that I was a Guinness man, and it was a heady thing to take on that role, to wit:

What's Guinness For? It's For Me!

> I can't be without
> My Guinness stout,
> The foam that wouldn't die.
> You can take it from me
> (Not my Guinness, hee-hee!)
> I can not tell a lie.
> Guinness forever!
> (The froth lasts that long.)
> Morn, noon and night it pleases:
> The sight, the taste, all the senses
> Guinness enhances, or at least entrances.
> From Malarkey to Blarney
> I will tout
> My Guinness, stoutly,
> Devoutly. Guinness,
> I bow to thee
> And to those others
> Under the table
> Who were not so able
> As I to hold you,
> O god of brew,
> Within the brain
> And belly too.
> So what's the brew? Ha ha!
> It's Guinness, for this bloke,
> Joke or no joke!

Truly, I was flying high on ambrosia, the elixir of the gods. That was good enough for me, pub or no pub. I remember seeing on a news program the face-off of finalists, flown to Ireland by Guinness for a game of darts, winner take all, i.e., take possession of the pub itself, in a little town in the Emerald Isle. I wasn't jealous, much. Darts wasn't my game anyway. I'm better at pingpong or tennis than at darts. I was willing to wait till next year.

In due time, a year later, I saw the Guinness ad in *The New Yorker*. "Win a pub in Ireland. Write a poem about your most memorable pint of Guinness." Or words to that effect, so said the ad.

This one would be even more of a joke than the last one. The premise seemed ridiculous to me, and I wondered to what extent Guinness was making fun of itself. Why would they laugh at themselves? Humanists are supposed to do that, not brewers. It was right up my alley, for sure. I would really have fun with this one. I'm a wag of wags, to my way of thinking. It would be tongue in cheek, ironic, with a twist at the end. Much ado about nothing. Wispy as Irish mist. Nothing but bubbles, evaporating foam from a heady draw. I could pull it off, to my own satisfaction anyway:

My Most Memorable Pint of Guinness

Ah, distinctly I remember,
'Twas a lovely day in September,
Just like the one in May,
(Or was it last Saturday?)
My Guinness, my love, in hand.
'Twas memorable, you understand.
But the most memorable, I think,
May be the next one that I drink!
Let's see, shall we?

Here was one that Guinness could actually use in an advertising campaign, I thought to myself. A compelling invitation to drink. I congratulated myself also on the ultra-subtle allusion to sex tucked into the text. I thereby invoked the classic theme of "wine, women and song," but avoiding the sexism of gender-specification in my presentation. Would the contest judges at Guinness be so astute as to perceive the double edge of "My Guinness, my love, in hand"?

"My love" is of course, for present purposes, my Guinness, but also implies a hand embracing your human love-object while hoisting aloft the brimming brew in the other hand. One hand on your Guinness, the other hand on your lover. Alternatively, "my love" could be a noun of direct address to your lover, your intimate audience.

I doubted, though, that they would get it. They would probably miss, also, the literary allusion in the first line. It was to Poe, a verbatim quote from *The Raven*:

> Ah, distinctly I remember,
> It was in the bleak December,
> And each separate dying ember
> Wrought its ghost upon the floor.

Its context was mystery. What was tapping at the chamber door? What bold surprise would leap up and out from the dark night to thrill every nerve? What pain or pleasure of love awaited after hours? What intriguing stranger would intrude into our world? All this dramatic tension and incipient suspense is set up in the first four words of my rendition. To no one's delectation but my own, no doubt. A delightful little secret, nonetheless. Something for literary critics of a more sensitive ilk to appreciate. With all that layered subtlety though, no hope of winning this one either.

The next drink-thinking contest I put in for was closer to home, a Saint Patrick's Day poem for *The Wilmington Star-News*, Wilmington, North Carolina. You had to mention a girl named Mary or Kathleen or Kate, mention a drink of beer, wine, or whiskey, and tell a story in verse. Pretty general criteria, just right for a loose drinking song.

I set to work right away. This poem would be for the ages, the definitive Irish drinking lyric, an instant classic, to be hummed and mumbled by any imbiber through time immemorial. I could already hear America singing my Irish thing, if it could make it past the Great Green Swamp in our own down-home state first. If this poem were to be universal, it would have to apply to all Irish wine, women, and song. It would speak to every occasion, express the double Irish tradition of dissolute hooliganism and irrepressible spunk. It would be all things Irish to all the world.

A tall order, of my own instigation, but I didn't have much to lose either. I would at the very least teach and delight myself and my wife until the rest of the world was ready to pick up the beat.

I Will Be Merry

O I will be merry with Mary,
And I'll make a date with Kate.
I like to be seen with Kathleen.
Any one of 'em's good for a mate!
 Here's to us, here's to them,
 Here's to you and me!
 First you let yourself go to hell,
 Then you set yourself free!
There's wine and beer and porter,
And also some liquor that's quicker!
I drink just as much as I oughter,
Though my tongue gets a little bit thicker!
 [Refrain]
When it comes to women and whisky
There's not much distinction, you know.
To fool with each gets a bit risky,
But take 'em and let the rest go!
 [Refrain]

I don't recall what the prize for this contest was, but it wasn't a pub in Ireland. My guess is that the judges likewise in this case failed to pick up on the quadruple-entendre in my use of words such as *mate* in the first stanza. "Any one of 'em's good for a mate" means 1) good to make a wife of; 2) good to have as a close friend; 3) good for a quick round of sex; 4) good for a jolly fellow such as I. Bet you missed at least one of those, eh? It's just as well if they didn't get all of it. Wouldn't want to offend anybody. Actually it's tame yet spicy. Its time will come.

Enough of strong drink. Food for thought coming up, food for creative thought, for creative writing, for oodles of stories, novels, poems, also for a poem by me in that delicious and tempting unfettered form, free verse. What is the role of luck in life? Does God play dice with the Universe? Why do you suppose it is that so many games are played in a season of baseball, specifically 162 in the Major Leagues. Because it doesn't matter how hard you hit the ball, it depends on where and how the ball bounces, and the bounces are either lucky or unlucky. It takes many games for the lucky and unlucky bounces to even out.

It's like that in life, too. Hardly anybody gets killed by a stingray, but the expert wildlife guru Steve Irwin did. Hitler got lucky when the bomb under the table gravely hurt others but not him. The rest of the world got unlucky as a result, for another year.

It's up to the poet to make sense of all of this. Plato's theory was that poets were mad, loony. But because it's a mad mad mad mad world, it takes a touch of madness to get in touch with it and go with the flow of it. In both work and play, Lady Luck plays a big part. On the World Poker Tour, the big winner never does it without getting lucky, on any given day. Almost all recreational games are a variable mix of skill and chance, making them a lot like life overall. But the stakes are smaller, thus the fun. You won't die of cancer if you draw the short straw in a game.

Is there a game that involves almost no luck, good or bad? I think there is. What do you think? Any game played with a ball takes crazy, unpredictable bounces at times. Games with cards or dice are subject to laws of probability but are unpredictable on a given draw or throw. Such games are like life in that you don't necessarily deserve what you get at any given time, good or bad.

There is at least one game, however, where you always get what you deserve, good or bad. It is the game of chess. I find it paradoxical that one of the greatest chess players of all time, Bobby Fischer, was probably certifiably insane. Increasingly an anti-Semitic, anti-Everything exile, even at his prime he was not only antisocial but perversely so. He was thus an unfortunate example of a superior grandmaster of one of the purest games in existence but an idiot and outcast in the larger world outside of it.

That's one of the anomalies of the human brain. There are multiple insights and multiple misreads in any one human mind, the luck of the biological draw and of the dicey environmental factors subsequent to it.

In general, I like games that are simple in rules and interpretation, though challenging in play. I prefer tennis to basketball for that reason because, rule-wise, tennis is absolutely straightforward. The only grey area is line calls, good or bad, in or out. Pretty simple, much easier than calling balls and strikes in baseball, for example. In basketball the problem is fouls and calling of fouls. A highly variable variable depending on who's doing the calling. Same to a degree with football—holding and interference calls, etc. But chess is less problematic even than tennis.

In chess there's no ball as well as no calls. No luck of the bounce, no fouls, very few exceptions to basic rules, and no grey areas. As for luck, there are no elements of chance in the setup of the chessboard or the prescribed movement of pieces. That leaves as variables only the two players. Do you feel lucky? Tummy feeling crummy? Distracted by family matters, love quarrels, financial worries? That may affect your play, but the board and the pieces are subject only to you and your opponent, independent of manufacturing defects, playing surfaces, wind and weather. The game is thus isolated from most of what constitutes human life. It constrains the result to skill, meaning that the outcome is a fairer test of ability on any given day than other games are. It is not a simple game, of course, quite the contrary. It offers an astronomical variety of choice in moves. But with its being so purely geometric and mathematical in its scheme, the day is fast approaching that no human will be able to beat the most advanced computerized chess program. The triumph of machine over the human mind that created it. We have outwitted ourselves.

There's an easy remedy for that. Just dumb down your computer when you play on it, to a level that you can beat or at least play-even with. When you're playing with a real person, though, you're on your own. Justice will be done to you or for you that day. You are master of your fate for perhaps the only time in your life, the time that you spend at the chessboard. It's good to know that human ingenuity is clever enough to provide all of us that opportunity, regardless of our lot in life otherwise and elsewhere. It's just too bad that hardly anybody I know plays chess anymore! Except that, disembodied in cyberspace, clacking and cackling away at unseen foes, hovers somewhere in the Great Void the shade of the Fischer King himself. Maybe even he would have liked my little poem about his game:

A Game of Chess

> They say that in ancient times the Queen was not
>   all-powerful
> The way it came to be around the fourteenth
>   century
> When this game came into the lasting perfection
> It still retains. It's not that this play of carved
>   wood
> Or stark ivory or fancy plastic or many microchips
> Is lifelike exactly, for the only chancy element
> Is, will he or she pick up
> On the goof you made, or not?
> It's the only game
> Between you and another human (or machine)
> Without interference from
> Lady Luck
> Who is the reigning Queen
> In many another
> Game of Life.
> Which means that justice
> Is almost never done
> Anywhere—
> Except on this little checkerboard square
> All in Black and White.

From love and music to food and drink to games and philosophy we move to Ultimate Reality itself, the subject of my own first poem as a love-lorn college freshman, and our final subject here of creative contemplation. Karen and I both grew up in churchgoing families, hers Presbyterian, mine Episcopalian. Karen was existentially precocious. Most kids go along with their parents and siblings to church, like it or not. Karen went, didn't like it, and struck out on her own road early. She was a rationalist even as a pre-teenager. Didn't believe everything she was told, very little of it in fact. Liked to observe natural phenomena, down to earth like worms and snails. Noah's animal story seemed contrived. Did Noah infest his own ark with worms, snails, all manner of bugs, a male and female of each, and of every creeping thing of that kind that creepeth upon the earth? What about hermaphroditic worms? Just one of each of those? There were too many unanswered questions, wormholes in the old book.

Karen lapsed early within herself from the Presbyterian Church and outwardly as soon as she was on her own. She went to Wooster College, of Presbyterian affiliation, because not only was it a fine school in the liberal arts tradition but that's where her parents paid tuition plus room and board for Karen and her three younger sisters in turn. At Wooster she met and eventually married a Presbyterian. The church at that time seemed to the two of them too materialistic and out of touch with cutting edge social issues. They together turned Unitarian. The nonsectarian nature and humanistic outlook of Unitarianism were in tune with Karen's eclectic views.

In adulthood Karen attained a mystic dimension to her thinking. God is to be found within as well as without the self. Nature, as in the Romantic view, manifests an overarching sublimity bespeaking a force that "rolls through all things," as Wordsworth put it. After Karen was widowed, she continued to attend a Unitarian Fellowship. Seven years later, when Karen and I became a couple, we attended it together. Eventually I reverted to Episcopal, after our relocation to North Carolina, and Karen kept me company in that switch, not worrying too much about what actually went on in church.

She believed me when I said the whole thing could be taken symbolically, like a poetic metaphor of the spiritual dimension beyond one's individual slice of life. It was an easy sell. Gave us a chance to sing old standby hymns in the neighborhood church choir, including many hymns in the early American folk tradition, African-American spirituals that Karen is enamored of, and the like.

My religious views underwent a sea change following my traumatic injury of May 1990 and the consequent loss of the bond of my marriage to Barbara. My prayers about my hearing crisis had gone unanswered. My former life was overturned and shoveled under in my attempt to dig my way out. The new garden path that opened up was an Eden of forbidden fruit. I wavered and fell in grasping at it. Why would a higher power unveil to me a forbidden way which with all the help and the best will in the world I could not and would not deny despite the injury to those dear ones I was sworn to uphold, which was bound to torture me and tear me apart, turn me upside down and inside out? Clearly, whichever way I went I was toast in my own eyes. Damned if I do and damned if I don't. I couldn't make sense of it in any way consonant with my upbringing. I would have to tear all the old matter down and build something else up from the ruins according to a design of my own making.

My religion became more abstract, less guilt-driven. It seemed I was victimized by my dutiful conventional life, the injury in the line of duty, which I had to transcend by extraordinary means, a redemptive earthly love. That trashed my old set of beliefs—nose to the grindstone and reap the harvest—which I had steadfastly relied on. Karen resurrected me.

Something was at work here besides traditional religion and I had to figure it out. I wrote it out on reams of paper to test the limits of the power of the pen. The journals mounted high, interspersed with poems and jokes. I would drain the swamp of my mental morass to get to the bottom of things, hit paydirt, find the underground fountain of waters. It was venting on a cosmic scale. I had struck into the writing well, and was writing well. Something had to give: my world, or the underworld, or the realm of the gods, maybe all of the above.

In the end, the joke book and the poems showed me the way. Do your best and forget the rest. "First you let yourself go to hell, then you set yourself free." I enjoyed life when I was around Karen and didn't when I wasn't. So I chose joy. Joy came by surprise to C.S. Lewis, as his book *Surprised by Joy*, inspired by Wordsworth, tells. It came to me because I came to it, to her. I was damned in my former world by my chosen path but damn glad of it nevertheless because I had saved my life by losing it, if I may turn a scriptural phrase around a bit.

Existentially I began to think like a Unitarian, though I hated some Unitarians' intolerance of and even contempt for Christian terminology and their ironic religious bigotry in the course of doing so. If a Christian believer stumbled into our Unitarian Fellowship, he or she was on occasion obtusely shunned, spurned, chastised, and overall thoroughly rousted. "God" and "Jesus" were treated almost like cuss words or anathema, not to be uttered in the presence of the Fellowship or holy hell might break loose. I was appalled by this reverse inhospitability and glad finally to retreat to the comfortable refuge of an Episcopal church in our new home of Southport, North Carolina.

This last compromise resolution, my nominal homecoming in religion *pro forma*, was not done before I had earlier acquiesced to rewrite, by request from our local Unitarian group in Cumberland, Maryland, the gospel song *Shall We Gather at the River*:

> Shall we gather at the River
> Where bright angel feet have trod,
> With its crystal tides forever
> Flowing by the throne of God?
>
> *Yes, we'll gather at the River,*
> *The beautiful, the beautiful River,*
> *Gather with the saints at the River*
> *That flows by the throne of God.*
>
> Soon we'll meet the shining River,
> Soon our pilgrimage will cease,
> Soon our happy hearts will quiver
> With the melody of peace.
> *[Refrain]*

I was supposed to make it inoffensive to Unitarian Fellowship ears, by deleting all reference to God, angels, saints, heaven, or any other such bugging things snagged afoul by the interconnected web of life that includes everything and everyone except anything or anybody that smacks of old-time religion.

Yes, I made a Unitarian hymn out of *Shall We Gather at the River*, fit to be the theme song of the entire U-U world. The words are all-encompassing, luminous, ethereal. It dances around the edges of a great void, the unmentionable Black Hole of traditional religion that sucks so many saints and sinners into its vast vortex for better or worse, good or ill. I wonder if someday Julia Ward Howe may be in effect excommunicated after the fact from Unitarianism for daring to utter and record for posterity those zealous words, "Mine Eyes Have Seen the Glory of the Coming of the Lord," although that was not only real religion, it was eloquent poem, stirring song, and living lyric all rolled up into one thing great and good. I believe in my hymn too, Bowdlerized though it be. It says it all in a mellow way.

When you try to say it all, all at once, there's a flattening out like the roll of a river. But the water analogy is powerful, huge like the Mississippi, which must know somethin' though it don't say nothin'. And the Eternal River just keeps rollin' along beyond it all, less gritty than its earthly cousin The Big Muddy, which is likewise a wellspring, in full flood, of many a stirring song of the soul. Whatever works for you, just let it flow.

An Eternal River

> Life is an eternal river,
> Building force from streams around.
> Each stream flows into a river,
> Every stream swelling its sound!
> *Yes, we'll meet at the river,*
> *The beautiful, the beautiful river,*
> *Tributaries to the great river,*
> *The shining sea the world around.*

When a stream meets the river,
Two waters merge into one.
When all waters meet together,
The stream, river, ocean all are one!
Yes, we'll meet at the river,
The beautiful, the beautiful river,
Tributaries to the great river,
Bright in the moon, the stars, the sun.

15

Wanna Be in Our Video?

THIS STORY COULD BE EITHER fiction or real experience. The real experience version of it is more mysterious and less sordid, so that should suffice nicely. It was a near walk on the wild side. I've told this true version of the story to my wife, who found it alluring. The fictive version may end up never being told, a loss to the annals of non-true crime.

For ten years I took part in the workings of a semi-secret organization. It didn't purport to be secretive, it just operates that way. From 1994 to 2003 I graded Advanced Placement (AP) exams for the Educational Testing Service (ETS) of Princeton, New Jersey, the same people who produce the Scholastic Achievement Test, or SAT, which determines the fate of so many hopeful college-bound high school seniors. Designed to give high school seniors a jump start in their freshman year of college, the AP program provides the opportunity for high school seniors to earn college credit for special college-level courses offered as approved in high schools and then certified for each student by a test administered by ETS after completion of the course.

The tests are graded in June, following the final semester of high school, at several sites around the country. A few hundred high school AP teachers and college professors grade stacks of these exams in a week-long sojourn, six eight-hour days of speed-reading slave labor, one such week's sojourn for each AP subject in the ETS repertoire for that year. It's all finished up by mid-June, thousands of papers, hundreds of graders, half a dozen grading sites.

My subject was the AP English Language test, which meant student composition of (presumably) literate essays of analysis and interpretation in response to a reading passage, three essays per student, one on each of three readings a page or less in length as reproduced in a small type-face. The students had twenty minutes to write each essay, an hour's worth of work on their part for that part of the test. Each subgroup of AP graders was responsible for reading one of the questions, or one essay per student, an assembly line setup in the mode of Henry Ford. A decent grading speed for turning over these stacks of student essays seemed in our case to be about two minutes per essay: to read, digest, inwardly critique, and assign a numerical score of 0 to 9.

Although the hundreds and thousands of essays that we read at our little table, six or seven of us professionals hunched on our elbows flipping through endless pages hour upon hour, tended to cluster around a handful of familiar cliché-type answers, making the work numbing to the brain as well as the behind, the subject matter was worthy and the responses occasionally humorous or even hilarious, both wittingly and unwittingly.

The reproduced literature that the students were writing about varied through the years from love poems by John Donne, essays by satirist H. L. Mencken, passages from novelist E. M. Forster, Victorian art critic John Ruskin, classic and contemporary American authors like Nathaniel Hawthorne and James Baldwin, and historically fascinating works including Frederick Douglass's autobiography and poetry by colonial writer Anne Bradstreet.

Curiously, one year included two letters of correspondence between officials of two large companies: Coca-Cola and Grove Press. The executive letter from Coca-Cola complained about Grove Press's use of the phrase "It's the real thing" in its advertising for a book, *Diary of a Harlem School Teacher.* The letter in reply from Grove Press urbanely suggested that "those who read our ad may well tend to go out and buy a Coke rather than our book," so that Coca-Cola had nothing to fear from Grove's use of the sequence of words, "It's the real thing," in its notice about *Diary of a Harlem School Teacher.*

Some student essays sided with the complaint by Coca-Cola, but generally the better papers applauded the satirical rejoinder from Grove; a few students hedged: "It's a harsh world that responds more willingly to cruel sarcasm than to mouse-like respect, but it's the real world," offered one cleverly sensitive student. Another astutely noted, "Cola is not actually real—it's made of chemicals and artificial flavoring." Nonsensical student responses included a comment that "without the first letter, the reply would have nothing to stand on." A witty conceit by a student writer about the almost infantile nature of Coca-Cola's complaint pictured the "pitiful wailing by this corporate colossus wanting his bottle back." Here was a poetic venturer in the making, one who never met a metaphor he or she didn't almost like. Me neither.

I must have liked something about this intensely compressed job to have not only put up with it for ten years, one week per year, but to have actively sought it out and continued to re-enlist. One incentive was pay. A thousand dollars or more for a week's work at a posh college campus or other luxurious location, plus travel expenses and meal allowances en route. In addition, there were special social and cultural events during the week--an evening reading by a famous novelist or poet; maybe a barbeque and dance with music by "Thunder Ridge," for example, whoever they might be; sometimes a field trip to a nearby historic attraction or a museum or a minor league baseball game—lots of good company among kindred spirits, colleagues known and newly met.

Overall it was a stimulating, high-powered experience despite the drudgery. And I energized myself during the day's routine by playing mind games to get through it in good order. I established goals and quotas for myself, for example. An overall goal might be 225 essays for the day, in line with the two-minute per essay pace that I had established by observation as being a slightly above par rate. Then I could break that down by hour or half hour to keep myself on track throughout the day. A good essay was usually at least two scrawling pages long in the oversized exam booklet but, because

I found satisfaction in being quota-driven, I secretly rejoiced when I got a one-pager or even a half-pager because that speeded things up regardless of its being symptomatic of below average or failing performance—another body, mind, and college career down the drain, hooray! Good for the quota stats!

Thus inwardly compromised in this jaded view of my role as educator and adjudicator for purposes of this enforced experience, I may have sown the seeds for other forms of depredation after-hours. Time and chance would tell that story. One of the mind games I liked to play was a numbers game. It was considered good form to spread the scores over the spectrum of grades to produce a bell-shaped normal distribution overall: most grades bunching toward the middle, in the four to six range, but a good representative scattering in the fringes, a nine-score for each one-score (very few of either, the outer extremes), eights and twos equalizing, somewhat more frequent, and a reasonable quantity of sevens and threes, solid passes and solid flunks respectively. So it was discouraging to me, the objective grader, when I found a packet of twenty-five essays turning out entirely within the four to six range. Proof that mediocrity is alive and well in this country, even among those pretending to an education.

Contrarily, it was a joy to behold bizarre or unorthodox patterns of scores shaping up in a given folder of twenty-five exams. I'm particularly proud of one folder of mine in recent memory where without overt manipulation on my part the grade sequence 1, 2, 3, 4, 5, 6, 7 came up. Don't think that the 8 and 9 materialized, but I also recall sometimes noting backwards sequences of 8, 7, 6, 5, 4, 3, maybe even crowned by a horrible 2 at the end! Lovely! Yes, a mind is a terrible thing to waste, both for that 2-point essay student and for me, his or her congratulator to fulfill my rarely patterned sequence.

By the end of another long day of 225 sequenced and nonsequenced essay grades, I was ready for some better, less number-bound diversion. For reasons that may have pandered to some crass economic motive, or if not to some innocuous need for more space, the grading venue starting in the fifth or sixth year of my AP grading career had been relocated from the Garden-of-Eden-like campus at

Trinity University, San Antonio, to a hotel on the strand of Daytona Beach, Florida, a raucous contrast to Trinity U.

Trinity University was an esthetic delight: flowering landscape, odiferous trees and shrubs, artistic statuary, well stocked bookstore, historic aura, the Alamo and more. The San Antonio environs even featured an authentic ghost town nearby enough for a field trip—full feel of the Old Southwest. And there was the Riverwalk honky-tonk and the best of Tex-Mex all around.

San Antonio was hot as hell during daytime in June, but the air conditioning was set on freeze, so we had to dress in sweaters to keep from shivering in our boots, high-heel or otherwise. I swear that the air conditioning in Trinity University buildings must have had only one setting, that of refrigeration. Don't know the explanation for that in our high tech society, and at an institution of higher knowledge and high-tech learning.

For the ten years of my AP grading experience, the same freezing environment applied to all workaday buildings in whatever locale, Trinity or otherwise. Roast outside, freeze indoors. It all evens out, I guess, but there was no middle ground temperature-wise, unlike the bell curve.

Being a semi-secret outfit, ETS never explained their move of the English Language test from Trinity University to Daytona Beach. The ambiance of Daytona Beach is not just low-class, it's low-crass. Some of the hotels on the strand were nice, some less so. A couple of times I got to stay in Adams-Mark, the chain with the illiterate X mark as its logo. Nicely symbolic of the one-point and two-point essays we had to put up with in a day's work. On one side of the hotel was the beach, open to vehicular traffic, which in my book no beach should be, particularly one with swimmers, waders, and sunbathers on it. On the other side of the hotel was the thoroughfare, one never-ending stream of motorcycles. You could hear the racket of the roaring cycles from inside Adams-Mark at all hours no matter how deep below ground you had to go to enter the enclave of exam-grading rooms.

The beach by the hotel is beautifully broad and inviting to appearance, were it not for its being compromised by a narrow-eyed predatory underclass. We felt the pinch. One year, on the day of our departure from Daytona, a collegial friend of mine from Butler University had his wallet, his money, and his thick-lens glasses stolen when he momentarily turned his back on them, stuffed under his towel, to take a quick splash in the surf. Not only was he deprived of his money, glasses, and identity papers, he instantly almost became a nonperson unable to board an airplane, or even see his way around. ETS liaisons intervened and managed to get him back home to Indiana, at great length and trouble to all concerned.

Nevertheless, at the end of any grading day during these week-long experiences, all of us graders were itching for some kind of action other than pushing papers, pens, and pencils, even if it meant walking the plank along the beach. All in all, we still considered the whole experience something of a lark.

Most of us were in these days and evenings brimful of confidence. We had been hired and rehired in successive years by ETS, hadn't we? None of us had ever received in our own person any kind of evaluation of our job performance at the end of the week's work or anytime thereafter. A rehire was your only indicator that you did okay, and you had to wait six months to find out if you got a rehire.

One was never told what a standard quota or pace of grading was. One was never informed as to the propriety of his or her grade distribution. Their machines had data in detail on all those measures of performance, but we never got to see such data. The better to hire and fire in secret, my dear, I thought to myself. I wanted to learn the inner workings of this Star Chamber out of my own curiosity, if I could.

The only way to do so was to get to be a table leader. If you could make it through seven years you had a decent shot at a promotion. Rumor was that seven years was a standard tour of duty, although that was never stated or confirmed either, being company-confidential. You could readily surmise it though, by attrition and body-count over a period of time. After eight years I got the call. A new table leader was needed, to replace a last-minute dropout.

So I led a table. I was ushered into the inner sanctum of grader-graders. I got to see the data, spy a few ETS secrets. I answered the call to the secret sessions of table leaders during the day where progress and crises were assessed and addressed. I got to know who the movers and shirkers at my table were, based on numbers, curves, formulaic expectations. I became privy to the abnormality flags and asterisks that popped up beside particular names for my table. I was master of their fate. I could in effect fire for the future any one of my charges, or several (the gum chewer, the knuckle-cracker, the know-it-all?), or the whole bunch, with a stroke of my pen.

This was heady stuff. But I swore to myself that this power would not corrupt me, or at least not corrupt me absolutely, realizing too that this power was not absolute. I wasn't high in the hierarchy.

Still, this particular year, a table-leader year, I was particularly full of myself, ready to attack head-on if need be any beachcomber bums, tattooed goons, and the like.

My pals and I liked to refresh after a hard day by walking on the beach, checking out the sights, the carnival sounds of the thrill rides, bungee jumpings, dare-devil rocket type launchers of humans cannonball style, and the latest fashions in beachwear décolletage.

The worst of the beach-side rides, "Wild Thang" the sign said, catapulted their captive customers two hundred feet upward in the air in an open capsule contraption that eventually pulled them back down on an elastic tether which then devolved into a bungee-fall experience with a bounce-down within a few feet of the ground, back up and down, to a final shakedown and retrieval at the starting platform. The g-forces had to be enormous--astronaut-grade stuff. It cost each patron twenty dollars or more per ride. I figured such rides could easily cause brain damage or spinal injury. Perhaps the riders were not college material. Or maybe they were. Like the one-and-two point essay writer type of college material, not good enough for AP course credit anyway, small consolation to me.

After ogling all these wonders, we might expand our ramble to the throughway where the restaurants, shops, and clubs clustered. Might indulge in an ice-cream cone, always vanilla for me. Maybe a beer back at Adams-Mark to top off another lovely evening of another long, dutiful day. Then would come an accustomed nightly ritual of mine, a rollicking moonlight run on the almost deserted beach towards the witching hour of midnight.

By that time the cars, utility vehicles, mopeds, and other mechanized menaces had mercifully vacated the shore, and I could be more or less alone with my thoughts to clarify my mind and bolster my body, by pounding along the fine sand of this wide strand under the stars, the breeze created by my forward charge cooling my forehead and sucking the sweat off my skin up into the vaporous night. It was 11:30 on this uniquely fateful evening.

So far, as usual, it was my high point of the day. No motorcycles, no air-conditioning freeze, no two-point essays. Just the infinity of sand and surf. But existential stick in the mud that I am, I was goal-oriented even in this freed-up atmosphere. I would do two miles out and two miles back, twenty minutes each way. That would earn me sixteen points on Ken Cooper's aerobics scale, more than half the thirty points weekly minimum, all in one short evening's workout of less than an hour. At that rate, sixteen points per day, five or six days of exercise a week, I could get close to a hundred points in this week if I continued regularly in this wholesome effort to see me through the challenges and stultifications of the daily grind. Would this plodding attitude serve to steer me through and beyond the path to perdition that unbeknownst lay just ahead?

I set off at a gallop, out the back entrance of Adams-Mark, swerving left to parallel the cresting waves, whose whitecaps shone in the moon. The surf crashed and sent up into my face many microdrops of the ocean's spray, tangy to my taste and zesty into my skin. I wore red swimming trunks, white socks, and blue-striped running shoes, that's all. It wasn't a topless beach exactly but that didn't apply to me. I had no shame. Maybe I was vain, even. Diana, eternally young goddess of the moon, was looking down at me, getting a chaste eyeful. She was far off, in both space and time. All I could see from my vantage point was the Man in the Moon, a full round visage most like to Charlie Brown. Sex was not on my mind, unusual for me actually. But there was nobody eligible in reach to arouse the sexual impulse that continually flows in me, even a thousand miles distant from home, for my own dear sweet wife, bless her soul.

Suddenly, from out of the blue, or out of the black of night actually, came at a run, straight at me though from an oblique angle, a sweet young thing, to speak in euphemistic terms. She was a young thing, anyway, and Mr. Man in the Moon had lit his lamp showing her the way to me. She was trim in hair and figure. Two-piece bathing suit, string top whose contents flopped up and down agreeably. I could see her well enough in the light of the silvery moon, could see that her hair was raven-black, with bangs in front, which flopped agreeably too. There seemed much about her that was agreeable. But why was she heading on a beeline toward me, and in such great haste?

I didn't at once worry about the reason for the intrusion. I was content to observe and admire the charm of the encounter. After all, I was an experienced girl watcher. Have never tired of or shrunk back from that pastime. I like watching girls, from a respectful distance.

Here now the distance boundary was becoming rapidly violated. I was being accosted! I had already sized her up in an instant at first glance. Comely enough for a Coppertone commercial. Could have been a model, maybe she was one already. Medium height. Body by Thunderbird—sleek and racy. Skin luminous in the moonshine. Who was I to question all this? A gift to me from the gods, obviously.

I sensed she was up to no good, that this bizarre assault on my space was libidinous. Guys know these things, I guess, just as girls must. Doesn't happen to me all the time. Actually, it never happens. Thus the intrigue, intensifying the incipient thrill of it all.

She had emerged from a small group of similar young things who were sitting or kneeling in a circle just up from the edge of the surf, apparently planning an escapade of some sort, or so I imagined. Although I had taken in, processed, and analyzed all the detail of this enchanting scene, I had not broken stride in the measured pace toward my goal for the evening: four miles, forty minutes.

She was upon me. Half breathless, starting to take up stride with me, she intoned into my ear from a distance of no more than a couple of feet, "Wanna be in our video?"

There it was. A proposition. It was not only against expectation, it went against all preparation and education in my background. I had never heard any come-on so direct. Never end a sentence with a proposition, was the stock advice that I expected others to adhere to as well, particularly sweet young things that I was accustomed to watching in all innocence. What was I supposed to say?

It was a yes-no question. My fate was in my mouth. One word would do it, either way. I was caught off guard and maintained for a moment a stunned silence.

Meanwhile my ego and superego engaged in a mute dialogue between the front and back lobes of my brain. What does she see in me? Do I look studly in the dim light? She can't resist my sex-pack abs? She goes for the athletic type? My profile strikes her as interesting, the turn-on of intelligence for a discerning wench? My sleek physique belies my middle age enough to qualify for her exhausting romps? Yes, all of the above, of course. She has searched me out and found me. I am the one and only man on the beach, at this ungodly hour, available and active enough to perform for her video.

The chance of a lifetime. Every healthy young man's dream, every muddling middle-aged man's fantasy, every old fogey's hallucination. I can be a playboy tonight. What better entertainment for men can any man want? What self-respecting idiot would ever turn that down?

So naturally I said, "No, thanks." And continued on my unseen way, four miles, forty minutes.

I admit to having had second thoughts or second reactions, at the time. I half-hoped I would see this wondrous coven of witches still conclaving in the sand above the surf upon the homeward leg of my run back to Adams-Mark. Would my answer be the same? Would I resist the almightiest of temptations twice in the same night?

Thankfully I was spared this dilemma. The girls had gone by the time I passed that way again. All I could do now was speculate about this unique road not taken.

What would have become of me had I taken the bait and bit? Would I have chewed and savored it? Or been chewed and spat out, left to weep and gnash my teeth?

My considered judgment is that I got lucky. And smart. For me, getting lucky happens with my wife. I'm a lucky guy.

Do I wonder about their video? How could they pull it off without me? Did my refusal scuttle the project? Apparently not. There's a sucker born every minute. The only thing that Daytona Beach has more of than motorcycles is strip clubs. There's sleaze aplenty there, more than its share. Yes, I think the video was made, even without my aid.

I happened upon it in a video store in Southport, North Carolina, a year or so later. There it was, bold and bare in the title: *The Girls of Daytona Beach.* I glanced at the cover cursorily. It was of the "Girls Gone Wild" ilk. If I had been in it I might have rented it out. As it was, I wasn't, and I didn't.

So my Daytona Beach experience with ETS had a darker tinge than the ETS experience at Trinity University. Not only did I get into the inner workings of the secret side of academe that ETS presides over, its carefully guarded evaluation procedures and hiring and firing practices, but I got a glimpse into the underworld that moved on the periphery of the hotel scene, the secret nighttime doings of Daytona girls gone wild. They're nice enough, at a distance, which is about all the girl watching they'll get from me, it appears.

16

What's Up, Doc?

IT'S GREAT TO BE YOUNG but tough being a kid. Particularly if you're a kid with an overactive imagination. I was one of those. It was sickening. I remember making notes to myself, before going to bed, of symptoms I would claim to have in the morning as an excuse to stay home from school: sore throat, cough, sniffles. Although that list wasn't too creative, I did develop a genuine case of hypochondria and have endured bouts of that throughout life. Phantom diseases can be as debilitating as the real thing. Hookworm, polio, heart disease, kidney failure—I have suffered from all of these though having had none of them.

Two books on my shelf compete for my attention, one wholesome, one lugubrious: *A Dictionary of Symptoms* is the bad one for me. The good one is called *Take Care of Yourself,* which omits most of the diseases known to mankind, those that hardly anybody ever gets, such as *neurofibromyalgia* (generalized pain in nerve and muscle tissue; like everything hurts for no seemingly good reason). But the *Dictionary of Symptoms* includes all that nasty stuff however extreme or unusual. It makes for horrid reading, so I reach for it only as a last resort. Preventive medicine has been my credo in adult life. I became a health nut, having had a head start as a bit of a nut anyway. Obsessive-compulsiveness is a boon to a health nut. Means you can have the same things for breakfast every day, and for lunch every day, leaving dinner as the only variable assuming there is a significant other in the household whose needs for communal dining need to be accommodated. So I yielded control over dinner to my significant other, my first wife, then to my second wife. Breakfast and lunch were my province alone.

Breakfast became my main meal of the day, a multi-course, multi-minute affair. Standard advice is to strive for five fruits in a day's eating. I figured I could meet or exceed that in one sitting and be all stoked up for the day fruitwise. It was straightforward: a glass of orange or grape or grapefruit juice is one fruit. A banana with cereal is two. A half-grapefruit or orange on the side is three. The other two fruits could materialize by expanding the cereal component of the menu. First cereal course—Kretschmer lightly toasted wheat germ with the aforesaid banana. Second cereal course—no-sugar-added Grapenuts, with a handful of almonds or dried cranberries. Third cereal course—old-fashioned, i.e., big-flake oatmeal, with raisins. Repeat all this once a day, every day throughout the year and the years. After this extensive sort of breakfast, lunch was an afterthought by comparison. A bowl of tomato soup and a tuna sandwich would do. And anything for dinner would likewise suffice. I will not swear that I have followed this regimen to the letter day in and day out throughout the decades, but I have remained true to the spirit of it—a boatload of fruit and cereal to start the day, and with any luck see it through.

So that simple formula took care of my daily nutritional requirements and then some, into perpetuity. The second criterion of any health maintenance program is regular exercise. My guideline in this aspect was the aerobics guru of the 1970's, Dr. Ken Cooper, author of two treasured, dog-eared paperbacks prominent in my bookcase: *Aerobics*, and *The New Aerobics*. The obsessive-compulsive attraction of the Cooper aerobics system is the weekly point count. Thirty points per week keeps you in shape. More than thirty keeps you in better shape. Simple and elegant. Not just a formula, almost a magic formula. Fitness is only thirty points away, every week.

The quickest and thus relatively the easiest way to thirty points or more was, and is, by jogging or running. A ten-minute mile, which is about my speed on a good day, is worth four points. Eight measly miles per week is thirty two points, more than enough. When I first began to run for exercise, in 1980 or so, it took me a month or two to build up the necessary aerobic capacity to do a mile without strain. I discovered to my delight that distance running at a moderate rate can be relatively painless, even relaxing during the doing of it. Your body gets attuned to it, achieves a steady-state of energy output with little discomfort, almost like going into automatic pilot.

I should have learned all that much earlier in life, because I had worked out with the cross-country running team in high school a couple of years. But since that was before Ken Cooper's book came out I didn't know that running could be non-excruciating. When the cross-country team practiced, I and my friends, none of us serious runners, hung far behind the pack, together, merely talking and wisecracking as a kind of lark, a happy-go-lucky after-school activity. Then when at length we reached the last practice leg, a stretch of open ground across the girls' field-hockey field, we would sprint like mad and fling ourselves breathless across the finish. We never made the varsity or the traveling squad at this rate, and to the extent that we did any running over the two and a half mile course it was wheezing and gasping all the way, complete with constriction and chest pains. That was my impression of what distance running would inevitably entail in any form that it was pursued.

Having in the full bloom of adulthood gotten wind of an exhilarating approach to running as both health and recreation, I took in this new breath of life inspiring me to the goal of aerobic fitness. As anyone who runs habitually can testify, however, one runs risks when one runs. There are routine hazards and extraordinary ones.

The routine hazards are muscle aches and pains, including the risk of injury especially to legs and feet, and disabling injury to joints, short or long-term debilitation of those. Happily, pounding the pavement also toughens muscles and joints so that, if luck holds, the joints become accustomed to the abuse and resistant to pain and perforation. Belatedly, however, I discovered that running on the slanted sides of roads or even along a sloping beach strains knee cartilage and can set one back a few weeks or months.

More serious than that, though, is the occasional encounter head-on with a motorized vehicle, even a big one like a car or SUV. My rugged Staffordshire terrier ran head-on into a moving SUV, bounced off and somehow survived. It happened to me too, once, with a passenger sedan.

A good many of us have been in a vehicular accident of some kind at one time or another. In a serious circumstance, such an occurrence invokes an altered sense of time and space. There is the suddenness of the onset of the incident. Your normal world in an instant has evaporated. In an interval of perhaps a few seconds the future is suspended. You enter a new dimension of experience, a dislocation that is both thrilling and chilling. I will recount first a close call and then the real thing.

I have learned that a small economy sized car can go forward in the usual manner rolling on its wheels and can also go forward at right angles to the pavement, sliding sideways as if it were not on wheels at all, like a brick being shoved broadside down a chute. It is easy to accomplish that. I have done it myself. Here's how, step by step, believe it or not!

Drive seventy miles per hour on an interstate highway, suddenly jerk the steering wheel a hundred degrees to the right or left, and then hold it in that position for the next two seconds, being careful to straighten the wheels out by returning the steering wheel momentarily to its upright position as soon as the sideways slide begins to be achieved, meanwhile taking your foot off the accelerator for the moment. Your previous momentum is sufficient to maintain high-speed progress in the original direction regardless of the spinning of your drive wheels and your new orientation sideways.

As you proceed at a glide speed of sixty miles per hour, with your shoulders now aligned parallel with the road, you can briefly glance up across either the adjacent lane or the median strip to receive the startled gaze of passing motorists who don't understand that you are attaining a state of equilibrium in your sidelong manner, and then you try twisting the steering wheel back and forth to create a workable balance in all this discontinuity.

Because the car has been blown off its track by your first sharp turn to nowhere, it will likely continue in the revolving pattern of torque momentum initially established regardless of what you do with the wheel.

Within a few more seconds your vehicle will revolve 360 degrees, returning to its original forward-pointing straight-ahead position, at which point you cease gyrations of the steering wheel and resume normal travel as if you had control of this odd in-lane swerve all along.

You may then congratulate yourself on this remarkable reprieve, and relax by checking in the rearview mirror to note the sixteen wheelers close behind in your path, whose greedy grill-jaws you have just managed to evade.

This strange twist of things happened to me, in that sequence and time-frame, on Interstate 70 southbound between Hagerstown and Frederick, Maryland, one fine autumn morning a number of years ago. I had passed by a car in the right lane, which, before I could return into the right lane in front of it, accelerated and passed me on the right and without warning veered hard left into me as it began to overtake me. All I could do to avoid a collision was jerk the steering wheel to the left, the maneuver that initiated my full circle spin in place at speed. A couple of years earlier, in suburban northern Virginia, I had done a 360 degree turn with my car on a rotating skid, but that was on ice along a quiet rural road at low speed. No big deal, by comparison.

Now we turn to an episode that occurred with my feet on the ground, at least they were on the ground to begin with. It was a dark and stormy morning. The rain had yielded to a drizzle, then vaporized away to a mist. In brief, it was foggy—pea soup. I donned my grey sweatsuit and loped out the front door to begin a four-mile run. My accustomed route in those days, a number of years ago, was simplicity itself. Out and back, out and back.

The little road we lived on was a horseshoe half-loop. I hated the prissy name of the street—Grandview Drive. But yes, the view was grand, out back across U.S. Route 40 hidden in a cut at a distance of six hundred feet beyond a low treeline bordering our sloping property. On the horizon were the Allegheny Mountains several miles off, with a glorious notch through which one could spy the Cumberland Narrows, where the sun rose up as if in an inverse image of its path over the fulcrum of the heelstone of Stonehenge on solstice day. The orange ball of the sun was the target of your eye at sunrise through that oversized peep sight. The grey sides of the eroded Appalachians complemented the brilliant skyrise colors, muting them so you never had to shield your eyes or avert your gaze. The colors changed with the time of day and the season, so you didn't take the view for granted. Each day was a new scene, when you looked over that way.

Today, this morning, there was no point in looking because everything was socked in. So right now Grandview Drive wasn't even Goodview Drive, which was the name I would have preferred for it, since nobody has ever thought to name a street Goodview Drive to my knowledge. It's less pretentious, not a cliché, much less of a canned ring to it. And it sounds goofy, befitting my gadfly manner. But now there was no view at all. You couldn't see ten feet in front of your face.

I knew the road well, though. The half-loop measured exactly one mile from my next neighbor's driveway, around in a long horseshoe curve to the stop sign at the extension of Barnard Street. I would have liked to rename Barnard Street too, as Barnyard Street, nice rural connotation, just as I preferred a change of name for nearby Crestview Acres to Crestfallen Acres. I like to play mind games when I run, and name games are a good recreation in that mode.

At the start of my run, my first challenge was to get past Summit Place. That was most easily done by avoiding a left turn up to the summit, which I accordingly did. Just beyond the Summit Place intersection, a new challenge began to loom. It was a single, round, white light moving in the fog toward me, slightly to my left, now closing rapidly. What could it be? No motorcycle noise accompanied it.

Oh, yes, a car with a dead headlight, and there it is now, emerging from the fog. Well, what do you know, it's coming straight at me! Right now it's only a dozen feet out, smack head-on. Iceberg, dead ahead! I see the hood, slate grey, and the driver behind the hood. It's a young woman, red hair.

I'm already beginning to respond to the danger. Apparently the vehicle is incapable of evasive or halting action at this short range, so it is all up to me. From out of the fog and the car is doing about twenty-five miles an hour. A dozen feet at twenty-five miles an hour takes about three-tenths of a second. I have three-tenths of a second to fight or flee, though at this moment I don't pause to do the math in my head.

I spring—to my right, being right handed and right-footed. The car has me dead center in its sights. In one giant jump I try to shoot the several feet past the left grillwork and dead left headlight of this huge menace, in my less than a third of a second of allotted time. I don't make it. Luckily there is no figurehead of a hood ornament projecting its nose or protruding breasts howitzer-like to impale me on the spot. Unfortunately, there is the aforementioned hood. And a logo on it. DODGE, it says, in capital letters. How appropriate, I should have thought, had I had time to think.

I dodge, it doesn't. It bangs into a bone of my upper body, at the junction of the collarbone and shoulder blade. Metal against bone. A hooded car against sweatshirt-hooded flesh. It makes an impression. I do have one thought at that instant. Wow, that hurts! It is the extent of my cogitation but not my perception.

The third of a second that elapsed in this encounter had stretched out in a visual sense like a panorama, in cinemascope like the unfolding of a collapsible telescope. The sequence progressed like a series of stop-frame action shots, yielding a succession of a few hundred micro-intervals instead of a short quick segment. Kind of like your brain takes a picture and then modifies it by degrees, so the focus can more studiously ponder the scene.

Whatever process was at work, it enabled me to alter the point of impact. My visual sense had been quick frozen but not my muscular response. My legs and midsection had escaped a crushing blow, by this means. The impact of the top edge of the hood with the top edge of my body, the left collarbone and shoulder, my feet and legs off of and more or less parallel to the ground below, spun me into and through the air, clear of the road in an arching, twisting trajectory over into a ditch on the roadside fifteen or twenty feet from the point of contact.

The ground was moist and much less unyielding than the car hood had been. The sharp intense pain of the hit against the hood was not replicated by impact with the earth. I found myself lying on the ground after a quick rollover, not much of a bounce, and found that I could pick myself up, stand, even walk. And then I began to run again, after the car, which careened away as if scared by a ghost, its taillights receding into the mist, briefly flashing hotter red at the end of the short block before turning right and off at a lurch down Barnard Street.

A hit and run, it was. Without going back into the house to clean up I retreated to my car, drove to the local police station, bleeding through my clothes at the shoulder, to report the crime. Then I went to the city hospital, was given priority at the triage desk. As things turned out, I was bloodied but unbroken.

The doctor mollified me by observing, "You know, pedestrian strikes under the conditions you describe are fatal something less than fifty percent of the time." So the odds had been in my favor, but barely.

Time had stood still at that moment. It seems that my Olympic-brand watch with the gold-painted metal wristband had been flung off my wrist by the impact and been tossed an indeterminate and unrecoverable distance. It was lost somewhere in the ocean of tall grass in the neighboring field.

But the culprit was found by a quick police search. It was the young teenage daughter of a resident in the neighborhood. The dead headlight had been a dead giveaway. I talked it all over with her father. Went to their house to discuss it. She was a new driver. Panicked. Chickened out. Did I want to press charges? No. She was in good hands. Father knows best. All the comforting clichés came out from me to their aid. I merely wanted due compensation. My wristwatch back plus whatever insurance money was coming my way.

I learned from a lawyer friend that the formula for bodily injury recompense is the amount of medical bills times three for pain and suffering. The emergency room fee in those days was twenty-five dollars. So I splurged for a seventy-five dollar watch. Twenty years ago, according to my book seventy-five smackers bought a lot of watch.

I figure I came out ahead. All in a day's play. The wound was at or just above the spot where recently now I have had a pacemaker implanted. Timing is everything. In another twenty years the hit would have totaled the pacemaker. I would have had a lonely heart in that case but I would also have had the additional pain and suffering as a bonus in my complaint. It's good to know that pain and suffering is worth something, after all.

I used to think I had diseases I didn't have, like hookworm and silicosis. More recently, I've had things that doctors didn't think I had, even in the face of direct experience or examination, basic things like a broken arm. Diagnosis is art as well as science because appearances can belie reality. We know less than we know, that is, there's more we don't know than we know, as it's usually phrased.

When we think how strange and even horrible some of what we know is, like serial murder, mass murder, genocide, plus the more innocuous, less intimidating News of the Weird type of strange, akin to tabloid stories like "Man Eats Pound of Nails and Rusts to Death," it boggles the mind further to realize that what we don't know can be weirder still than what we know. If we hadn't learned about JFK's escapades after the fact, for example, who would have believed it? How was it possible that Rock Hudson could be gay? Or that Monica's spinach dip could spill the beans?

On the more microcosmic level is the labyrinth of the human body. It took eons for homo sapiens to emerge from primordial slime, but just the twinkling of an eye on the timeline of life. It seems that, evolutionarily speaking, our human race is almost an accident. Biological explanations for our evolution are insufficient to trace the track fully. It would be illuminating if the DNA coding mechanism became common knowledge, but its workings are so abstruse as to attract little interest in the attention span of the common person.

It seems we all love a mystery. Most of us are content to accept as a given the conundrum of existence without having to fully fathom or take issue with it. Such was, alas, the case with a doctor of my acquaintance, whom I met in a game of tennis.

My maternal grandmother judged doctors on the basis of appearance. The more a doctor looked like Dr. Kildare or Marcus Welby, the better that doctor was. If she was referred to a specialist, she refused to follow up afterwards if in her judgment he or she looked "insignificant." Insignificant could include too short, too young, too casual, too homely. A doctor should be male, graying at the temples, slender, tall, and have an air of calm, comforting authority. In short, be a clone of Robert Young. So having found such a doctor or two, she stuck with them throughout her ninety-five years of life. It worked for her, obviously.

With me, sometimes the most significant-looking doctors are the worst. When I was injured in a job-related accident affecting my hearing (chronic ringing in the ears caused by a misplaced loudspeaker at a graduation event), Workers Compensation forced a fine-looking quack psychiatrist upon me to testify that the ear-ringing didn't bother me because I continued to function at work.

In order to denigrate and discredit me, he put down in writing that I came across to him as "disheveled" and unprofessional (I had gone to his office in blue jeans, with a three-day beard, and in need of a haircut). For his part he was of medium height and build, wore a neatly pressed business suit, and had a trim haircut highlighting the graying of his temples. What a fop! Well, I guess I showed him a thing or two. I collected a cool $250 for my pain and suffering despite his trashing of me. So take that, quack!

The tennis player doctor I met during my first year playing 3.5 USTA league tennis was insignificant looking for a doctor according to my grandmother's terms. He looked more like a tennis player: T-shirt, baseball hat, elastic-band tennis shorts, white socks, tennis shoes. He was, after all, on a tennis court. A young buck. Sheepish grin. I didn't know at that point that he was a doctor. My subsequent acquaintance with him was likewise entirely on the tennis court, but eventually I learned that he was a practitioner in internal medicine and had an office in town. A number of my friends and acquaintances had him as their family doctor. They all swore by him as to his competence and compassion. I was duly impressed despite his medically insignificant looks on a tennis court with T-shirt, baseball hat, and the smirking grin. He was also ruthless in that arena.

The ultimate portrait of mild-mannered pose and seething interior is Superman masking as Clark Kent. Just don a pair of geeky eyeglasses and presto, a ninety-pound weakling is perceived. Other dual personas, especially those in real life, can have equivalent appeal because of the pleasing irony.

One of my favorite examples is the former all-star football player Pat Fischer. He played cornerback for the St. Louis Cardinals and then the Washington Redskins in the National Football League. He stood five feet, nine inches and weighed 170 pounds tops. Went up against running backs and wide receivers well over six feet, two hundred pounds and beat them more often than not. Not only beat them but beat up on them. His rule was, if they catch the ball they have to pay a high price for it. If they run in my territory they will regret it, will limp back to their huddle in great pain because of my toughness and tenacity, because of the pounding they take from me on every play that I can get my hands, elbows, shoulders, and helmet on and into their chest, gut, bones, and innards.

Fischer was adept at enforcing his rule because he was not only tough but smart. Calculating that a runner or receiver requires two feet to run with, he invariably managed to catch, lift, and hold one of their feet off the ground and thus useless for traction. Thereupon the runner would quickly crash to the turf. Quickness of body and mind, intensity, resilience, hard but honest contempt for the antagonist lifted him up to trample upon any foe.

He hailed from and resided in rural Nebraska. Wore glasses off the field. And out of uniform he looked exactly like Mr. Peepers—short, slight, bespectacled. In conversation, as during interviews, he was gentle of voice and manner. Seemed like your neighborhood librarian sharing an afternoon of light verse with you over tea and cookies.

My tennis compatriot, Dr. Tee, betrayed a similar incongruity—mild off the court and in the office, a terror in the throes of athletic competition. His forte was to monopolize the net, from one alley to the other on every point. If you didn't hit it high enough over his head, your shot would come back at you either on a line or on a high bounce at ninety miles an hour. So I relished the opportunity to play on his side of the net as his partner in doubles, recreationally at the neighborhood park and also as a teammate on occasion when we had been recruited for the same roster in the USTA league.

One Friday morning in mid-summer we were playing a neighborhood round robin type of game and I had him on my side. I was playing on the deuce or right-hand side of the court, receiving serve, and he was on the left, at the net. The serve came in to me, I shot it back cross-court and low, the server got to the ball and lofted a high deep lob in my direction, to the extreme right corner of the court. I retreated to take the ball in the air before it had a chance to bounce at the baseline and carom out of reach.

As I ran back I turned sidelong, facing the right sideline, and called out my claim on the ball, "I've got it!"

I heard the same call of privilege from behind me. "I've got it," the second voice shouted in echo to my own.

It was too late. I had committed positionally and muscularly for the stroke and had already begun to swing, still on the move rearward in the backcourt. Into my back came leaping and swinging and crashing down, on top of me, my partner, Dr. Tee. I was already almost airborne from my own impetus, but the collision from behind sent me flying like a pinwheel or helicopter propeller, a horizontal spin face-up, at least one complete circuit before impacting the concrete surface of the court, hitting the ground with left wrist and full backbone simultaneously

It was my back that bothered me most at first, that is to say, immediately. Despite the pain and shock I was able, after some initial writhing about, to move up to a sitting position and then shortly to stand up again. My left hand and wrist, however, did not resume their accustomed state in which there is flexion of the wrist and mobility of the hand. I discovered that I couldn't bend my wrist although I could bend and manipulate my fingers as before, and my shoulder and elbow moved normally. So although I was stiff-armed in the wrist, I could still hold a tennis ball in my left hand and toss it up, which is all that tennis requires of the non-dominant hand unless you're a two-handed stroker, which I wasn't.

I continued to play out the set, and when my turn to serve came, I served, tossing the ball up stiff-wristed from my left hand. My wrist did hurt but was not obviously swollen, distended, or at a bent angle.

To my complaint of pain in the wrist, Dr. Tee came over, looked at it, and advised, "Put some ice on it when you get home."

After we finished the set, I went home and put ice on the wrist. Within an hour or two the wrist swelled to double its normal size and at that point I could hardly move my fingers or left hand at all. My wife drove me right away to the local hospital. I got to see the x-ray on the spot. The radius bone of my left arm was fractured about an inch above the wrist.

There was an obvious gap between the two sides of the bone bordering the fracture, and the bone was held together by just a sliver on the margin at the side of the bone perhaps within a quarter of an inch of having been completely sawed in half. I got it wrapped up and began the six-week process that bones take to heal themselves. And it was not until some months after the lapse of the six-week mending period that I began to regain normal flexibility in my left wrist.

Dr. Tee had not examined or diagnosed me professionally, so I should give him some slack for that. I conclude that in the heat of competition, in ultra-high gear, compassion plays second fiddle. I'll still take him on my side when we play. Heed his call behind my back "I've got it!" And not pay much mind to any advice beyond the game at hand, which demands our mutual, obsessive focus on the hated enemy without distractions of a personal nature.

The only other bone I remember breaking was my chin. A colleague of mine lent me his copy of the Canadian Air Force fitness manual. It had an entire chapter on pushups. One kind of pushup explained was the clap-your-hands pushup. To do such a pushup you lie prone on the floor, push yourself up by the arms, balancing your midsection and legs by means of your outstretched toes, just as in an ordinary manly pushup. But each time you push your chest and head up in this manner, you take on the challenge of agility and legerdemain, at the top of your push, by releasing your two hands from the ground, clapping them together in front of your face, and then returning your hands to the floor to support your uplifted torso, neck, and head as before.

So I tried it. It might have worked for me once or twice, but before I got many reps accomplished it all came to a grinding halt. In clapping my hands on an upward thrust, I failed to fix them rapidly enough in place on the floor after the clapping, so my chin crashed to earth with the weight of my upper body bearing down on it.

The mishap chipped a piece of bone off from the extreme forward tip of my chin. I could feel the chip floating free under the skin. My chin is big enough to withstand the loss. It doesn't look obliquely sliced or anything. Eventually the piece of chipped bone got absorbed by degrees into the bloodstream of my body. So I can't amuse myself anymore by pushing it around under my skin during idle moments.

I also gave up pursuit of the Canadian Air Force's manual method of quickness and fitness. Kenneth Cooper's Aerobics methods surpass all that. At the end of the day, Dr. Cooper takes the prize in my book as my favorite physician, bar none. I wouldn't walk a mile for a Camel, but I'll run four miles for Dr. Kenneth Cooper, and for myself, any day rain or shine, even fog or, preferably, no fog.

17

Valley Boy

IT'S NICE TO HAVE A place, outside of or beyond where you live, that's special to you, a haven that your mind can retreat to even when you're not there. Such places don't go away. They're there when you need them. That's particularly true the more remote, vast, and wild the place is that you pick to be your special place. This place is bigger than life, bigger even than your life—big enough not to fade with time, an immovable object with irresistible force, an essence worthy to live for until the day you die.

To me, Yosemite is such a place. I go there at infrequent, irregular intervals, but the contemplation of it underpins my sense of the grandiose in creation and symbolizes all fulfillment in human striving. And Yosemite does this for me even though it nearly does me in when I go there. Yosemite both humbles me and bolsters my ego as I participate in its wonder. We all need Yosemite, or something like it. To my mind, though, there isn't anything else quite like it.

I first went to Yosemite in 1962, to work for the summer as a busboy, my vacation between my junior and senior year in college. My father got me the job through a friend of his at the Department of the Interior. I started working the late shift at Yosemite Lodge, 4 p.m. to midnight. There's a knack to being a good busboy. I didn't have it. Seems I was too slow, too distracted, basically out of it. Management was nice enough not to send me home in disgrace. I got kicked upstairs, to the hotel at Glacier Point (a few thousand feet above and overlooking the Valley), because the pace there was less hectic. I still had a job, if I could make the grade up there.

Glacier Point is a mile from Yosemite Lodge, straight up. By road it's thirty five miles. I settled into the hotel there with my compatriots in toil—mostly college students on summer break. We lived in the basement: housekeepers (all female); busboys, dishwashers, garbage men, the "Firefall" man, refreshment standers, bellmen, night watchmen (all male). There was also a fulltime French ski instructor, lying fallow for the summer, Rober(t).

My duties and schedule were varied. I got to unload the pantry, bus dishes, and wash pots in scalding water with deep, expansive rubber gloves. Occasionally, if I stuck my arm too low in the sink while scrubbing pots, my oversized rubber glove filled with boiling water, my arm and hand still inside. My reaction time improved considerably each time that happened, in instantaneously flipping off the boiling-water filled glove before I got steamed hard red like a lobster.

After-hours my quickened, hot hand served me well at the ping-pong table. I even won the in-house table tennis tournament, but in such a low-key way that nobody bothered to award me the pre-announced prize and I was too modest to claim it.

But the epic scale of the surroundings emboldened me. With my busboy-hardened legs I would after a month or so climb Half Dome solo, on July 4, up the hiker's ladder on its soaring back, which looks impressively steep in photos, several hundred virtually vertical feet. Perhaps I was getting the hang, making great strides, leaping and bounding from stumblebum to adventure-sportsman.

I made a couple of all too brief visitations in 1980 en route to and returning from California, including a quick ascent of Half Dome, but it was not until thirty years after my first exposure that I again sojourned in Yosemite for an extended stay.

Glacier Point Hotel had burned down in the interim. In its place was a parking lot for sightseers, making it a melancholy reminiscence for me. My wife Karen and I stood on the precipice where my ping-pong buddy Dan cast the Firefall down off the cliff every night during that summer of 1962.

All day he would stoke and burn down the coals on top of the cliff. At dusk, in response to a yodel from below, "LET THE FIRE FALL!" he raked them over in a thirty-second cascade, a spectacular attraction in those days. But now the Firefall too was no more, having been discontinued as a hazard.

The Point itself was the same, the best view in the Park. Yosemite Falls across the Valley to the left. Half Dome in left profile dead ahead, shooting its shorn face five thousand feet straight up from the Valley. Farther to the right, the snowy spiked spine of the Sierra spanned the horizon, 13,000-foot Mt. Lyell and its hundred rippling white-and-tan dappled companions.

Straight down off Glacier Point was the Valley floor, a sheer drop of over three thousand feet. Thirty years ago I had walked down and up that cliff twice, on two contrasting trails of different pitch. The first experience was the 4.4 mile trail looping around on the left from the top, a sunny, dusty hot trek. I walked it down one Saturday and celebrated at the bottom with a can of lemon-lime Teem from a lodge vending machine, which complemented the first lemon-lime Sprite I ever saw or drank, that same summer at a bus station in Fresno (my effervescent post-teen years were at the cusp of the soft-drink explosion age).

This cliff also showed up my own split entity, namely a chunk of stolidity spliced with a streak of impetuosity. The 4.4 mile trail was too circuitous to my liking, an oscillating switchback four or five steps across for every step down. On the way back, or up, I would try a more direct approach. I had heard rumors of a one-and-a-half mile trail up the cliff, a one-way trail up only, forbidden in the down direction.

No one I knew had done it, and apparently it was an obscure and little known or traveled thing. Supposedly it started near the base of the Firefall and just went up rather directly from there to the top. The hike down 4.4 mile trail had taken all afternoon.

Twilight was now approaching. I could walk the 4.4 miles in time for a nice all-night weekend game of matchstick poker. Or I could try my blind luck, straight up in the gathering gloom and get back sooner or never.

Not that I hadn't already encountered first-hand the formidable forces of Nature. At the basin past the foot of Lower Yosemite Fall, where the water seems to drift into a pool, I had waded and nearly been pulled under at first step. Booby traps were everywhere. Above Nevada Fall I had chuckled at a warning sign on the bank of the Merced River a few rods upstream of the brink, which invited passersby to throw a stick in the water and watch it "go by," that is, go bye-bye, as if imagining it to be you and to beware by self-proof.

Now, contemplating my incipient climb, I may have remembered, though I did not take it to heart or give due respect to it, the warning given by direct word of mouth to summer employees at our orientation: "One or more persons will be severely, perhaps fatally injured during your time here while walking or hiking around this Valley and its cliffs. It may be someone else or it may be you. Be advised and be smart. Don't take stupid chances."

All this was clear and plain enough. I could even translate it into my own post-adolescent vernacular: "If you screw around with Mother Nature, Mother Nature will screw you." But I hadn't yet learned that a joker is also a fool. I guess I was enticed by the prospect of learning about Mother Nature hands-on.

I headlong made my way to the foot of the Firefall cliff directly below the overhang of Glacier Point, as the sunset waned. No trail in sight. I figured it must be on the cliff somewhere nearby. If I started up the cliff, maybe I would run into the trail as it made a lateral pass along some crevice. It all seemed pretty one-dimensional in my mind: If the trail goes up, so can you.

So I just started climbing up the slope. It was a scrambling slope, no ropes or pitons required, but more of a grope than a ramble. This was a cliff rather than a hill, more up than forward. Solid granite in composition, rocks and boulders of all sizes and many facets. Sparse vegetation. I worked my way upward, apelike in posture but not in speed or agility.

It was dusk, the sky taking on the color of the granite, the landscape and airscape becoming more colorless each minute. I seemed to be on a direct and fairly expeditious ascent to oblivion, to all appearances.

I had an awareness of being foolhardy. It didn't change what I was doing. I guess I was on an unspoken dare with myself. "This is stupid, but so are you. Just blunder on."

When you're climbing a high rock, the landscape below miniaturizes with amazing speed even if you're proceeding upward at a haphazard pace. The Valley floor was quickly diminishing to view by this means, especially in the gathering dark. I was by now several hundred feet up, and it would be nearly as problematic to retreat as to continue on. I was dangerously approaching a point of no return.

Actually, I hadn't even thought about backing out of this particular gamble. Deliberation was not a hallmark of this expedition. Mind-benumbed, I plodded ahead. At this point I didn't have much of anything substantive or encouraging to go on. A few feeble yellow lights glimmered in the postage-stamp-size parking lots. But the upside to this situation is that as darkness increases, your eyes adjust; they get used to the dark. I was, however, lost—and not particularly well adjusted to that feeling.

Just before panic fully set in, as I continued to crawl, trip, and slide upward, my newly educated pupils perceived a streak of color just ahead painted on a granite boulder—orange, linear, terminating in an arrowhead pointing right. By accident, just before being overwhelmed in the dark, I had stumbled onto the trail. Though it occurred to me that I could conceivably continue straight up, the most direct way to the top, I turned right to follow the trail.

As I followed my salvation, I began to figure out the strategy of this marked route. It traced an incline along a natural fault that had allowed evergreens to grow in its cracks. They made a sheltering overhead cover, a zigzagging gauntlet-corridor through rockslides and past precipices. I instantly became a tree hugger. The moon was now up, so I also had enough moonshine to go on and if need be last me through the night. I could see the trees, and that was enough.

At intervals the "trail" continued to be marked with orange or at times with blue paint, just a few sporadic arrows to reassure that it was going somewhere other than over or off. The track continued up to the right at what seemed like a thirty or forty degree angle oblique to the face of the cliff. What in daytime would have been a strain with moaning and groaning was in these blessedly thankful circumstances a walk in the park. My own impetuous nature had become channeled and directed by the work of earlier trailblazers, and the mountain had become user friendly, accessible to the upwardly mobile young urban pioneer.

The trees eventually yielded to a dry-cascade bed, which meandered just enough to avoid being a waterfall in the spring snowmelt. You could pick and go for any size of granite boulder to hop, step and jump to and from—footstool size, table size, keg size, basketball size—in a dancing game, a hard-rock jig. I knew this waterless channel would take me to the top, to the source of the same fountain of waters that fed Vernal Falls, Nevada Fall, and the Yosemite Falls themselves.

The closer to the top I came, the steeper the incline. The last hundred feet was an almost perpendicular grope, but one that I could do with no fear of falling because of the cozy angles and cushioning vegetation.

I was home. I ambled past the moonlit-grey empty refreshment stand and onto the redwood porch of Glacier Point Hotel, ghostly dark. I had come like a thief in the night, stolen a couple of hours of illicit bliss, defied the odds and the mountain gods.

I hadn't yet learned proper respect for Yosemite's dangers and wonders. I was ignorant, I was blissful. But I was learning to test out clichés for myself, getting to put a little spin on them, seeing that the reverse also can be true, like, in my case, what goes down must come up.

And more to the point, you don't necessarily get what you deserve, lucky for all of us! Maybe I had advanced just to the point of Half-Dumb. That was my next inspiration—the projection a mile high, straight over in the middle of the Valley, that magnificent face I gazed into each lunch hour over half empty tea glasses and tinkling silver—that wonderful rock I would leap up and onto and look over off of, above all the world at its feet, five thousand feet below my own.

That year, on Independence Day, I walked from the bottom of Yosemite Valley over to and up the backside ladder of Half Dome to the top free and easy, my rite of passage as a Valley Boy.

So, at least in the little world of my own mind, I had become a Mountain Man. Thirty years passed. It was now early summer of 1992. I had told Karen about the mile-and-a-half trail up Glacier Point. I invited her to reenact the ascent, to celebrate my thirty-year waiting-anniversary with Yosemite.

After scouting the summit, the ghost haunt of vanished Glacier Point Inn, in the morning sun we drove the thirty-five mile circuit to the Valley. On foot, we canvassed the rock wall, a three-thousand foot vertical vault, from a bit of a distance to get perspective. It covered the horizon from end to end and the sky almost from bottom to top. You had to stretch your neck back till it hurt, so as to see the overhanging cliff-line, a mass of dark-ribbed ebony, jamming your forward and peripheral vision into a smooth opaque oblivion of igneous black, a vista of night-in-day.

We retreated in awe, farther back into the meadow. The soft and varicolored grass there had its own enticement. You can rest your eyes in the more familiar world of diminutive flora and fauna, or overwhelm them with the merest glance back to the forbidding blank terror over and above.

I found a Monarch-size butterfly, flitting and fluttering helplessly on its back at the edge of the two-lane Valley road. It seemed to have a broken wing membrane. Something in the human or natural world had ravaged it perhaps beyond help. I picked it up gingerly and set it upright on some friendly looking grass blades, hoping to help revive it or at least ease its struggles. It gasped in miniature trembles. I fantasized that the healing power of Mother Nature might intercede even within the little space of time allotted to this evanescent thing. I then left it alone to its destiny and turned again to the larger world around us.

At this farther distance, the overarching wall revealed some internal features and geometry. Its centerpiece began to unfold to analysis, as if it were a triptych in my mind's eye. Karen and I could see its Euclidean aspect. The trail line, or what protected it, emerged to our view. As you look up, facing the cliff, from the top the trail traces down and then angles back to form two sides of a right triangle, obliquely downward to the right, then down leftward. The hypotenuse in this scheme is an imaginary straight line plunging three thousand feet from top to bottom.

The upper diagonal is a shattered boulder line slanting down rightward to an extended fir and redwood traverse which angles down left, paralleling the steep dry creek bed that descends to the Valley floor somewhere over by the Firefall's foot. At one time this ghost of a trail had a geographical designation, true to what it used to be, namely, the Staircase Falls. Even now, perhaps it's still more a "fall" than a trail, for any who may stumble upon it. In modern Google legend it is called The Ledge Trail.

The comforting thing about this revelation was that we now understood the plan of the path and we could appreciate how relatively sheltered it was although traversing a vertical face. The trail had in fact been designed by Mother Nature, with merely some dabbling in paint by the directional hand of mankind as testimony to the company of civilized creatures. We couldn't see the orange and blue makeup from below. We had to be on the face, be part of the almost virgin countenance, to know its features remained hard and unyielding.

We were ready to give it a try. I still wasn't exactly sure where the trail began at the base of the cliff. It was a mightily broad base. All telltale charcoal traces of the Firefall that once besooted the side had long since washed off. The creek bed at the top, however, had to at some point reach the bottom, and since the tree line and creek bed forming the trail had to intersect, one could go up the creek (and thus be up a creek without a paddle).

We found the creek bed at cliff-bottom near the timbered tents of Camp Curry. Then began the boulder hopping. A couple of hundred feet up, the dry creek began bending farther to the right than we wanted to go. We started to bushwhack through some mossy rock-cover in search of the high trail of the lonesome pines. And another couple of hundred feet up, we found some faded rouge-marks and azure pockmarked patches on a boulder here or there; the tree-line trail was still in evidence, angling up to the right. Time to stop, take a break, take a look around.

The Valley floor was, at a guess, a good five hundred feet down, fairly straight down, though at no time did we seem in danger of a direct fall into nothing, or worse, to a hard rocky doom. It was a bright blue day, tons of sun rearward, on the Valley side. It was early afternoon, no worry about running out of time or light. Now that we had found the real trail, we perhaps were thinking that we already had it made. But Mother Nature overarches both humans and cliffs. She has programmed them both to fall, to tumble down, one way or another at some point.

There was no doubt in either of our minds that we would go onward and upward rather than back out or go down. We were being adventurous but not, to our minds, foolhardy. We didn't consider it a battle of wits. My head, I knew, was smaller than that of other males of my age and size. It's been that way ever since I was a kid. My baseball hat was always too small for my friends—size six rather than seven. Karen, being a smallish woman, also has a smallish head. In short, here were two puny humans up against one much bigger super-non-human Mother. Not just puny humans, pea-brained humans.

We were not aware of what we were getting into on this slippery slope, this vast impersonal granite apron. What would be the result of this mismatch? Would we get tripped up? If so, how far would we fall? That would be a telling experience in itself, for survivors.

With our advance, we gained an increasingly wide and inspiring vantage over the scene below, which remained open to our gaze and a good excuse for frequent halts and breaks to take it all in: the Valley floor, the incomparable vista of Upper and Lower Yosemite Falls in half-full flood over across the Valley, the placid intervening mead-owland, the tingling sun copper-toning all of that while tanning our own hides. We turned our back on the sun and pressed along the marked trailway.

Not many meters along the newfound path, a weathered metallic sign on a rusty post blocked the way. Its letters were incised into its unpainted surface: *Abandoned Trail. Danger. Rockslides. Do Not Proceed.*

We read but did not heed. I knew the way, didn't I? I had done this before, hadn't I? It's trees and creek, isn't it? All these cogent arguments went unheard by Mother Nature.

We proceeded. We did not abandon the trail. We were treading on spectacularly dangerous ground, the more dangerous the more intriguing. Like, what would George Mallory do? But we all know what happened to him. (For reference, Mallory was a pioneering mountaineer of the 1920's who in an early attempt of Mt. Everest, in little more than a T-shirt and leather jacket, made it to the Second Step at 28,000 feet. His frozen-solid body was found just recently, eighty years later.)

We followed the tree line. These trees were six or seven times our size—reassuring rather than intimidating. Lots of friendly Douglases to keep us company. They would no doubt be sufficient protection against mishap. Just as we remembered from our distant visual survey, however, the tree line gave way to the creek bed at a high point, three-fourths of the way up the cliff.

As we approached this nexus, the cooling shade and reassuring cover lapsed into open sky and hot, bare rock. I must confess at this point that I am a known acrophobic. I avoid looking down deep stairwells or shudder when I do look. Even looking out from the safe insides of the glassed-in observation deck of the Chicago Sears Tower makes me not only uneasy but queasy. I have fear of falling, at altitude. Karen did not suffer from such an affliction.

Once when we were hiking in the Colorado Rockies near Telluride, we encountered at eleven thousand feet a path-traverse across a sloping shale apron that, on the open side, shortly plunged into a direct drop of several thousand feet. The trail within the angled shale was a foot wide. She walked across it straightforwardly. Easy Street. Then she had to walk back to me when I stood behind, on Queasy Street. That was the end of the trail for me on that hike, far short of the intended terminus, because I was chicken and had to turn back.

The concourse of boulders in the adjoining creek bed here had tumbled into a fragmented jumble of loose gravel-like stone and dusty shards. There had been, on one or more occasions during my thirty year absence, rockslides and landslides obliterating any former trail or dry creek bed. In short, here was a fossilized avalanche. Nevertheless, despite all warning and the obvious new hazard, I still considered this cliff trail to be user friendly.

I ventured onto this granite cascade, Karen at my heels. Soon we could be above the fallen stretch (a hundred yards or so) and back on solid ground, or solid rock of varied configuration.

I was making good progress up this slope, when Karen fell. She fell bodily straight down, her feet having slipped out from under her as if pulled straight out behind her by some fiendish magician, into the intervening air. She landed headfirst, directly onto the rocks that we had been treading.

In Don Berry's novel with the unlikely title *Trask*, set in the Old Territorial Northwest, a cliffside walk eventuates in a calamitous five-hundred foot fall by one of the party, a tragedy which in those pioneer days had to be shrugged off and the expedition resumed without too much interruption or lingering reflection. Karen's fall was a hundred times shorter than that particular one, but it nevertheless gave us both much to ponder. As many a close shave tends to do, one's appreciation of the waking moment gains sharpness and savor. We got a reprieve and were going to make the most of it.

Karen had fallen straight down five feet six inches onto her chin. The bruise was immediate and deep, a subcutaneously cleft chin instantaneously. It was blue-black, already changing color into vermillion tinge, a large and irregular hematoma, but only chin deep. It looked like hell.

"Are you okay?" I offered, concerned, worried, and upset.

"No," she said.

But she picked herself up and without much assistance scrambled beside me to the top of the rockslide and safety.

We continued up the creek-bed boulders. Toward the cliff-top, the going was much more impeded than it had been years earlier, for a dense thicket of brambles had intruded into the path. Near the summit, a guarding phalanx of wasps began to murmur and stir. Karen is allergic to stings. We couldn't back down.

I charged through the offending nests, she followed in my slipstream. We scampered and clawed over the top, past the stinging barrage of flying fire. And so, still in the gleam of early afternoon, we were atop Glacier Point.

We walked into the parking lot adjacent to the overlook. Too bad, none of the cars was ours. Nothing to do but go back down again, this time on the 4.4 mile trail and take in the scenery at leisure, drink it in, get high on it for life. And we were already sky-high, thousands of feet of sky.

Karen had taken Glacier Point, taken it on the chin, and survived to tell the tale. But since she's busy planning our next trip to Yosemite, which will take place well before the thirtieth anniversary of her deep scrape and narrow escape, I'm the tattletale of Nature's secrets for now.

Yosemite is not one of Nature's secrets, but it will tell you all of them, if you want to know.

18

The Seventy-Five Dollar Grapefruit

IT IS GOOD TO CULTIVATE your own garden to the extent that you are able. Don't believe that late nonsense about a tomato thus derived costing sixty-four dollars in an inefficient attempt at husbandry. My brother makes sauerkraut in his basement, takes just a couple of months to ripen and is guaranteed to kill all pathogens upon ingestion in the human gut. I pledge to do sauerkraut myself, or as a family project under the direction of my wife, the gourmet of our household. She grows tomatoes at the rate of sixty-four per dollar, as demonstrated just last season. Actually, they grew out of our ears, so fast we could hardly give enough away to avoid trampling them underfoot.

The seventy-five dollar grapefruit that I produced is a different matter altogether. It has not to do with gardening but with life in general, and with any aspect of life that one may pick out of the air. We always bite off, in one way or another, more than we can chew. The part that we can't chew is the difference between seventy-five cents and seventy-five dollars. It's the practical demonstration of the uncertainty principle in quantum physics. You can never know what's exactly in store for you in any particular endeavor. The strand that you follow intertwines to paths unseen and unseeable as you thread through the labyrinth of each day's work and play.

I have long been fond of grapefruit. In bygone years I used to have half of one every morning at breakfast. I got to appreciate various distinctions between the yellow and pink kind. The pink kind not only had a blush on the surface, they sometimes bled within. I started to suspect that a contaminating dye was responsible for that maraschino-like effusion and came to prefer the uncolored type of grapefruit—no blush, no blood, no shame, no blame. A purer experience of delectation, fruit clear and simple.

I liked to cut a grapefruit in half and admire its neatly sectioned partitions, each one just bite size. What a perfect setup. I tried to figure out an efficient way to take advantage of Nature's convenient parceling of these fleshy morsels.

It requires both a knife and spoon, knife to slice and spoon to scoop. After some trial and error, I discovered there's more than one way to slice a grapefruit. For a while, using a sharp pointed and bladed knife, I meticulously separated each chamber from its flesh by poking down on both sides of each membrane that divides flesh from flesh, proceeding section to section.

It took an exacting touch to isolate the dividing membrane on both of its sides away from the two sections of flesh it bordered. And then after doing all that I would poke down at the outer periphery of each divided section to separate them at the back from the horny outer rind. At last lay before me twenty discrete morsels of succulent fruit, ready for scooping up by my spoon. But that was a lot of work. A bit tedious.

I found I could get nearly as good a result in a fraction of the time by making just one incision of the knife per membrane. No need to separate on both sides of the membrane, nor to bother slicing away the back edge by the rind. Sixteen quick pokes and both it and I were ready to eat, the grapefruit passive, myself active. Sixteen strokes instead of forty-eight. I congratulated myself on being perhaps the first person on earth to be privy to that process and that discovery.

Alas, eventually I had to forgo all that pain of preparation and joy of partaking of my favorite fruit when, despite my healthful grapefruit regimen, I developed a heart arrhythmia requiring a medication that forbade grapefruit. Other citrus was allowed, so I stuck to orange juice. Oranges themselves are somewhat too small to be fit subject for exacting early morning surgery when the knife wielder is sleepy-eyed. I stuck with orange juice too, even in the face of warnings by a professor from Yale University, pontificating on PBS-TV that orange juice's natural sugars were an early morning no-no and that a conscientious health nut should have salmon for breakfast. I took that caveat with a grain of salt and eventually learned to ignore it. Don't believe everything you hear, even from a Yale professor. He can't know it all. I'll pick and choose what works for me, and OJ does work despite my detestation of its notorious knife-wielding namesake. Would that the shadowy OJ had restricted knife wielding to bits of grapefruit flesh.

One day during my grapefruit and knife-blading years, I discovered that the refrigerator bin was bare of my requisite grapefruit or even half of a grapefruit. I had to have it. So I decided to drive out to the grocery store a few blocks away for some grapefruit.

It was an overcast, dreary early morning. I revved up my little Hornet and scooted off down the block, then over and down the steep little hill on Victoria Street to Main Street. At Main Street and Victoria was a stop sign. I stopped, waited for traffic to clear, and then entered Main Street for a right turn toward the store just a little piece down that road.

Just as I turned right, into Main Street, the left edge of my front bumper went bang. I glanced again to my left and saw to my amazement that I had engaged the right fender of a passing car with the left edge of my bumper. How the hell did that happen? I immediately pulled off to the right side of the road and my victim did likewise.

We surveyed the damage. A dent to his right fender. Not a scratch on my Hornet. We exchanged names, phone numbers, insurance data. Because the damage was minor, I suggested to him that we could settle up privately without involving claims adjustors or gendarmerie. He agreed. He would get an estimate or two, let me know the price of the repair bill, things would be fine again and no one the wiser, except maybe me.

After he went along on his way, I figured out how the accident had taken shape. Victoria Street ends at the stop sign on Main Street. There is no continuing road directly across Main Street. But just a few feet down Main Street, on the left obliquely across from Victoria Street, another small street emerges onto Main Street opposite though askew from Victoria. In checking traffic on the left as I was to enter Main Street from Victoria, I had failed to notice in the gloom of dawn, yet no headlights burning anywhere, a surreptitious vehicle sneaking into Main Street catty-corner down across from me. That turned out to be my unseen antagonist who momentarily encountered my left bumper with his right fender, and vice versa.

I continued on to the grocery store, chastened and subdued but more than ever in need of breakfast to soothe my jangled early morning self. The grapefruit cost seventy-five cents apiece or so. I bundled it up, took it home, and slashed into it with even more than usual gusto. It paid the price for my crackup. And then I waited a few days.

A call came, the estimate, and the bill. Seventy-five dollars. That was in the days when seventy-five dollars was seventy-five dollars. Today it would be $750. My grapefruit had cost me seventy-five dollars, plus seventy-five cents, that morning.

I'm not too good in math, but that's the only way I know to calculate the cost of that grapefruit. I wouldn't have paid seventy-five dollars otherwise. When we consider the unseen factors that apply to any transaction, we never quite know the true cost of anything, do we!

19

When Friends Drop Out

SOME OF MY BEST FRIENDS are people I don't know. The search for kindred spirits is a wide one. Sometimes I'm not sure who my real friends are. I've been dumped and bumped often enough to have become existentially leery. I take friendship where I find it, enjoy it for as long as it lasts, and go on when I get crushed. I don't expect friendship to fail and am always bewildered when it does. And I've managed to avoid becoming shy or gun shy, don't ask me why. Friends can hurt you a lot more than enemies can, because you're more vulnerable to them. A punch in the gut when you're not expecting it will kill you inside, just like happened to Houdini in his prime.

I can find safe alter egos and kindred spirits, people I don't know who inspire and uplift me, as role models that I idolize, and such icons sustain me when flesh and blood friendship fails. Steve Irwin was such a friend. So, now, is Jimmy Carter, and Doug Williams, and Kenny Lofton. Steve Irwin found love in the terrible splendor of animal life. A savannah monitor, which, as Steve cuddled it, his hands under its lower jaw, would bite his finger off if it got a chance, is a gorgeous "ripper," whose poo yields a treasure trove of interesting insights such as the guts of whatever it's been eating.

When Steve searched the Outback to encounter close up the most poisonous snakes in the world, he climaxed the program with number one, the "Fierce snake," whose venom would do anybody in, even Dixie. On a desolate stretch of sunbaked, rock-littered, shrubless plain, he caught up with one, which looked to be six feet or so long and a couple of inches thick. Always on foot, and in shorts, he rustled it out from under a random boulder. "What a beauty!"

He chased it around for a while, deftly grabbed it up by the tail and let it sway back and forth in a hissing mode, with its head waving and hovering just beyond Steve's quick swiveling hip, in a true snake dance on the part of both.

He put it back down and let it slide away a few yards, to quiet down and go again to rest in the sun. Steve got down on his belly too and crawled, actually slid, around to meet up with the beauty head on for a face to face encounter, to develop a more intimate personal relationship with the most deadly serpent on earth. Steve smoothly stroked up, as if swimming on land, to within five or six feet of the uncurled reptile, who maintained its position, as if defending its little corner of wasteland.

"You're all right, mate," encouraged Steve, with heartfelt rapture, savoring the moment and the rapport building in proportion to the tension and suspense.

After a minute or so of this mutual sizing up and interchange of vibes, the snake began slowly to slither again, this time toward Steve, who was stretched out prone, head up, arms wide and flat on the sand, a static, swan-dive posture. The snake's tongue flitted in and out, as if sensing every nuance of Steve's aura. "Criminy, fantastic," mused Steve, as the silent menace approached.

Steve froze in suspended animation, all the time whispering encouragement to the viper and addressing his video audience in dulcet tones second by second, a blow-by-blow account for the ages in real-time. "This is the real thing, deadliest snake in the world, he's got a bead on me, woo!" And still, "Easy now, you're all right, you beauty!"

The Fierce one advanced coolly, measuredly, smoothly toward Steve's exposed, upturned face, within two feet, continued gliding directly in, then angled about two degrees to the side and brushed with Steve cheek to cheek, not missing a beat, no quivering, jerking or wavering on the part of either protagonist. Forked tongue still oscillating back and forth, it scooted on past Steve's left flank, gained momentum and disappeared a few seconds later under a small outcropping. "That's about as close as I want to get to you, Mr. Fierce Snake. Cheerio, old mate!" Steve rose, brushed himself off, waved two fists in the air, and beamed a signoff grin to the camera. "Fantastic! Number One! I love it, yes!"

The audacious ostentatiousness of all this struck no false note with me. Steve was in tune with all creatures and spilled his blood, laid his life on the line, for their sake.

He charmed snakes, and they could tell he meant them well. In other words, he was and still is, even beyond death, a true friend. And because I believe in Steve, I believe in true friendship, that there is such a thing in this world, that Steve is my uplifter too even if he didn't know me, for he loved each creature—snakes, stingrays, and all, and me included. He remains a role model and kindred spirit.

Jimmy Carter has this spirit too. It's no existential accident that his initials are JC, as in Jesus Christ, pardon the blasphemy. Some dismiss him, saying, even as he takes a long overdue Nobel Peace Prize, "Well, he's been popping off for years."

My wife and I went to his Sunday School class in Plains, Georgia, almost ten years ago, introduced ourselves after Sunday School and got our picture taken there, just us with him and Rosalyn. I still remember the thesis of his lesson that Sunday, based on an Epistle of St. Paul: "Be eager to do good."

And every day before and since our visit, he has demonstrated his lessons in his life, to the hilt. He doesn't know me, but he's my friend.

Doug Williams, superbowl quarterback champ of the Redskins, is another friend of mine, because, for example, he doesn't wear gold chains. He doesn't know me, though I drove through Zachary, Louisiana, saw his house, left him a phone message. I read his book, and I could have written it myself (it was titled *Quarterblack*, but I would have called it *Soul and Heart*).

Kenny Lofton (of the Cleveland Indians, Pittsburgh Pirates, Chicago Cubs, etc.) wears gold chains, but he's a friend of mine too. In this age of the multimillion dollar shirker, he's the one who runs out every ground ball to the hilt, the only one I know of that does so.

That makes him my friend. I will be the other one who runs out all the ground balls of life.

Turning to people I do know, we will have to come down to earth a bit. I have my share of friends, and my share of friends that do me in, those who all of a sudden turn on me and momentarily shatter my faith in friendship until it is revived by Steve, Jimmy, Doug, and above all old faithfuls like my relatives and friends David, Barbara, Marian, Barbara, Rich, Tom, Mary, Dan, Joe, Joellen, Bill, Sophie, Lisa, Dean, Debbie, Ed, Billie, Bill, Jeannie, and my wife Karen.

A couple of recent examples will illustrate the evils of the day. When I retired two years ago and moved from western Maryland to Southport, North Carolina, I needed a few friends. Karen and I started playing tennis much more regularly than we had during our "working" life. Three, four, five times a week. We joined two leagues and signed up for several tennis ladders. In addition to singles and men's and women's doubles, Karen and I played mixed doubles in partnership with each other. We fought a bit at first when in competition but eventually settled down and into a tight pair on court, just as we have matched each other off court.

I began to play tennis so often that I was able to dispense with other exercise such as jogging and stationary bike riding, unless it rained for a week straight. My shape kept straight and firm, my weight held steady or dropped a bit, down from 160-165 to 155-160. My first serve improved and double faulting began to subside, maybe because of a compromised second serve. A forehand slice and backhand twist sufficed in lieu of topspin on either stroke.

I was intrigued to learn that "tennis" derives from French *tenez,* meaning "Take that!" Good for working off aggression, latent hostility, any tension of the day. Just say inwardly as you serve out your aces, "Take that!" to the unlucky slobs on the other side of the net.

However, sometimes I'm the unlucky slob on the other side of the net. I signed up for a men's senior doubles team in the Wilmington USTA league, as well as a regular adult team in the same league, above beginner but below expert. Having played at tennis for over thirty years I'm still no expert but at least not a beginner anymore.

On the senior team (fifty or older), during the first practice I encountered Joe, and we hit it off right away, got off to a five to zero game lead in the first set against our opposing teammates. We lost the next seven games and the set but maintained our newfound friendship through the entire season and beyond, usually insisting on playing with each other against any opposing doubles team and ending up with a 5-2 match record for the season

Joe is my age (sixty plus) but looks ten or twenty years younger than he is (just as I hope to do someday), even when he takes his hat off to reveal a receding, incipiently bald pate, like my own. Joe has quirks like always needing to be the one of us that serves first in a set, and needing to rely on me to keep the score straight. He's a nice guy, the inside of whose house I, at the time of this writing, had yet to see (after an acquaintanceship of almost two years), though I went to his house a number of times to drop him off and had a tour of his side yard. He always calls me "buddy," which is enough for me.

In summer, after the spring competition (February to May) had ended, we engaged in some lessons with a tennis semipro hired ad hoc by our team captain, Leon. One morning during a warmup prior to the lesson proper, we were dinking to each other at half court, slow speed, as is customary before beginning to hit in earnest.

I dinked one medium high over the net to Joe, who proceeded to whack it back with all his might. The smash bounced once at my feet and then (while I vainly tried to cover with a quick downthrust of my racket) directly up into the tender spot from below. Stunned and numbed, then seared with excruciating groin pains, I doubled over, tossed away my racket in anguish and disgust, and after a few moments' recovery stalked off and out of the court, trying to walk off the hurt and contempt of the unaccountable ambush.

A few minutes later I walked back, sullenly, to apologies by Joe: "Sorry, but it was right in my sweet spot!" Same goes for your dastardly return, I thought to myself, and went through the motions of the lesson without the customary joy or love of the sport, nursing my bruised mental and physical self. It was a low blow, requiring time for emotional recovery from it. Overreacting to extremity, I rushed out that night to buy an oversized codpiece type of athletic protector such as worn by rodeo cowboys and was six months weaning myself of the use of it. Of course I wholeheartedly forgave Joe for his lapse which contrasts dramatically with his true self.

So a friend can do you in, in a careless moment. The same friend can also save your life, in a caring moment.

Exactly one year after the painful incident just considered, Joe was Johnny on the spot when I needed a guardian angel. I was captaining a senior (i.e., old guys) team, which had finished the regular schedule 16-2, won the city championship (Wilmington), and was competing in the State Tournament to determine the champion of North Carolina. Joe was my teammate and sometime doubles partner during this successful run. Our team was in the second day of tournament competition, having managed to win the preceding day's match. We needed a win on both the second and third day to advance further.

Joe and I were scheduled to play the third day. I warmed up with the team for a half hour on a neutral court in the heat of midday an hour before the start of play the second day. I was glad the weather that day was a typically blistering North Carolina coast mid-June scorcher, ninety degrees at least. "Some like it hot, and I do," I said to the group as we pounded the ball at each other ahead of time.

I knew our team had an advantage under these conditions, since many senior types tend to wilt as a hot match goes to a second set or beyond. Our team was spryer than most, I had noticed during the preceding weeks, we being on the whole less superannuated seniors and less lard-loaded.

Each match consisted of three courts. Court one went quickly to our side, 6-4, 6-0. Court two was nip and tuck. We lost the first set 6-4, won the second set 6-2. In lieu of third sets in state tournament, ten-point tiebreaks are played. Halfway through the tiebreak on court two, I felt my heartbeat go irregular.

When we lost court two on an ace at match point, a bolt like an icicle dart hit me internally in the upper chest and I fell straight down from my courtside bench, my legs flat out in front, my backside bouncing on the concrete berm.

I picked myself up and lay down on the bench, turning on my side to face court three just opposite, where play was continuing in a similarly gut-jolting way.

The match and our tournament chances hinged on this third and last court. The opposition (Winston-Salem) had won the first set on court three, 6-4. Our players, Jim and Dave, got down 5-2 in the second but scratched their way to 5-5 in games. It seemed, and I was hoping, that the set might go to a seven-point tiebreak, which we might win, and then the match would be decided by a subsequent ten-point tiebreak in lieu of a third set, per tournament rule.

During the course of this denouement, I was lying on my side or back, bending or turning my head to catch the action at crucial moments. My other teammates, watching, thought and bantered that I simply couldn't stand the tension and was protecting my sensibilities from the excruciation of too much excitement. Actually, I was trying to protect my body from interior hemorrhage or the like.

Finally, after three match points against us in the last couple of games and numerous deuces in the twelfth game of the second set, we lost it all on a sharp angle shot by Winston-Salem, skipping parallel to the net, bouncing out of reach.

Now emotionally crushed as well as physically queasy, I bobbed up, went over to Jim and Dave, shook their hand without irony or sarcasm.

"Good game, guys. You played really good," I consoled.

"Too many errors," muttered Dave, and added, "Well, now I won't have to beg you about putting me in more."

I walked together with Joe from the courts toward the parking lot. Just as we were passing by the door of the clubhouse, I fell bodily to the walkway, headlong, breaking my fall with my hands and arms.

I had collapsed, not stumbled. Yet I immediately picked myself up from the concrete, as Joe stopped and blinked at me in astonishment.

"What happened? Are you all right?" he asked me.

"Yeah, I'm okay," I offered, and immediately went into the clubhouse to the men's room. Inside the men's room I peed and washed my hands, and then went outside to rejoin Joe.

Still concerned, naturally, he wanted to know what was up with me. I tried to brush off his queries, and we proceeded together to the parking lot. I assured him there was no need for concern, got in my car, and drove off, planning to rendezvous with Karen, as I had pre-arranged, at a neighborhood restaurant. I got onto Oleander Drive, a main and busy thoroughfare through north Wilmington.

A couple of miles down Oleander, my breathing faltered and my field of vision began to implode, shrinking concentrically in a gradually collapsing circle. "So this is what it's like to die," I shrieked inwardly. "This is it!"

With an ultimate, clutching exertion of will and concentration, I depressed the brake pedal and ground to a halt in-lane, in the middle of my side of that busy road, not able to consider whatever massive vehicular menace was behind me.

Having stopped, still conscious, I glanced up into the rearview mirror. Only distant traffic, funneling by a red sports car behind me as if forming a protective bubble around me on the left.

I managed somehow to slowly ease over to the right and into a small parking lot to stop in front of a shop. I grasped at the lever under the driver's seat to let it down so I could recline and try to recover my senses. Joe appeared at my left window. "Hey, buddy. You better let me take you where you're going."

Without my knowing it, Joe had followed me to make sure I was all right. He had run interference behind me, keeping the trailing traffic at bay. When I had stopped, he had pulled up to safeguard and shepherd me so I could pull over. I left my car in the little lot and got into his fire engine convertible.

"You were weaving," he said.

"Maybe I'm high on life," I ventured. "I'm a lucky stiff. Thanks for saving me!" (If I had had my wits fully intact, I might have added a punchline: "You know who are the unlucky stiffs? Dead people with rigor mortis setting in after a crash.")

He drove me to the restaurant, helped me out and toward the front door of the place. He held my arm, but I fell down on my way to the door. He got me in and to the table where Karen was.

"He needs something to eat, quick," he joked to Karen.

"Thanks, man," I said.

Wishing me well, he then left. I went to the men's room to wash up, and there I collapsed again. I went back to the table, plunged my hands into the chips bowl and then the chips into the bean dip. I opened up the menu and tried to focus on its contents. As I was moving my eyes back and forth and up and down over the menu page, my head fell flat with a splat on the hard wood of the table.

I was in the hospital three days. Although during all of those faints I had retained semi-consciousness, it might have been total lights-out except for Joe.

Upon my admittance to the hospital they measured an intermittent heart rate of fifteen beats a minute. Seems that I had an episode of bradychardia, similar to a few occurrences under safer circumstances two decades prior. The cure for me, I thought at the time (prior to an eventual pacemaker implant), was merely to run four to six miles daily to keep the heart rate regular and reasonably up to speed.

That I am still able to do that, however, I owe to Joe. When I dropped down and out, he didn't. He made my day, and my life. It was a near thing. I owe him more than one. I owe him everything.

The second character in this court drama is Leon, the previous team captain. I had been told he was looking for a player on his senior team and so I called him up, wanting to be on two teams rather than just on a younger "Adult" team as in the preceding year. He didn't commit himself but said I could try out at the next practice, which I did, the one where I met Joe and almost beat the old regulars first time out.

Leon turned out to be short but well proportioned, swarthy of complexion, face furrowed either with care or with years. But he tittered in almost everything he said, spoke with a cultured European sounding accent, and wore a beret even while playing. He had a good groundstroke when it cleared the net, which it often did though not reliably. When I played as his partner in practice, he asked me to call it to his attention and correct him when he attempted a windmill-type stroke, but I couldn't muster the audacity to criticize when he flailed away in vain. The misstroke was obvious to all, even him.

He seemed to take a liking to me while tittering taunts or joking insults. I have had a solar *angst* since removal of a squaymous cell carcinoma on my right thumb several years ago, and so I slather on sunblock, button up my tennis shirt to the Adam's apple and turn up the collar, creating a bit of a scene.

He belittled me for it and said I looked nothing like a tennis player, but called me his "secret weapon" against unsuspecting foes not used to my curvilinear shots, which is all I can manage since I never was taught or coached to acquire an orthodox style, a classic topspin, or the like. Because I can't hit it the right way, the oblique bounces I impart will throw many middle of the road tennis players off and will fool even some good players for a time.

He liked to address me by the monicker "Ricky-Ticky-Tavvy," which seemed to me a charming epithet. I was, in effect, his pet freak. He let me play with Joe against all comers or else pair me with a top of the line smasher type as a complementary, formidable duo. He said to me once in practice, "You don't waste energy like other players do on themselves when they miss a shot. Your stoic plodding eventuates in bad play on their part."

Many people consider my sloth-like rhythm of life and flinty face a vice more than a virtue. I was charmed by his flattery, his charitable insight. I felt appreciated and inwardly applauded Leon's grudging respect of me. I considered him a friend.

Leon himself had a problem winning, that is to say, not winning. Whomever he teamed with, he lost, at least this particular season. So he tended more and more to watch from the sidelines and let others play. Sometimes somebody wouldn't show and he would step in, and inevitably lose. Once he stepped in with me, we lost, and I got lectured for fifteen minutes afterward.

I rationalized this as displacing of self-anger onto me rather than any erosion of friendship or respect. He continued to be nice to me, cordial, jovial, complimentary in the main. At one of our summer practice sessions with our instructor, I was paired with Leon for some drills. We were practicing some switching routines to cover for overhead shots in the backcourt.

I joked that one casual player I know thinks he owns one half of the side as his territory, not to be encroached upon by his partner. He will, for example, say "This is my side!" and "You're over onto my side!"

One cannot play tennis at all well with such an attitude. There are such things as ball hogs, but tennis is foremost about mobility and switching lanes with partner as needed.

Leon reacted to my joke about the "You're over on my side" player with the remark, "And you have some problems with that, like missing the fucking shot on my side!"

I don't like to be cussed at. I tried to laugh it off and patted him on the shoulder: "Leon, you're pretty intense, but, actually, intensity is good!"

We muddled through the session. That Sunday, on the morning of the weekend's ordinary team practice, I sang in my church choir as always, left immediately after the service, and got to the afternoon practice, thirty five miles away (the distance from Southport to Wilmington), about as usual, at 1:10 p.m. Players would typically drift in between one and one-thirty on Sunday.

This time, two players arrived earlier and two later than me. So then, four of us played a set while the odd man sat out and then was rotated in. Several sets were played in this musical chairs manner, which was working well.

I was due to rotate out but another player asked for a bye instead, so I obliged by staying on for the next set. Leon intoned, "If you screw up practice by coming late and dare to keep playing, well, I've had enough of this shit, I'm leaving," and he stalked off court.

I protested, "What?"

"You heard me," he said.

"You're being irrational," I offered.

"You can't expect to get away with what you're doing," he spat back.

I ventured, in exasperation, "Leon, you're a nut," and then I threw the gauntlet, "I quit."

He was unmoved. Leon's infamous last words were, "I'm supposed to care?" And then he drove off.

So a nurtured friend was precipitously lost. This little rupture was beyond repair. I recalled after the fact something Leon said during the last match we played together and lost. It was a historical anecdote. "Lord Nelson had a crew member who failed to secure a canon onboard, which broke loose and endangered the crew but was then fixed in place without consequence. And that shipmate outshone all others in bravery and success in boarding the enemy ship during battle. Afterwards Nelson declared, 'I now acknowledge and decorate your gallantry but will nonetheless hang you for your offense,' and he did so." Leon said this to me after I had made a winning shot on "his side" of the court.

So I guess somewhere in his secret self Leon, for obscure reasons, held a grudge against me, perhaps for winning even while he was losing. But I lost too, as Leon's quirky behavior took hold of him. I'm no longer his secret weapon, his pet freak. I've been dumped.

This sample of a couple of casual relationships with their embedded unexpected hurts serves merely as an emblem of relational disappointments. Much larger and deeper are the rifts that happen with those we get quite close to, yet ultimately lose. Best friends, blood relationships, spouses, even seeming soul mates can come and go of their own volition, even without warning. Sometimes they do, sometimes they don't. I lost a wife, a best office-buddy or two, and a favorite dentist friend in this manner. We all know the feeling. Still, one can get lucky. I've gotten a soul mate, as sometimes does happen, praise the Lord! So don't forget Steve, Jimmy, Doug, Kenny, David, Barbara, Marian, Barbara, Rich, Tom, Mary, Dan, Joe, Joellen, Bill, Sophie, Lisa, Dean, Debbie, Ed, Bill, Billie, Jeannie, Joe, and Karen.

Explanations to the traumatic breaks can be either learned too late or forever unfathomed. The suddenness of the reversals is sometimes uncanny. In a two-way relationship we are not in control, nor can we be if the other is to be free. And, unfortunately, for the other to be free means, sometimes, for them to be free of you yourself, who is the one, kindly, you should love the most anyway.

20

The Life of Really

INDEPENDENCE DAY, JULY 4, 2001, found us in Southport, Brunswick County, the historic backwater of North Carolina. The land is sand, i.e., nonproductive. Thirty years ago the area was undeveloped, underpopulated, malnourished. Now, however, it is a subtropical Mecca. Long stretches of timberland pine intertwine with medium long stretches of golf course communities.

Our own development, Arbor Creek, is an enclave, golfless, surrounded by the tentacles of humongous St. James Plantation, a gated, mod community. Arbor Creek is mod but not gated.

I didn't know until several months after we moved to Southport how "South" we now are. We are at the thirty-fourth parallel, the same latitude as Atlanta. Southeastern North Carolina dives triangularly south into the Atlantic to an apex at Cape Fear. To get to Raleigh you drive due north for three hours. On a beeline straight west, one encounters more Deep South: Columbia, S.C., Athens, Ga., Anniston, Ala., Tupelo, Miss., our thirty-fourth-parallel sister cities.

In "winter" we had one-half of a snow day, but the flakes were puff. Winter is tennis season. Karen and I joined USTA (United States Tennis Association), got rated (as yet we're not "ranked"), and got involved in team tournaments. Beats golf aerobically and economically.

One of our first "house guests" was an alligator. It showed up just after the September NYC terrorist attack, taking over outside while people were hunkering down inside. For ten days it inhabited our "lake" out back, a.k.a. pond, swamp. It's a watery vista we share with a half dozen neighbors—a young, artificial body of water, new but not pristine. It's got fish that swarm at bread crumbs, and two permanent decoy ducks. After the alligator left, a young, orphaned grebe flew in and adopted the decoys as parents. The decoys bob with the waves and look real, to us and to passing stray fowl. While the alligator reigned, the fowl flew overhead without testing the waters.

Big Al liked to float in the exact center of the pond, snout and surface-piercing eyes visible. It had, at the very least, a sizable head. We figured overall it was around eight feet head to tail.

I tried to sneak up on it a few times, from a distance, as close as I could get at the water's edge. The lake pinches a bit in the middle and I hoped to catch Al napping there in midstream for a close look-see. I snuck along the marsh-grass margin. Al's snout and beady eyes bulged up and out in his siesta. I closed in, trying to get an eye-shot head-on. I was within thirty feet of the beast when, without so much as a thrash or snap, he (she? hish?) slunk under the ripples and out of view (I'll take a shy alligator anytime and leave the other kind to Steve Irwin and company).

This sneak and look, duck and run routine was repeated daily—my attempt at getting close to nature as long as it didn't get too close to me. Then one day the green monster was gone, snuck off in the night to the vast pastures of St. James Plantation, hungry for golf balls or for something in range to eat rather than just look at.

Southport is in the heart of hurricane country. The big blow of 1999 swept away most of neighboring Oak Island beach—the best and nearest ocean beach (five miles away). They've pumped sand at it for two years and it's usable again. I started a routine of running four miles a day on the Oak Island sand in summer. Did it in sneakers at first, then said to myself, sand is for bare feet. So I ran naked-footed a couple of times, until I landed on a protruding rock, hidden in the surf, and suffered a "bruised sole" (a physical rather than spiritual injury, merely a temporary, temporal impediment). Now I run in appropriate footgear, along the Intra-Coastal Waterway, on Fish Factory Road (I used to think only God can make a fish, before I saw that sign). Fish Factory Road has not only fish but marsh grass, blue herons, sea gulls, the whole bit; also some nice sunsets at the right time of day. This road, to my mind, is heaven on earth. And, if you're my type of runner, the best thing about the landscape down here is it's flat.

We had no hurricanes this past season despite dire predictions. We haven't quite run out of money yet and Social Security will be kicking in before long. Looks like we're here to stay!

What I'm learning from all of this is my natural life-rhythms, according to my own existential almanac. Late to bed, late to rise. First task of the day is simple fun: do the Jumble in the *Wilmington Star-News*. I love this low pressure lifestyle. Always plenty to do of what you choose. So I 1) read, 2) get immersed in classical music, 3) sing in church choir and neighboring chorales, and also mutely in my own head night and morning, and 4) write stories about my observations and adventures, from memory and experience, on all subject matter, from terrorists to tourists, on all places from Yosemite, CA, to Bald Head Island, NC.

Breakfast can take a couple of hours if you want it to, and I do. Then I decide whether to drive to Fish Factory Road to run the Intra-Coastal or walk to our Clubhouse half a mile down the access road and use the weight and bike room for an hour.

On the access road, adjacent to our own little lane, I pass by the tennis courts at a lagoon inhabited by a family of fourteen mallards, often watched over by a great blue heron in a trance-like stance on a gazebo rail as if fixated in time. Next to all of that is the little turtle pond (but the turtles in it are big!). On a recent visit to a neighbor's house at Oak Island, we sat out back overlooking the Intra-Coastal and watched two huge Great Horned Owls perch on a lonesome pine almost within arms' reach. In our own backyard, goldfinches flock to our feeder in a fluttering frenzy, chirping their heads off on high for us, in their own paradise, the young live-oak grove in our domestic, mixed forest.

Best of all is the timelessness of this place, its seeming immutability within the cycles of Nature. One isn't supposed to build a house on sand, and here that's all there is, but there's no prohibition on a sand castle. When I ask Karen, as we finish off our daily tennis workout, "What day is today?" we realize that the seamless nature of this reality is a fulfillment, not an emptiness, that our wonderment introduces us not to Al Zheimer but Al Gator. Like Big Al, we loll around our pond, gaze, laze, and snap up whatever strikes our fancy.

They say that in the dark of a cave, where time seems to stand still, a volunteer recluse will stretch waking hours to a routine of 20-30 hour work shifts in a lengthening sunless cycle. But in the light of a new day, a new outdoors, dreaming and waking keep each other company all the time, deep down, in our own Southland. It's pretty nice. Hurricanes can wait till next year. Y'all come down, y'hear!

21

Where Did the Time Go?

EACH OF US IS A locus of creation and destruction. Those two contending forces also whirl about outside of us. Material body and ethereal soul intertwine inextricably until the moment of dissolution. The will is theoretically free but circumstantially constrained because it is impinged upon and as much dependent from without as dependent within. Although, for example, your body is toned by you it is not entirely owned by you, being Nature's product. Your life *in toto* is not all a do-it-yourself project. Nobody can do all that needs to be done. We can't always be in control.

Sometimes we have to acknowledge our limitations. I tried operating on myself once, with a knife. In my late teenhood, I tried to remove what seemed like a cyst on one of my legs. I was too immature to get professional help. My cut and paste job inflamed the offending limb. I finally got it repaired by a real doctor, who marveled at my initiative in taking the knife to myself. "What were you thinking when you did that?" he mused. I should have replied, "You know what they say, 'Suture self!'" Laughter can be a good cover when ignorance shows. Humor is an acknowledgment of the funny predicament of our being the playthings of the gods.

Surgical intervention is also a continual reminder of our mortality. Most of us undergo such indignities periodically. Sometimes the cutting is superficial, sometimes deeply penetrating. I've had a bit of both. A benign fibroma on my left thigh, the remnant of a boil in childhood, which lumped and abraded against my swimming trunks, was nicely sliced out and stitched over, leaving a beautifully flat and smooth spliced patch. And one morning a few years ago I awoke to a kaleidoscope of incandescent orange tinges on my right thumb. It was squaymous, a second-degree skin cancer. The skin doctor deep froze it, it blistered up for a week, doming into a little ampitheater of subdermal viscous micro-action, eventually morphing into a white inkblot-shaped arid area behind my thumb knuckle.

And I bite my tongue. Not because I say things I shouldn't. It's because my teeth don't know where to go. They clamp down dead center on my tongue at random times during the act of eating. Never happened when I was a kid—only lately, in late middle age. All of a sudden I had forgotten how to chew.

Chewing is normally subconscious, like moving your legs when walking or your lips when talking. The doctors looking at my lacerated tongue suggested I think about my chewing when eating, to be deliberate about chewing. I tried that for a while despite the inconvenience, unnaturalness, and distraction of it. Sometimes it worked and sometimes not. And also, imagine someone at table saying, "What are you thinking about?" as I stare at the tablecloth. And then the reply, "Chewing." Almost rude, definitely crazy!

One cannot long think about such things if one is to get through the daily round. Anyway, I still occasionally took a bite out of the middle or sometimes the side of my tongue, enough to draw blood. It was pretty scary for a while—humiliating and intimidating. Eating became a fearful event rather than the casual joy it should be. More recently, however, I seem to be growing out of this latterday disability. Shows never to give up hope. The old can not only learn new tricks but relearn old tricks that were forgotten for a while. Like chew your food, not your mouth.

Meanwhile I had had two lumps cut out of my tongue professionally, and then later an additional new tongue-lump cut out. The maxillofacial surgeon couldn't figure out how they got there, though I surmised it was my tongue's protest at being chronically abused by me. He was surprised that these lumps consisted of "gristle." This whole gristly episode of my life is, I hope, now mostly a thing of the past. I learned from my tongue doctors that tongues heal fast because they are vascularly enriched, that is, lots of blood vessels, thus their healthy pink glow.

One thing that doesn't heal is a hernia. I started working on getting a hernia at a young age. I've always preferred handpowered lawn mowers to motor mowers. Nevertheless, I used a power mower for years, hating it all the time. Once I caught my foot in one by accident while mowing. The blade sliced off the front of my tennis shoe and left parts of two toes dangling down in chewed up chunks, which were then surgically stuffed back into the skin and stitched at the emergency room.

But it was the handpowered mowers that I used when young and more recently in my later life that seemed to precipitate and then aggravate what became for me an inguinal hernia. I don't mow short grass. I wait till it's a healthy length, otherwise (I would say to myself) why should I bother? Higher grass tends to bind hand-mowers sporadically. When the mower binds, the person pushing the mower tends to continue forward momentarily, sometimes bodily into the handle of his or her mower. If the handle is held low enough, it strikes the human mower in the abdomen, jostling the intestines. Over time, jostled intestines may protrude into fissures between jostled muscles, creating a hernia.

So I got a hernia. It started out small. I showed it to my doctor. "If it doesn't bother you, it doesn't bother me," he said. I let it go for a couple of years. Hernias don't go away. They get bigger. It's a matter of time.

On a subsequent visit, my doctor told me, "Actually, you've now got two hernias." And one of them was almost starting to hurt. Having something (other than a few vanity pounds) that you have to squash down or back in order to have smooth skin is, eventually, esthetically intolerable. I got a referral to a hernia doctor. I didn't like his bedside manner. I was concerned about the possibility of testicular injury during the operation. He said, "Haven't done that to anybody yet but you know the law of averages will catch up with you eventually."

I didn't care for that philosophy, at least not out loud. And I had to sign a paper stating I was aware of such an operation's possible side effects, one of which was death.

So I looked around for another hernia doctor. And I found one, just what I was looking for. Dr. Rock, solid name, solid approach. Surgery without cutting: laporoscopy, by which hernias in the groin are repaired through a microcut near the belly button, via a kind of snake-scope. Just what the doctor ordered, I thought to myself. I signed up for it right away. Double hernia, double repair at one stroke with one small poke.

It was an outpatient procedure—in and out in one day, i.e., do all your hurting and healing at home. Sounded good to me. I showed up at the hospital at 11 a.m. as scheduled. The operation was set for 1 p.m. I couldn't have known in advance that this would be a mind-altering as well as a body-mending experience. It gave me a new outlook on the universe and a new insight into the phenomenon of human mortality.

I was made to feel at home as much as possible in this inherently alien environment. Nothing but good vibes and good feelings all around. First came an informative consultation with the anesthetist. I told him that I have a congenitally irregular heartbeat. He could sense from my lean frame, although I looked like a ninety pound weakling, that I was in pretty good cardiovascular shape. We discussed my exercise habits (stationary bike and casual jogging). He said I qualified to be sedated, that I could go into it feeling good that I was presently fit, regardless of the outcome. In due course I got flat on my back on a gurney, in my flapping hospital surgical chemise, was hooked up intravenously and wheeled into the operating room. It was crowded with nurses and doctors but had high ceilings and a spacious, relaxed air about it. I was as much at ease as I could be under the circumstances.

Dr. Rock was nowhere to be seen. I wasn't worried. Dr. Rock inspired confidence. His name, his look, his looks, everything about him gave me assurance that I was in good hands—that I was right in willingly entrusting to him the preservation of my life, of the ostensible aspect of it as well as the private parts. He is a brown eyed handsome man, chiseled features, stiff upper lip. Nerves of steel. No problem too knotty, no intestine too entangled for quick dispatch by his steady hand guided by his keen eye. I could feel his calm, benevolent and competent presence in that operating room, behind the scene, in control. But what I saw now was two aides hovering over the intravenous bottle feeding into my vein.

They made small talk. "How are you feeling?"

"Fine, thanks. How long will the anesthetic take to take effect?"

"Just a couple of minutes. You won't have to wait long."

I began to wait for the not very long wait they had promised. I expected there to be at least a period of waiting. I anticipated a blow by blow description of when and how the sedative would begin to be administered, but before I got any such report, I was off and under.

Then came the surprise and the revelation. I became a time traveler, into the future. I skipped across an expanse of time, a chasm of potentially infinite and bottomless dimension, instantaneously. It was a time warp, a space fold, a transcendent moment. Without pause or lapse, I journeyed from "You won't have to wait long" to "Hi, how are you feeling?" Was this a trip backwards in time to where I had started out in the OR? But it was another face, another voice though the same question. A female voice, as before, and a female face, but one with red hair, not a white surgical cap. It was not the OR. Call it the RR—recovery room, rest and relaxation, reality railway, whatever. The thing was over and done before it started. Lunchtime all of a sudden was suppertime. Several hours of my life had disappeared, leaving no trace except a half-inch scar by my belly button.

"What time is it?" I wondered out loud.

"About four o'clock," was the answer.

"How long was the operation?"

"About twenty-five minutes.

I had been unconscious for three hours. Not asleep. There's a universe of difference between the two. When I'm asleep, I know it, either during or after the fact. I'm in time, dreaming or not dreaming. Time passes, and I know it. This new experience was altogether different. Time had not passed. It was obliterated. An eventful segment of my experience had been spliced out of my awareness even as it occurred. It had transpired without me, at least in the Descartesian sense. I was not. I did not think, was not aware, therefore I, to myself, did not exist in that stretch.

This sort of thing had never happened to me before. I had my tonsils out when I was nine, just young enough not to notice such things as now impinged upon my mind. No doubt the same phenomenon had occurred then, but it had not occurred to me to wonder about it or perceive its implications. For now it seemed to me I knew one of the biggest secrets of all time, or at least one that isn't common knowledge because I never heard about it before in all my born days (notwithstanding that the experience of anesthesia itself is a common one). It's in one sense similar to another paradox—the familiar puzzle about sound not existing if nobody hears it; for example, a landslide on Mars makes no noise. But in another sense it's a conundrum of a different order because it affects us, or at least me, existentially. It goes a long way to explaining some fascinating improbabilities.

The three hours that passed instantly, seamlessly, became for me an emblem of infinity. For that "nonexistent" three hours could have been ten, or thirty, or thirty thousand, and I could have awoken from that extensible span just as instantaneously as if the indeterminately long time had not existed.

I suppose that extended time-leaps of this kind happen to people who arouse from comas, and also could happen cryogenically or in various other modes. When I was a kid, my friend Billy Baker told me he once went to sleep at night and immediately opened his eyes to find that it was morning already.

More recently, I unknowingly rolled up a tree toad in an awning one fall and unrolled it the next spring. It was bleached and flattened and fell onto the deck planking, where it lay without my bothering to give it a decent burial. Yet within a few minutes it turned green (which is good for frog-types), hunkered up, and hopped off almost before I noticed it again. The same instant time-lapse must have recurred for it but without any philosophizing on its part.

I will speak mainly in empirical rather than religious terms in these musings, yet with a mystical tinge coloring the argument.

Existentially, what this actually familiar phenomenon of time-lapse means for me is that in effect we have "eternal life" in the present, whenever that present exists for us. Since we are not aware of the times that we are not alive and only aware of the times that we are alive, in effect we are always alive as far as we're concerned.

Has there been any time in your conscious experience that you have not at least vaguely been aware that you were alive? And isn't your experience always taking place in the present? In the future, will you be aware of any time that you are not alive (do you suppose)? Did you get bored not being alive in all previous epochs of time prior to your advent?

Time does not exist, for us, when we don't exist or when we are not either conscious or subconscious. Our life is an infinity of its own because we were unaware of its inception and it has continued without terminus. We are everything unto ourselves within the few moments of time that we are here. We feel that we have always been alive, even though we know there was much time when we weren't alive. We inhabit our own personal universe, in an infinitely small yet dilated microcosm of our own time that seems always to have existed.

We exist in the here and now because we are only conscious in the here and now. Since we, presumably, can never know that we are ever dead, we will know only and always that we are alive, and thus, to ourselves, we will always be alive, whenever that may be.

These realizations, some the material of cliché, others not, lead to a corollary of extension which seems beyond everyday or even "scientific" awareness. Is individual consciousness of the human order, or of any order, a continual thing beyond a given lifespan? The odds would seem to favor that hypothesis.

Look at the odds against your, or anyone's, existing at this moment, or at any particular moment in history or prehistory. Although to yourself you have always been alive, there is almost no mathematical chance that you, or that any particular individual, would be alive for any given span of any finite lifetime in the run of the cosmos.

It's easy to do the figures regarding that premise. The universe, most cosmologists say, is about fourteen billion years old. Take any biological lifespan—human, animal, or vegetable, up to say a few thousand years for the most durable plant (like the creosote bush). It's quite a long shot for any individual living thing (relatively short lifespan) to exist at any given moment during a span of several billion years.

To get to the heart of the matter, a human life is at most a hundred years or so, let's say a hundred years for convenience. Homo sapiens has existed for a maximum of about a hundred thousand years. So the chance of a particular hundred-year lifespan existing at any given time during the hundred-thousand year domain of our species is about a thousand to one.

Consider, however, the present moment, which is what we all live in, like it or not. It is extremely unlikely that any one of several billion human beings who live and have lived in the course of human history and prehistory would be alive, within the aggregate hundred thousand year lifespan of the human species, at any given moment. How long is a moment? For convenience, let's be generous and say half a second. Divide a hundred thousand years by half a second and you get an astronomically high number. It is a near certainty that any given half second will not coincide with any potluck moment within the last hundred thousand years, that is, the existence of any particular moment, configuration, dry-frozen scenario, any actual snapshot of life at any time (even of this very instant itself), defies the odds.

It was highly unlikely, for example, that the ice cubes in your drink of choice should float to exactly the microposition that they occupied just a moment ago, even though it did happen. Every moment and every configuration we experience is, in this analysis, improbable in the utmost (given the quotient of any finite time or event divided by the near-infinity of cosmic measure). And yet each moment, each scene that has happened, did in fact exist for those who were there.

Still, the chances were overwhelmingly against any particular person, such as you or I, being there or being alive at any given time in human experience (such as now!), unless we postulate that our consciousness may not be time-bound in a linear sense. If we look at it that way, what is going on now, or something like it, was bound to happen sooner or later.

Though this conjecture may sound something like the multiple universe theory of recent vogue, that all things possible that could ever happen will happen, given the infinity of time to fulfill the infinity of possibilities, I find this "all and everything" hypothesis a bit much to swallow. I think choices are real, not random, and I believe in direction and progression rather than an eternal merry-go-round.

The seeming randomness of many things may be an illusion that we now see "through the glass darkly." Form (structure, order) seems to be a plus, a creative force in itself against the dissipater, Chaos, which provides a backdrop and an endgame. Nothing much could ever have arisen from eternal entropy. By its own definition, Nothing can not "exist," therefore begetting something in the exposed vacuum, thus yielding "all things visible and invisible" *ex nihilo.*

So having a hernia created a hiatus in my bodily fabric and also my fabric of space-time. Briefly becoming "nothing" seemed to make me more inwardly aware of "everything," of the significance of my consciousness to me (once I began thinking about it deliberately!) I got "something from nothing."

For example, it occurred to me that Consciousness (that is, awareness), particularly in company with its best relations, conscience and conscientiousness, is one of the higher manifestations of "Form," which is the basis of everything meaningful. In short, there is a purpose to things: Things "matter."

The lugubrious cliché "Nothing matters" disproves itself: When nothing "matters," something becomes of nothing, again *ex nihilo*! Emblematically, we have tunes and music (creative constructs) which are "meaningful" (pleasing, engaging) imposed upon a background of noise and randomness which are not creative in principle.

Just so, the art and music that is based on form and structure (beauty, shape, harmony) will endure; "art" or "music" not so grounded is insubstantial, ephemeral, blown away with the wind. It's why a painting created by a mind and hand can last, and why one done by driving a car over paint splashed under tires can't (even though that's been tried); and this esthetic phenomenon can serve to demonstrate how Everything (formed creation) inevitably supersedes Nothing (formless lifelessness). Existence cannot be denied. Nothing, by not existing, cannot rule. Substance and essence triumph over the null and void.

It seems capricious that any particular consciousness should inhabit any particular body. But what conscious inhabitation of a body does is exclude habitation of any other body by that consciousness. Thus we can only be one conscious entity at a time. That seems to be the only materially demonstrable limit on our potentially continual run from life to life.

Even if you have only one finite life, for you that life seems forever. That's why you're alive now. But since we have always been aware of our existing, that is, to our consciousness our existence is more infinite than finite, we could nonexist for a thousand, ten thousand, or ten million years and it would seem to us as nothing. If we did not remember, as seems the norm, what went on a thousand or ten thousand years ago, it would seem again, a thousand years hence, should the human race persist so long, that if reborn we would again be eternally alive. And so on, and so on.

It seems logical to assert that we will never be aware of being "dead," and therefore we will always be alive in our own awareness. Because the odds of our being alive at any particular time seem so small, the odds of our being continually alive at indeterminate times seem to increase.

What form will this hypothetical continually renewing consciousness take, or what forms has it already taken? What will the next trip be like? We may have to wait a long time to find out, but it will seem like no time at all.

So now I have a repaired hernia, with safety netting internally sewn, virtually guaranteed to last a lifetime. I moved south to a pine needle lawn that needs almost no mowing. I'm almost "set for life," as the saying goes. As Orson Welles, who is given the last word in *The Long Hot Summer*, with Paul Newman and Joanne Woodward, is inspired to say, "Sometimes I think I'll just live forever!" What a hopeless philosophy, and yet, how full of hope it is!

22

The Ghost Crab of Trinity Center

I WOULD NOT MAKE A good god, nor a good boss in the classic sense, nor a good farmer. I don't like to cull or weed, or kill chickens. I'm a nurturer by nature, not an enforcer. Haim Ginott is my guru. Instead of saying to your bumbling kid, "Don't spill your milk," you say "Milk is not for spilling." Likewise, mud is not for slinging, people are not for killing, etc. The premise is, thus, that you and others are not no damn good but are works in progress, continually if sporadically on the rise to the high road.

Recently I was crafting a log of my life's voyage from the tumbling seas of early childhood to the meanderings of middle age and beyond. While working on this dreamy pursuit, seaside at Trinity Center, Salter Path, North Carolina, in a workshop conducted by Mabel Dolan (pen name), poet and professor, Mabel and I were returning from lunch at the dining hall across the road from Pelican House, our locus on the beach for this writing retreat. On the dirt drive access to Pelican House we encountered a meandering ghost crab, apparently exiled far from its beach habitat which was a quarter mile or more away beyond a heavy tangle of maritime forest. "Look, it's lost," bemoaned Mabel.

I had never before seen a ghost crab up close like this. It's antenna eyes hung out an inch or more above its shell, swiveling to and fro like some miniature Martian menace from *War of the Worlds*. It seemed to me a vulnerable feature, those eyes, as if ripe for plucking by some predator.

Silly me, I was moved to rescue the creature and give it back to its beach. Mabel and I undertook to do so. "All Shall Be Well," Dame Julian of Norwich said long ago, and "All *Shell* Be Well," I liked to echo in this seascape, in tribute to her.

Ghost crabs are so named because they come and go like shadows, in sideways bursts of up to ten miles an hour. This one was, appropriately enough, a pale white, about half the size of my palm, just the right shape to pick up, hold, and maybe even cuddle, I fantasized, though not without apprehension, noting its pincer-like claws the size and shape of small pliers or wire cutters.

I managed to corral it next to a tree trunk, ventured to pick it up, whereupon it promptly pinched me and drew blood. "Ouch!" said I, quickly dropping it by reflex.

Mabel went up to Pelican House and returned with a jar. We carefully cajoled the ingrate inside the jar and, while Mabel went back into Pelican House, I began to negotiate the quarter mile zigzag path through the dense dune-forest, past twelve enclaves at intervals displaying wood-carved Stations of the Cross icons fixed upon stubby myrtles and scrub oaks along this *via odorosa.*

At length, my bug-eyed cargo still staring up and out at me through its glass mobile-house, I emerged from the forest into an open area behind the beach forest dune, not yet accessible to the ocean because of intervening fenced-in property between the beach and us (ghost crab and me moving as one).

I strode briskly along the dune bank another few hundred feet to the planked boardwalk and its weathered wood stairway that led over and onto the beach itself, approached near to the surf, and with a triumphant flourish set down and opened up the jar to free my captive ghost-guest. It scurried out, scudded away at ten miles an hour sideways to a fresh refuge almost quicker than my own, non-oscillating eyes could follow.

I turned around to go back to Pelican House by retracing my circuitous route, to behold on the north side of the horizon a blackened sky, a tornado factory. The sky-gods were angry, but why? Thunder and lightning all of a sudden, my just-traveled Stations of the Cross effort notwithstanding. Scared but inspired now to save my own skin, I rushed up and over the boardwalk stairs, along the nether side of the dune and back into the sheltering wood, to the safety of its canopy in the comfort of that latter-day *Via Dolorosa* within it, thence to the regenerative haven of Pelican House itself.

Later on, Mabel shared with me some on-line literature about ghost crabs. Seems they are the little beasts of the beach, devouring everything they can get their claws on in a speedily ruthless way. Most excruciating of all to me, they are the sworn enemy of sea turtle hatchlings, whom I and my wife Karen have just recently pledged to watch over in nightly vigils while they incubate below the sand, and ultimately we usher them into the waves when they emerge slipping and floundering from the nest.

Sadly, it's a crab eat sea-turtle world, and perhaps at some point vice versa. I wouldn't have set things up that way if I had had a say in the cosmic scheme of things, but what do I know?

I'm just a hatchling myself, shuffling at the margin of the bounding main, living on the edge. And as any maturing sea turtle (and many another sentient being) should sense, it's a rough childhood through sea and seaweed, at length to find the way back, as if by instinct, to the native shore. It helps to try telling that old story anew, *A* to *Z*, searching the Alpha and Omega or the Oblivious Nullity: Taking the night train through the Twilight Zone to the Far Side, Close to Home, and finding the Word and the world within ourselves. Beginning, Middle, and End. Our life's accounting. Our own story book.

Maria Sharapova, model tennis player, advised commercially, "Make every shot a power shot." I like the ring of that. And so I'll close in a similar vein with a wave and a smile, saying, make every word a telling word.